I LOVE YOU MAGGIE

Phillip Good
75,500 words

Prologue

When wild woods have found a way to outrun fences,
And hawks fly higher than a frightened gun,
Fleeing from hovering eyes and hands
Truth bursts through preconceptions,
Then I'll come . . . like a Navajo
Across the burning desert.

Nothing is satisfying: Noises?
Dead brown-green images burnt in the retina?
The coastal hills are green and brown;
Just before twilight,
The sun paints the hills with chiaroscuro touches
And the eucalyptus blaze.
I watch the sunset (glimpses of it)
Through a mesh of branches.
I want something, I've never experienced before
. . . Oranges, apples? Cookies raisins-in?
I came charging. (English is boring and Latin is dead
and the song of the cookie-man runs through my head.)
. . . In the bins of avocados, spotted yellow gourds,
Humped and twisted, shiny and shellacked,
On the shelves of brand names,
Regular or jumbo, old not new,
The instant kind?

(You can run, run as fast as you can,
But you can't catch me . . .)

If it is not here, it may be there.
To the supervisor of my division, room 200:
I thank you for your attention,
Your time, and your forgiveness.
My trip will not entail important business.
I am content enough
And yet the Welfare State cannot imagine,
Could fulfill, I grant you, any reasonable request;
But cannot imagine:

2

New higher causes wait, new Helens in the western isles.

I came charging . . .
The saddlebags caught fire just outside of town;
Toilet articles dribbled the length of the road;
Car wheels crushed razor, canteen, and freshly toasted bread.
The rearview mirror fell off; the road was bumpy;
He took a wrong turn at night and buried the cycle in the sand.
Whimpered when it came time to look for a place to sleep,
Stumbled wearily from campsite to campsite
Looking for the right place.
Important to find the right place, not to forget
Anything; but he kept dropping, leaving things behind.
If he went back, it should be before he'd driven too far.
Turning back would be an adventure too.
He could not enjoy:
Scurried to lay out his bedroll,
Went supperless, unable to sleep because he was hungry,
Because he was afraid
Of being a trespasser, of being a victim.
He shut his eyes but the roar of the cycle persisted
While a filmstrip of the roadway unrolled continuously.
A sound!
An animal in the underbrush? Someone else, a man?
The stars sifted warily through the trees overhead;
The shadows did not move any closer.
"I will go on for one more day," he promised.

The next day, the desert road headed into the sun;
The glare from the stony flats seared his eyes.
The crash helmet, white and lined, stored the heat.
He stopped, wet the lining with a bottle of Coke,
And lay down beside the highway.
(Parsons and Barcus were for number one. Wood was merely
unaware of others, unaware so much of him was others, his
conversations someone else's phrases, the words as little
theirs as his. Though he knew the boundaries of his world,
the road's edge, the double solid lines one should not cross.)
The shadows gave the desert's colors context.
The inverted ocean's bottom writhed for fifteen living miles:
Whole fields of anemones among the pebbles,

Shadow of cholla where no cholla grew,
Life without form that invited hands to grope where eyes had been.
Wood wondered if he watched long enough,
If he would ever come to know,
Or if his first glances,
Colored by his experiences
Were in a mirror taken for a window.
The open view through unfocused light
Trapped a lizard
Shedding his skin on a jagged rock
A bird hunting him,
The shadow of the hawk's wings,
And the looming mountains.
Truth bursts through preconceptions . . .
. . Then I'll come, like an unshod Navajo across the burning desert.
The free ferry cut across the Gulf between marshy islets.
A cyclist in boots, black leather jacket, goggles
Back from the slimy beach, a final swarming of memories
Mounts his dented red cycle, the laughing message
"Jesus Saves" painted on the front fender. Bugs
Attracted out of the dust
Sweep over the handlebars into his face. Bug
Blood smears across Wood's cheeks and cakes the dust.
He leaves the oil cities Orange, Port Arthur;
Crosses the Sabine River;
Passes the rice fields, cotton fields, cane fields;
The rain begins just as the road widens.
He passes a dog, a colored man;
A horse leads a wagonload of cotton into Opelousas.
Speeds through oak-shaded streets, then
The highway Huey built through swampland
From Opelousas to Baton Rouge, New Orleans, along the
Mississippi.
The rain comes down in sheets.
The cycle loses all contact with the road.
No place to stop on the highway
And no way to stop. The cross winds
Threaten to blow him against the railings
or into the oncoming traffic.
Ridiculous: no way to stop;
The caked dirt dribbles beneath his undershirt.

4

The rain-swollen rivers thunder beneath the bridges.
A flock of Negroes crowd round to greet him.
Mademoiselle du Maupin, pigeons over Alexandria.
The town smells of perique and exhumed flesh, coffee and ripe fruit.
The cycle slips sideways in a failed U-turn.
A spray of oil mixed with water;
A cloud of steam from a muffler-scorched pant leg.
Three black faces, sullen and closed,
The only witnesses, other than Lafayette's statue.

He wheeled the two-banger for one block, then two.
Across the street, the entrance to the St Charles hotel,
A doorman sheltered under a long canopy,
Uniform embroidered with gold braid,
A coat that fell long and heavy past his knees.
Wood unlatched one scorched and sodden saddlebag,
Strode into the lobby, wet and filthy,
Ripped trousers showing a dirty, gray expanse of leg.
"Yassuh, Yassuh, follow me."
Wood asked for a room with a view.
Would he pay then or when he checked out?
(The bellboy took his oil-smeared saddlebag.)
"When I check out," Wood said.

New Orleans 1960

Chapter 1 (Mason)

Viewed from a historical perspective, there is nothing precipitous in the rise of a militant Negro movement at this time. I cannot quarrel with those of my colleagues who would posit, sometimes with unwarranted hindsight, its potential emergence some twenty years earlier. The responsible member of the White Citizen's Council who recoils from what he views as a conspiracy and the uncertain businessman, particularly the Jew, who cannot decide whether or not he wishes the movement to continue, do not seem to realize their relative helplessness before social and historical forces.

Students often suggest in the privacy of my office that petitions or a letter to the appropriate person in power might speed or halt the process. The mechanism for change is not quite so accessible. I must repeatedly caution these eager young students and friends as to the difficulty of focusing responsibility on any particular event or individual.

These explanations do not appear to satisfy them. I realize, of course, that students are not here so much for explanations as for the opportunity to express themselves. I have found in my teaching that students seldom want an answer to question one or question seven. No, questioning is just part of a game for them; they jockey for their positions on the field while still unwilling to learn the rules. Customarily, therefore, their queries will be followed by requests for my signature, my appearance at a debate, or in one memorable case, an invitation to join a student group picketing Woolworth's.

I can remember being in the cafeteria having coffee with Henry Starr, a former instructor in our department, when I was approached by the student delegation. For once, I was fully grateful for Henry's exuberant presence. He soon succeeded in convincing the group that he wanted to join their picket line. "What sort of clothes should I wear?" he asked, "How long should I expect to be in jail?" He'd even convinced me of his sincerity when he changed course abruptly and suggested they picket Dals instead. Now Dals is a quality department store, a store that advertises in the New Yorker without even a street or city address—just the name Dals and their trademark, the Georgian pillar. One wouldn't normally expect many colored persons among their patrons, but as Henry kept insisting to the student delegates over and over until they went away at last, "it was the principle of the thing that mattered."

I bought us a second cup of coffee (I was in a very good mood) and asked him, for he really was quite interested in protests and the integration movement, why he hadn't gotten involved. A frown almost suppressed the laughter from his fat Jewish face, but he said quite openly, "Life's too short."

That's it exactly. And when the students bring their petitions I can apologize, I can correct papers busily until they leave, but I can't tell them and they can't grasp the simple fact Henry bespoke that day, "Life's too short."

Each year, a fresh crop of students to make renewed assaults on my good will. I've often wondered why they come to me. I know of nothing in the content of my courses to encourage them. I teach and have taught British history for a number of years, and neither the basic course History 14B nor my advanced honors section contain any material relevant to the Civil War or its aftermath. They come to me I suspect because I lack the barrier of secretaries and the icy manner affected by certain of my senior colleagues. And perhaps they come because I am willing to talk with them. I have learned, however, to respond to students warily and with a large measure of caution.

When I began to teach, I had tremendous faith in my students and in my own potential as a teacher. I felt, because of the lengthy term of graduate study I had just completed, that I would not need to prepare my lectures. The lecture hour could be devoted to questions or a discussion of advanced topics. The students had been provided with a text and would have ample opportunity to review it on their own. Perhaps I would discuss my own research for several periods, give an assignment or quiz, and then comment on the results.

The approach might have worked, elsewhere, but not here, not with these students. I found no eager thirst for learning among them. Indeed they held an unfeeling disregard for me and for my subject. Whatever the nature of my lectures, whatever extra effort I made to whet their interest, they would respond, "How many examinations will there be?" followed by, "How much, (i.e., how little) will we be required to know?"

(What is required? It is required that they know the text; beyond that they need require, even as I, of themselves.)

My old thesis advisor, a man much respected for his theories on economic determinism, his discovery of the Hancock papers, and his teachings, had taken the trouble to write me at the very beginning of my career: "At first you may feel that your students are stupid, unintelligent. They are not. They are merely unlearned in the field in which you are teaching." Perhaps my students were not stupid, but they could be and often were ignorant and unwilling.

Soon, of course, I discovered the differences, the tremendous variance among them. It was natural to focus first on the bright ones who were so close to me in their aspirations, particularly as they so often drew attention to themselves. One or two would rise to speak on the slightest pretext, their interest in history lapsing as they heard the sounds of their own voices. A few would ask penetrating questions. Questions the limits of the course often prevented me from following through.

At first, I tried to answer all their questions. One young man I remember in particular; he would lean forward chin in palm whenever I would attempt an explanation, gradually twisting his face into a grimace as if he had nothing but contempt for me and the superficial nature of my comments. "Tell us the real story," that grimace seemed to say. Yet later, I discovered he was not even a real student taking my course for credit but a science major who needed a liberal arts elective.

I may have been obnoxious myself as a student. I suppose I was, we were. I have learned to look beyond the sneer to a student's potential and to answer snide questions politely but briefly even when they distract from the main purpose of a lecture. Again there are limits.

For the term must have a purpose, in part formal, determined by the syllabus, in part informal, determined by the students' varying needs. We cannot always follow to its end, material which, because of its very promise, is properly the subject of another semester.

I have learned to lecture watchfully.

When I first enter the classroom, I make a joking comment on the weather, take roll, and gather the students' assignments close to my side of the desk. I spot the chalk and brushes and any changes in the seating plan that they have created for themselves. Does the seat determine the individual? I am very careful to watch their faces throughout the lecture.

It became increasingly important to know who these highly variable individuals were and to anticipate their demands. Even an idle question from a less than diligent student requires careful consideration. For if a question requires a short answer, then I am to give it a short answer. If a question is inappropriate, I am to ignore, suppress or delay it. All for them! (Who is to tell what is appropriate? What new modes of thought might yield?)

The students have their own criterion. That is appropriate which is to be examined upon! Would that the criteria were as clear-cut from the teacher's point of view. Of course, the instructor has a basic duty to provide his students with a set of facts and theories similar to those provided other students who have taken the course. But oughtn't he to teach his students to think for themselves?

By my second or third year of teaching, I thought I understood the basic duty — I was and had been under a great deal of pressure from the department chairman to do so — and determined thereafter to confine my lectures to straightforward presentations of the core material, holding well in reserve the occasional stimulating lecture as a sop to the bright. Call it a compromise. Compromise is often an essential step when differences in understanding exist. (The bright are so varied in their capacity and approach, a talk designed to reach and share with them would have resulted only in confusion.)

Of course, a few students still evade me, incapable of grasping even the simple rote material I present, they sit smiling and fingering their pins. Our department chairman makes a point of their "reservoirs of ability." After all, they are in college! The fault must be mine; I require greater preparation, visual aids, and so forth! (Perhaps you understand now why I must always postpone another basic task, to know intimately the ninety students of my several classes.)

What if the students, themselves, are unprepared and past caring? If they do not even read the text! If they reject me, I reject them.

(Should I ask them, require them to sit and stare at a book that does not even begin to make sense to them? I have experienced failure with so many books, books I bought for reference, books I bought on a whim. Hard going, meant to be read and reread, I promise myself still I shall get to them someday.)

My schedule provides for office hours. I bring these to the attention of the students, particularly the ones who are in difficulty. I cannot dwell too long on elementary points in class. The majority will be bored and moreover we should fall behind schedule. Come see me during my office hours. Except one had a limited amount of time and, too often, these separate meetings mean merely a repetition of what has already been done in class.

To give them the attention they deserve is not merely a question of time but of involvement. I would have to give each one something of myself. To give them the heart to learn, I would have to be the heart beating for them, beating, beating, till their own hearts took on the rhythm.

I can give them attention. Understanding. Listen to their most rude appeals. But I am not prepared to give communion, a morsel of my flesh, three hours per week to each of ninety students. It would destroy me!

I arrived in New Orleans with my wife Violet to begin teaching shortly after we were married. We had Wendy almost immediately and Diane five years later. My family provided me with a second role, a very happy one, away from school. I discovered something in my relations with them and the community I had missed in my obsession with teaching.

It is not easy to reject one's students. But I must reject them or accept the part of them that is not me. It is only when I abandoned my vocation and reduced my work to its proper proportions that life became meaningful to me. Life is too short to do otherwise.

Chapter 2 (Mason and Wood)

Mason was just as anxious as his daughter that the meeting with her husband go well and that all of her cautions prove unnecessary. He remembered to lay his pipe and newspaper down before rising to greet the young man. Maggie smiled and laughed and hugged them both. She sat now in the corner of the sofa, watching, as if all she had ever wanted was for both of them to be together.

"I think I've seen you before," he said to Peter, for he remembered having seen the young man, not once, but several times in the Student Center, and once with Maggie. "Could it have been in the Center?"

"Possibly," Peter agreed, smiling bravely.

"You were talking with . . ." Dr. Mason was reminiscing as Maggie had feared he would, but Peter was occupied not with the words but with the mournful face of the man he still wanted to like him, a face thin, elongated, like a portrait of Lincoln without the beard. " . . . that integrationist fellow, what is his name? The one who is always getting arrested? I was sitting with Henry Starr having coffee. As a matter of fact, I remember Henry was particularly impressed with you."

"Oh!" Peter said trying to convey as much good feeling as he could in that single word.

Maggie, now Mrs. Wood, smiled at the two of them to indicate they were doing well. Though, unfortunately, they were behaving exactly as she'd expected, talking without listening, looking over to her constantly for encouragement in the manner of small children.

"As I recall," Professor Mason continued, "you sat down, Peter, with a group of students sitting near us and introduced this other fellow — what is his name, Zellner? — as . . ."

"Zellner?" Peter shook his head, uncertain.

"Yes, Zellner. Henry knew who he was-one of the local integrationist group-but you introduced him as the President of the Young Conservatives . . ."

"Oh, Lennie!" Peter interrupted, "Lennie Zellner!"

"Leonard Zellner," Mr. Mason repeated as if he were already somewhat tired of the anecdote. He gave a dry chuckle. "The German fellow at the next table began shouting and you all got into a terrible argument."

(It was all Lennie's fault. I introduced him as the President of the Young Conservatives as a joke, expecting him to play the old role; instead he began sounding off about integration. I tried to head him off and talk him round before my friends got sore, but dammed if those die-hard segregationists didn't start agreeing with him and picking on me. They couldn't have been listening to what Lennie was saying; they kept asking him what the Conservative Club was going to do about the niggers, and he kept making suggestions about intermarriage that should have turned their stomachs.

I was still trying to calm things down, when this fascist stood up across the cafeteria and hollered, "Go back to Russia" at me. Then everybody began yelling to Zellner to get rid of me. But he can't. I mean he's doubled up with laughter and not even trying. He's Leonard Zellner, the leading integrationist on campus. But all these rednecks are yelling at me and shouting that if it weren't for troublemakers from the North, the Negro would be happy. I still don't understand why things happened the way they did, everybody screaming, Zellner calling me a fascist, and this old geezer at the next table guffawing like a donkey.)

"Henry, that was Henry." Mr. Mason chuckled while Wood finished his mime. "It's true, you know," Mason continued, "a lot of the trouble is caused by people from the North who don't understand the situation."

Wood thought, "He doesn't understand it. He doesn't understand it at all."

Mr. Mason was thinking of Maggie. She was curled up in a corner of the sofa, smiling, half-asleep. "She doesn't want to direct," Mr. Mason thought, "She just wants us all, even this impossible boy, to be together."

"How did you happen to meet Zellner?" he offered.

"Lennie? I kept bumping into him in different places."

Pepe's is a pizza joint near campus. Always noisy, some drunk offering free beer to everybody from an empty bottle, and a table full of fraternity men singing dirty limericks. The place was jammed when Zellner walked by the window; everybody stopped laughing and someone at each table whispered who he was.

A chorus of boos and jeers greeted him when he entered the place and a beer bottle rolled to his feet. He looked around but nobody was going to move over and make room. "C'mon Lennie," I holler, "sit-in." He scuttled over to the seat beside me, but before he could order a coke the whole fraternity crowd rose and began to sing:

Glory, glory segregation
The South will rise again

Then the manager turned on a bright light over our table, and a patrol car parked outside the window hoping for trouble.

"I met him the first night I was here." Wood said . . .

The phone rang in Wood's hotel room and of course it wasn't the right number. "I'd like to talk to you anyway." Wood said.

"Why?" replied a warm female voice.

"Because you're a girl, and I don't know anyone in this city."

"How long have you been here?" A low voice. A brunette; five feet three or four, he guessed.

"This afternoon. I've been asleep. Say I've got an air conditioning unit in my room."

"You'll find them all over New Orleans. We can't get along without them. I'll bet you've also got a T.V., a studio couch, and a bed lamp."

"Right! Does the T.V. work?"

"My boy friend has the identical room under yours."

"Uh. Boy friend." Wood made a face, invisible over the telephone. "Have you got any girl friends?"

"To whom I could introduce you?"

Wood nodded eagerly, though again his gesture could only be inferred.

"I don't know about that. Besides I'm sorry but I do have to talk to this friend of mine; my cousin is getting married tonight, and he's here for the reception."

"Congratulations. Are you five foot three?" Wood asked.

"No, I'm five-five." she snapped. The line went dead. Peter was replacing the receiver when he heard her say, "Lots of food at the reception. You sound like you could use some food. Why don't you come?"

"Thanks. Where is it?"

"In the hotel. Don't worry about an invitation. We've five or six hundred guests expected."

"How will I recognize you?"

"You won't." She hung up. This time he was given no reprieve.

He snapped on the T.V., played with the air-conditioning unit until it was almost check out time, and then took another bath. He

13

packed the wet washcloth and a hotel towel along with his gear, dressed, and slipped out the side entrance. The cars on either side of his cycle had parking tickets; his cycle was safe and untouched.

A newsvendor with an armload of papers offered him two bits of advice:

"Don't worry about any of them damn parking tickets. Ya just bring him to me if you get one.

"When ya go into one of those striptease joints on Bourbon Street, order a Singapore Sling. She's a big tall drink, ya can sip it all night and watch the girls, and the bartender can't do nothing."

Peter reentered the hotel to look for the wedding reception and found it in a mammoth ballroom on the second floor. Several partitions had been removed to unite three large rooms. Guests in formal clothes were streaming in and out of the entrance along with tall black waiters bearing trays of drinks. Before entering, he checked his own black Dacron-wool, maybe wash-and-wear, against the clothing of the others.

Ignoring the discrepancy, he popped two steps inside. Six hundred or even a thousand people milled about in utter confusion. The odds looked favorable against detection. Purposely ignoring the groups shaking hands in the doorway, he strode toward the far wall, scuttling sideways between the tables of food.

Canapés and boiled shrimp were set beside carved blocks of ice. Carrot sticks, celery, olives, cheese balls, and still warm meat-and-vegetable-filled pastries provided highly edible alternatives. After eating his way through half an ice block of shrimp, he began to relax and smile at people and took a glass of champagne from a passing waiter.

"I see you could make it," the brunette said.

He jumped. "How d'ya do. How did ya know? How d'ya..." he stopped, started again: "All these people, very good food, uh, could I get you a drink?"

She laughed like the champagne. The most beautiful girl in the room, the most beautiful girl he'd seen since he'd started on his travels. The pampered teenagers he'd been admiring were reduced to little girls and the paint and rinses of the older women were artificial in the glare.

The bandleader announced over the p.a. that the first dance would be for the bride.

"That's my cousin."

With the next tune, a dozen couples took the floor and he asked her to dance with him.

Her upper body was lavishly endowed, her hips broad, her lips thick and sensuous. The lips were waiting for his judgment. "Do you like me or the dress?"

Embarrassed, afraid to reveal his thoughts, he tried to change the subject. "Uh, who's the groom?"

"Are you really interested? We've other things to eat besides the shrimp." She gestured toward the table where a waiter had just sat down a fresh tray of hot hors d'oeuvres

"Sure. Say, you're real aren't you." They had a glass of champagne together. He wanted to dance again.

"I'm sorry, I've got to stand in the reception line. Here's my address. Call me if you stay in town."

"I guess. But what's your name?"

." . . Although you'll be hard to explain to my father. Tell him you go to the University here. Eat all you want. Bye."

He fitted the fingers of his left hand with canapés and took a position where he could watch her in the reception line. Everyone looked so ordinary beside her.

"Queen Ester," said a woman next to him.

Peter shook his head, puzzled.

"My niece Miriam," the stout women repeated, pointing to the girl.

He tried to recall Miriam's huge Semitic eyes, lids lightly touched with greenish silver. The stout woman interrupted authoritatively: "Are you one of the groom's classmates?"

"I'm very pleased to meet you." Peter said promptly, pumping her hand enthusiastically.

"I don't think we met," the woman said doubtfully.

"Would you like to dance?" Peter asked.

"Dance, it's good for you," another equally stout woman coaxed her friend. Peter took his partner gracefully around a portion of her waist, holding her at conversation length, and began to create a step. They passed Miriam held still more sedately by a thin neurasthenic boy, and Peter winked at her. She looked sufficiently surprised and amused. Peter danced the Hora-bug allowing his partner to shake and have fun.

"The old outdo the young!" a spectator shouted, for the aunts and uncles had stolen the floor from the bride-and groom's friends following the lead of Peter's partner.

Peter danced the Hora-bug a second and third time till, leaving his partner breathless and gasping in the doorway, he collared a final glass of champagne for use in the street. The newsvendor was angry.

"Goddam uppity nigger," he said, pointing down the street. "Wanted me to call him a cab. One of those black bastards from Chicago. Christ, I shouldda chased him another block."

He gave Peter another piece of advice. "Always use a hammer on the bastards."

Imagine a Mardi-Gras parade, jostling people, reaching hands, dozens of decorated floats and their costumed riders. Hawkers on Chicago's Maxwell Street. The showgirls of Vegas on a revolving stage. Then walk along a deserted city street, long after the shops have closed, a light rain having hushed the dust and noises of the day, to run unexpectedly into the very center of the parade: Bourbon street! Dazzling multicolored lights, flambeau bearers, their torches singeing the walls, the sounds of a hundred competing bands, till wearily you reach the quieter, dimmer end of the street where it slips into the older Quarter.

Turning back, Wood saw individuals for the first time: a bearded man in a white chef's outfit astride a giant hot dog, three toughs leaning against a wall smoking, a waiter in black tux and cummerbund grabbing a quick cigarette in the street, girls walking, men watching, men waiting.

A midget grabbed his legs. "Mitzi on stage now."

"Buy one drink, stay all night."

The next barker caught him with his strident voice. "Take a peek," he offered, "Get your pecker wet. Show goes on continually nine to four."

"Twelve beautiful girls. On stage all the time. From Vegas, Chicago, Cincinnati, Houston, and bayous, Lola the swamp girl fiery Cajun blood on stage now!"

"Some like to dance, some like to fuck. Whaddya say?" The accents were not Southern but were from no particular time and place, toneless and harsh, like those of an automaton, crude and indifferent. (Watch them, imitate them. Pass like a shadow.)

Two sailors walking the outer edge of the sidewalk were corralled by "'Fraid we're goin' to cut your peter off?"

(Note how long the barkers hold the door open, when they drop the curtain.)

16

"Want to give your girl friend a thrill? Bring the little lady along."
An old carny gag, but the busload of tourists laugh anyway.

Pete passed as a shadow. Borrowing a cigarette from a barker, he leaned back relaxed against photographs of three of the twelve beauties until the smoke reached his lungs and he coughed abruptly. The barker gave him a funny look. Pete smiled as if it were pot not tobacco he was pretending to smoke.

The shine boys clustered round the doorway, platforms and bags full of polish and brushes. "Bug off you little bastards," the barker said suddenly and let fly with a kick. He caught one of the negroes in the tail. Pete laughed.

"Mind the door for me will ya," the barker said. "Close the curtain when the cops come. I want to catch a cuppa coffee."

Peter assumed the post. He waved inarticulately at the passersby. He opened the door a crack and mimed a routine; he shouted, "Bring the little lady along," at the people's backs.

"Where's Vic?" asked another midget down by his waist.

"The guy on the door?" Peter stammered, afraid of losing his job.

"No, the boss."

"He, uh, gone to Vegas."

The midget seemed satisfied with the reply.

Pete looked away, uncomfortable. The star attraction was on stage. She walked slowly along the front of the platform, dressed only in babydolls, ready for bed. "That's Ann," the midget said, "She's a fine girl."

"Hey sailors, get a load of this!" Pete shouted to let off steam. The crowd turned and Ann, her silhouette framed in the doorway, succeeded in luring them in to the bar. (I'm getting good at this, Pete thought.)

"Keeping you busy?" a girl asked from just inside the doorway. Her voice was husky from too little sleep. Like every other girl in the place, she wore too much makeup, but the long sheets of raven black hair made Pete look once then twice.

"Hi Dixie," said the midget. He lit a cigar.

"Hi Joe," she acknowledged before turning her attention back to Pete. "Taking Don's place?"

"Just for awhile," Pete said, stalling for time, trying to think of what he could say to keep their conversation going, "Uh, your name's Dixie?"

"Dixie Cupp. That's my stage name." She reached out her hand for Pete to shake, "I'm Dixie Mahone. C'mon in and buy me a drink after."

Too much of an intimacy for him to accept easily. "I'll run down the street and get ya a cup of coffee to go," Pete replied, brazenly.

Dixie did not seem pleased by his brashness. "At least wait till I go on stage."

Don came back. The crowds began to drift by in a thicker stream, groups as well as couples pointing and talking as they walked.

The midget said conversationally, "So Vic's in Vegas."

"Whaddya talking about?"

"That's what this guy said."

"Who the hell is he?" The two of them looked Pete up and down. He fiddled with his jacket, fumbled for an imaginary pack of cigarettes, found his sunglasses and put them on.

Dixie came to the door. "I'm on now," she said."

He followed her into a electric blue grotto whose dim lighting was supposed to make the girls look younger. A few managed to pass the test. Dixie hovered at the end of the apron, while a tryout frisked up and down the platform yelling "whee" and popping her cheeks. Dixie disapproved; a straight dancer, her dyke-style steps carried her in a series of promenades along the platform.

Her long legs already displayed to advantage in a translucent gown with a slit up one side, she removed the gown five minutes into her performance, revealing legs perfectly tapered, flesh still firm and vital at the thigh. Transfixed, Peter was unresponsive as the bartender, a male waiter, and a B-girl tried without success to get him to order a drink.

The B-girl pressed close. "How about a drink, mister?"

"I'm a friend of Dixie's."

"It doesn't make any difference; you have to buy a drink."

"Get him out of the doorway." the bartender said.

Dixie returned. She had changed her earrings.

"You are very young," he said, thinking of the Caesarian scar he'd seen across her abdomen.

Dixie's hand played with her earlobes. "I can't talk to you, if you don't buy me a drink."

Peter shrugged.

"Call me at home," she suggested and pressed her phone number into his hand.

18

Peter walked down the street whistling. He wasn't sure whether he was happy because he had two new numbers in his little black book or because he had made two friends in his very first day in a new city.

Chapter 3 (Mason and Wood)

Hands clenched behind his back, jaws working on the bit of his pipe, Dr. Mason glared for a few moments at his reflection in the window. A rhyme his dentist had taught him returned: "Lips together, teeth apart." Taught him too late, regrettably. The enamel had been worn away by the time he was twenty-five and he had to have all his teeth capped, first in plastic, later in porcelain and gold. The recollection distracted him; his hands tapped absently against the table and finally he turned off the light and sat down in his padded rocking chair, arms loose in his lap, the smoke from his pipe wreathing his head at intervals.

Maggie had not been home the previous night. He had been anxious but not seriously worried. Then the next day she missed work. The bookstore called him and his calmness had only added to the confusion. Half a dozen partial explanations had been relayed by her coworkers; nothing definitive.

She did not call for three days. When she did, he felt not angry but betrayed. He could not feel angry once he knew she was all right. She was no longer a child; he could no longer protect her. All he asked was she tell him beforehand what she was going to do. When he heard she was married, he gave them both his blessing and offered to send money.

Post cards were forwarded from New York, Niagara Falls, Chicago. They told him nothing about the details of her departure. Nor did he learn much over the phone. When she reappeared, it was without her new husband and, apparently, the need for any explanation. She would only say vaguely they had gone on a honeymoon and that Pete was still traveling.

"On business?"

She shook her head.

He remained calm. "Tell me about him. Does he go to college?"

Again an absent-minded nod.

He asked her for the name of the college and she spoke, finally, "In California," pronouncing the name of the state as if it were very far away and not worth thinking about.

For a week Maggie moped about the house. She went back to her old job in the bookstore, but she sat at home in the evenings. Mason was a little annoyed; he'd had plans and now felt obligated to stay home and sit with her.

Then, as abruptly as the original departure, her husband telephoned.

"Did you know he would be coming?" Mason asked.

"Hush, Daddy."

Her husband would be with them in five minutes, no, half an hour. They would have time to clean the house, time for Professor Mason to change his clothes. No, he was to sit still while they dusted around him. And change his slippers for his pipe. And promise to take his pipe out of his mouth before speaking ... promise not to say the wrong thing.

Well, it didn't matter. It was only important they all get to know one another as quickly as was feasible and then sit down and discuss the couple's plans for the future. But this proved impossible.

First, understandably, the lad was tired, travel-worn. He wanted to go to bed; he wanted to be alone with his wife. And then Dr. Mason had always wanted Maggie to marry Mike. Of course, that hadn't worked out. Perhaps it was for the best. Mike had gone on through college (Maggie had not) and was now on his way to being elected to the legislature from Baton Rouge.

This boy was something like Pete, the first Pete, the Pete Maggie had dated in high school, always underfoot and in trouble. Unfair, of course, to link the boy through a name, or compare him to someone like Mike. The trouble was you just couldn't talk with him. Did everyone out West talk the way he did, changing the subject half a dozen times and never answering a question? Being tired was no excuse for a lack of politeness and complete incoherence. Would the young man's conversation focus just long enough for him to tell them what he planned to do? And what right did he have calling Henry a donkey?

"How did you happen to meet this fellow, Zellner?"

. . . Wood wandered in and out of a series of bars buoyed up by his encounter with Dixie Cupp-Mahone. In most of the downtown locals, stony backs and an indifferent bartender greeted his presence. In one, he watched two old men playing dominoes on a checkered tablecloth, but they did not ask him to join them or include him in their conversation. Without being aware of the boundary, he wandered into a colored section where black men sat in doorways sipping beer and occasionally darted across the street to a bar to order another six-pack through the take-out window. The bodies leaning against the fence were hard and suspicious; he could not see the eyes of the men watching him. For a moment, he stood outside a colored bar listening to a warm black female singer's voice curl between the thighs of the sweaty dancing women; the eyes found him and he moved, drifted back toward the Quarters.

His second round of Bourbon Street was an avoidance tour. The doormen screeched their wares as if he were not a friend. In the bars on Royal where secretaries seemed to slip easily from lap to lap, he was ignored. In one lounge on St Philip whose focus was the barmaid, he was asked for an opinion. "I think he's right," said Wood hunched over a beer. "Ed, there's someone here who agrees with you." said the big-thighed barmaid. A little man who was sweeping the floor and fetching glasses from the table to the bar looked up when his name was called and spat in the sweepings by Pete's feet.

A beautiful red-haired boy tried to steer him into a gay bar around the corner. "I want to pick up a girl," Wood said thinking to discourage him.

"Oh, lots and lots of girls come in there, simply lots and lots of girls. I'll introduce you to one of them. I know everybody, all the sluts in the Quarter." The boy looked amused when Pete's face darkened at his use of the word 'slut,' then he apologized; "I didn't mean that. I know you don't need to pay for a girl. I'll introduce you to a nice one; you can even use my apartment if you like. It's right around the corner."

Two a.m., close to three: Wood returned to the quiet bar where he had watched the two old men play dominoes and found a crowd had formed outside. One of the hot-dog men had set up shop in the middle. The crowd on the street was merely the fringe of the mob inside. The place was wild, swinging jazz and swinging hips, and don't dare touch the local beer-it's lousy.

The proprietor shook maracas in the air over the bar, while the crowd swayed sympathetically with the few compressed in front of the jukebox. Pete let the tide carry him, looked for openings, found a girl who handed him her boy friend's beer. Sirens wailed, but they could have been part of the music. Pete wondered if he should dance, whom he should dance with. The crowd screamed as the police pushed their way into the bar. The police grabbed indiscriminately and heaved or kicked the crowd through a line of cops into the paddy wagon.

In the station, men and women were put into separate tanks; fifty in a room meant for half that number. No lights and no clear way of getting air. No one seemed to know why the bar had been raided. Every so often someone's movements would set the whole crowd boiling and people would get bruised accidentally with knee and elbow. The girls began to scream in their tank and one of the Mexican boys was crying in Spanish.

A curly-haired guy, standing next to Pete, seemed to think the party was still going on. "What'll we sing?" he asked. He slapped the Mexican on the back; the crying stopped. He moved freely through the crowd, despite the pressure, hollering and whispering encouragement. About twenty-four, an open-neck sports shirt displayed the thick blond pelt on his chest. Blurred masculine features, bushy eyebrows, a bent, perhaps broken nose. To Pete, the whole room seemed to be slightly out of focus. The face and the light disappeared in the dust storm.

(He'd slept on a sand bar. The girl woke him. The angle of the sun to the highway never changed.) "In the corner." the fellow said.

"I don't have any money for the fine," Pete whined.

Then someone pushed him and he snapped a vicious elbow back.

"Shut up in there." a stern voice said from outside.

"Aw fuck you," "Fuck you." scattered voices replied from within.

"What the hell, we're in jail," the curly haired boy philosophized at Wood's elbow. And he guided Pete into a corner where the crowd exerted less pressure. A wizened old man in a neat but spotted gray suit and a faded red necktie was already sitting on the floor there.

"This guy," the curly-haired boy began, "this old guy, just came in to get a pack of cigarettes for his wife when the place was raided. He lives next door to the bar. He's lived on Dumaine for how long?"

"Thirty years." the old man on the floor said.

"How old is he?" Pete asked sleepily.

"Seventy-two."

Pete nodded. Things weren't yet fully in focus. "Doesn't look strong enough to push the button."

"He asked me to get the cigarettes for him." the curly-haired boy said, "His quarter's still in the machine.

"I wish these guys would book us. So the old man could phone his wife." The blue eyes were full of pain as though somebody were hurting him.

One (three?) hours later, the police came finally, opened the cage and formed them into a long line. The curly-haired fellow said his name was Arnold Rosenweig and he lived at 2212 Carondolet. The sergeant wrote it down. The plainclothes inspector took a long look at 'Arnold Rosenweig'.

"And who are you?"

"Benson Brown," Pete said.

"Where do you live?"

"Same address."

"Same address?," said the inspector, "Sure. Hey, Rosenweig, what's this guy's name?"

"Brown, Benson Brown, B-R-O-W-"

"Get out of here."

Pete caught up with Arnold on the station steps; the sun was already high enough to be warm.

"Thanks Arnold." Pete said.

"Leonard," the man replied, "My name's Leonard Zellner."

Chapter 4 (Wood)

Alas, Wood and Zellner were not meant to be roommates. For one thing, Wood arose each morning, bright and early with the dawn, ready to eat his weight in eggs and pancakes. Zellner seldom got home before four or five a.m. and then he slept through until noon despite the steadily increasing heat.

For another, Zellner did not have an apartment but a single room off a littered courtyard. The one large double bed where Zellner slept filled most of the space and left Wood with only a few yards of flooring. And though Wood would much prefer to have slept near the huge rattling fan in the window that brought in an occasional cooling breeze, he was condemned instead to the foot of the bed, in the hottest most stifling portion of the room, to be woken each morning in the early hours when Zellner at last came stumbling in.

No food in Zellner's apartment, Wood discovered the first morning and rediscovered each evening thereafter when he renewed the search for nourishment as if somehow, inexplicably, a well-stocked refrigerator might have materialized during the day. Fortunately, food was to be had in the Quarters nearby, and Wood had coffee and doughnuts each evening before retiring, and fried eggs and grits and a huge glass of orange juice for breakfast, and coffee afterwards and a roll filled with pecans.

Once, the last morning he slept there, he found an oil-stained brown paper bag, still smelling of fresh hot doughnuts, pinioned beneath Zellner's hand, but the contents of the bag were an inseparable mass of powdered sugar, wax paper and macerated beignet so that Wood, though unaffected by the food's appearance, was unable to make the fulfilling meal he'd envisioned.

One other thing. Returning early to the room about six one evening—Zellner was not home, of course—Wood heard a knock on the door, and found a thin elderly Negro with graying hair and a slight stoop waiting on the threshold. The Negro peeked in expectantly, even took a step into the room, before Wood blocked his way. The man yelled "Lennar!" and receiving no answer hollered a second time, "I be back," or what sounded like "I be back" to Wood's untrained ear. In any event, Wood closed the door well before he was sure the man actually was leaving.

The visit was repeated the next evening at about the same hour, again shortly after Wood entered the room. Apparently, the light in

Zellner's window drew the visitors, for a seemingly endless series of visitors, followed. The last, a slim pockmarked brown girl, smiled, said nothing, then left after only a cursory glance at the Leonardless room. The next morning, Zellner having returned as usual singing just before dawn, Wood went looking for an apartment of his own.

With no particular plan in mind, he purchased the morning Picayune and looked through the classifieds, but the procession of street names only confused him. The street map he had severed neatly from the center of the telephone book offered endless possibilities. Here the Elysian Fields, there Lake Pontchatrain, and the muses—Clio, Erato, Thalia, Melpomene, Terpsichore, Euterpe, Polymnia, and Urania—one after the other on the way uptown.

He drove slowly along St Charles Avenue following the trolley line. The homes on one side of the tracks, toward the river, had wide set porticos and broad stairways. But the room he had seen advertised was on the other side, in a genteel slum where homes had been divided and divided again, first into duplexes, then into apartments, on and on, until, finally, they resolved into some fundamental quantum of space of which no further subdivision was possible.

Wood could accept the scuff marks on the walls and ceilings, for he was not really a very tidy person, but he was not prepared for a window that looked out on a window, or a floor that sloped away from beneath his feet curving into the center of the room, or the awful loneliness and the strange accents of the vacant-eyed people who lived in the houses on either side.

In the end, after a brief walking tour of the Garden District (for Wood prided himself on taking advantage of every moment), he headed the cycle uptown again still following the trolley line. When he judged he was close enough to the Zoo and the University to stop and look around, he had already gone past them, and was lost in a twisting labyrinth of residential streets that even the trolley car avoided. The sun was hidden in a steaming mist and the promises of early morning had given way to an endless brooding gray.

He paused, the cycle braced against one leg, and consulted his map. It told him nothing, perhaps because he no longer had any idea of where he was. The motorcycle's engine died. Wood tried the kickstarter, failed to start the engine, and tried again.

Everything is going to be all right, Wood thought. Be cool. The cycle would start. It had started before in Amarillo, Fort Worth, Shreveport, Opelousas. Just that ever since he and the cycle had left the breathless agony of Tehachapi Pass, 7000 feet up in the thin mountain air, the cycle had seemed to need more help in starting.

He bent over the motor with a wrench, not so much to repair it, for Wood's mechanical knowledge was limited to tires and spark plugs, as to hit smartly and firmly at the one spot—fuel line or electrical system—where the obstruction was hidden. At the moment when Wood felt he most needed to keep mind and body focused in the same direction, a young man only a few years older than himself emerged from the cellar doorway of an imposing mansion across the way.

Jacket over one arm and a half dozen books under the other, the young man exuded an air of confidence Wood would have given anything to match. Seizing the opportunity, Wood called out, "Do you know where I can rent a room?" and when the man did not reply added, "Are you renting a room here?"

"Why yes, I rent a room, downstairs," the man replied warily. He looked at the ground, at the doorway he'd vacated, at the sky, anywhere but at Wood's blue and gold leather jacket with University of California Wrestling stenciled across its back, anywhere but at the small red motorcycle with "Jesus Saves" painted on its front fender.

"The Vicker sisters live upstairs," the man continued just as Wood was thinking he might have lost his voice entirely. "Two retired maiden school teachers. They rent rooms. Two of us live downstairs. And a girl lives upstairs, I think."

Wood smiled eagerly.

"I don't think they have any more rooms though," the man added quickly. "How did you find out about the Vicker sisters? Did you hear about them at the University?"

"Can't be any harm in asking," Wood said, affably, ignoring the questions.

The man looked dubious.

Wood walked onto the wide front porch. Wide enough and long enough to hold three rooms the size of the one where he was staying.

Two huge chairs were set together before a series of closely spaced windows. Wood knocked on the big front door, using an ornate knocker half again the size of his fist. The curtains moved in one of the windows facing on the porch, but no one answered his knock. He knocked again. Still no answer. He knocked a third time and then walked the length of the porch, conscious as he did so that someone inside the house was tiptoeing from window to window ahead of him each time.

Finally, when he had reached the far end of the porch and was trying unsuccessfully to look past the curtains to the gloom within, the door opened behind him and a faint quavering voice said "Yeass?"

Wood bounded across the porch in the direction of the voice. The figure in the doorway, a slight elderly woman, immediately retreated, as one might step back in fear of a large and untrained puppy. "Can I help you?" she asked when she had regained her composure.

"I'm looking for a room," Wood said eagerly.

"Yes, we have a room," the woman replied. She spoke slowly and carefully, her slow measured Southern accents lengthened even further by the quaver associated with advancing age. "I'm not sure you would like it," she finished at last.

"It looks fine," Wood reassured her, "I mean the house looks fine. This is a great old house."

The woman seemed pleased. "It's a very old house."

"Our father built this house," a second equally ancient voice said from the doorway behind her.

A pair of women in their late seventies or early eighties stood framed in the opening, the elderly sisters the young man had spoken of. The one who had answered the door appeared shorter and frailer than the other, though presumably the braver, since it was she who first confronted the stranger. Tiny, dressed all in black, from her shoes to the tight ruffled collar at her throat, Wood guessed she could not have weighed more than seventy or eighty pounds.

"We taught history," she said unexpectedly, "to three generations of students."

"I like history," Wood said.

"Do you?" said the larger sister, "A lot of history is in this city. French, Spanish. Four hundred years. Our father told us so many stories."

"We taught history to three generations," interjected the elder. And as an after thought, asked, "Would you like to come in and sit down and talk to us about it?"

Wood stepped slowly over their threshold and into the front hallway, careful not to make any sudden moves that might startle the elderly pair. After some shuffling of chairs, the three of them sat down facing the porch, much he supposed as they had done sixty or more years earlier when a beau came calling. The two elderly women looked at Wood expectantly.

"I'd like to see the room," he said.

"It's a big one, a very big one."

"On the first floor."

"Just off the front porch."

"But you'd have to go through the front hall of course, to get in and out."

"That might not do."

"No, that might not do at all."

The pair continued to chatter, heads cocked at various angels like two particularly intelligent parakeets, but neither, Wood noticed after some moments, gave the slightest indication of wanting to go with him to look at the room.

"And you'd have to share a bath," said the younger sister, or at least Wood assumed she was the younger from the manner in which she deferred to the other, the frail woman in black who had answered the door originally.

"Father left us this house," the older one said.

"We already told him that."

"I'd like to see the room," Wood said.

"You'd want to see the bath too, of course."

"Of course." the older sister agreed.

They sat in companionable silence for several moments, planning the room tour, presumably, when the elder sister asked unexpectedly, "You don't take showers, do you?"

It was not really a question but a request, Wood surmised. He nodded agreement, though he had a sinking feeling this was only the first of many privileges he would be forced to surrender to get the room he wanted, the room he so urgently needed, the room he still had not seen. I'm desperate, he thought. But it is such a nice house. And all the other rooms I've seen have been so without hope.

"There's no way you could take a shower here," the older one continued.

"Not necessary," Wood said agreeably.

"And of course, we would have to find some way of signaling when the bathroom was empty."

"We live on this floor you see."

"That could be worked out."

"If he was agreeable."

"Yes, but he still might not like the room."

"I'm sure I'll like it!" Wood shouted, unable and unwilling to tolerate their chatter a moment longer.

The two women looked at him reproachfully. He had been much too loud. "I'm sure I'll like it," he whispered.

"We must ask Annie," said the younger sister.

"We must talk with Annie."

"Let me go and talk to her."

"She'll talk to Annie to see if it's all right for you to look at the room," said the older sister. The younger stood up slowly and, leaning on her cane, she shuffled from the parlor. The elder remained in her chair, hands folded in her lap, staring straight ahead unblinking like a museum mummy in its sarcophagus. Wood looked away. When he looked back her eyes were closed. Just napping, he hoped.

Five minutes or more passed and still the other woman did not return. Wood could not recall when he had last heard voices. He stood up. The older Vicker sister stirred in her chair. "I suppose you have to go now," she said. Had she had been awake all along? "I'm sorry we only had the one room. Perhaps some other time."

"Oh, but I haven't seen the room," Wood declared, indignant. He was not going to go until he had seen it and he hoped the determination showed in his voice.

She sighed as she must have sighed over a truly slow-witted pupil. "Let me show it to you then," she said, defeated. The elder Vicker sister led him slowly out of the front parlor and down a long papered hallway lined with a succession of suitcases and steamer trucks. Most of the doors to the hallway were closed, except for one leading to the kitchen, where a colored cleaning women, dust rag in hand, watched with amazement as he passed slowly by.

They halted finally at the entrance to a big comfortable room at the far end of the hall. The elderly woman made no move to go farther and he peeped inside over her shoulder.

Paradise. A bright sunny room, the opposite of all the life-draining accommodations he'd toured so far.

"How much a week is it?" Wood asked, and was conscious of his voice booming out awkwardly in the silence. He smiled nervously.

"Oh, you'll have to see the bath first," the old woman said.

He looked inside the bathroom. An old-fashioned toilet with its tank high on the wall above the throne, a sink, and a wooden clothes hamper. In the far corner next to the window sat the object of the earlier conversation, a deep porcelain bathtub perched on four legs. All was neat, the porcelain freshly scrubbed, and the room held a slight odor of disinfectant. What could the fuss be about?

30

"I like it," Wood took pains to say, since the bath appeared to be a point on which the sisters had to be satisfied.

He returned then to the bright airy room and made himself at home in a large armchair. The search was over. He had a place to stay, people in town he could visit, and he could easily find a job, perhaps teaching or doing some kind of research.

He heard a disturbance now in the hallway, several voices all talking at once. Three people came into the room, one behind the other as in a painting by Brueghel the Elder. An old colored woman, the one he had seen in the kitchen, led the procession, still wearing an apron around her waist and a kerchief tied over her hair. The two Vicker sisters stood at various distances behind her, the smaller and older sister in front, the younger and larger a few steps behind, just as they had been when he first met them. Both women, he noticed, were very careful to keep the cleaning lady between Wood and themselves.

"Mistah," the black woman began in halting fashion; she seemed to be missing several teeth or to have left her upper plate behind in the room where she was cleaning.

"Yes?"

"They's no room."

"Yes, I want to rent a room." His own voice sounded strange in his ears, like some character in a play.

"They's no room for you to rent." the woman said, although her words sounded to Wood's ears more like, "Thais nrumfyu too rennt."

"I'm not sure I understand."

"Tell him Annie," said the younger of the two sisters in a tone that suggested Annie might be deaf, "that we don't have any rooms for rent now."

"Not now," Annie said, "You go."

Wood went.

He stood outside, kicking futilely at the cycle's starter pedal. The man he had talked with earlier came back up the street and approached him. "Any luck?"

Wood told him the whole story, the visit in the beau's chair, the wonderful room, the three women repelling the male invader.

The man shook his head sympathetically. "I don't think they want a man living there. I think, and don't laugh, remember the times they grew up in, they were embarrassed about sharing the bathroom with a man. I told you they had a girl living upstairs before."

"But they're eighty years old."

"Well, that's the Vicker sisters. Chalk it up to experience. They probably embarrassed generations of teenagers the same way. I'd wondered how you'd heard about this place."

"Nothing downstairs?"

"Just my room and the other one's rented. Why don't you try at the University? I thought you came from there in the first place."

Wood thanked him. "Join me for lunch?" he suggested. He was not sure why, but he was reluctant to let go of this newfound friend.

The boy gestured with the books he held in one hand. His message was clear. He had things to do. Wood did not.

"Do you know how to pick up girls?" Wood persisted, raising a topic that interested him.

"In a general sort of way. I do O.K."

"What do you say to them? In this town? I mean, do you just walk up and say, 'Hi, you're beautiful.'" Wood's tone made it clear he was ready to accept the young man as his mentor in all things.

"I wouldn't be as direct as that."

"Thank you." Wood said.

Wood's cycle started at that moment, and two-banger and driver disappeared up the street trailing clouds of oily smoke. The young man shook his head in wonder. Above him, on the first floor of the mansion the Vicker sisters trailed Annie slowly through the house as she cleaned.

Chapter 5 (Wood)

Wood was terrified by the ease with which the morning and the early afternoon had slipped away. He had always valued his time, at least since he had started college, and felt obliged to use it productively, with so many miles covered each day, so many chapters read.

At school in California, he walked about between classes with a book in his hand. The book went with him to the cafeteria, to the laundromat, and to the play or the ball game to fill the time before the curtain went up.

For the last three or four months though, the book had remained unopened more and more, as if what happened in the theatre before the performance was as important as the play itself. And although he still believed every moment ought to be spent productively, often the afternoon disappeared into evening as he listened to the voices of the coeds walking by beneath his office window.

His walking tour of the Garden district that morning was experience, something to be treasured and recorded in his journal. But so too was the memory of an anorexic girl he'd met in a gas station in Tucumcari. She'd joked with him and said they were the only two blond-haired people in all of New Mexico. I should have stayed and talked with her, Wood thought. I should be meeting someone now, or out looking for a job, or off on my cycle seeing something new.

His first glimpse of the University cafeteria was of a dimly lit circular wasteland. Only after he had pushed past and through a heavy folding curtain did he view the part of the cafeteria favored by the after-lunch crowd, a serving area next to the kitchen that held coffee cups, trays, and a cash register. At the far side of the room, a swimming pool, glimpsed poorly through a mist-covered wall of glass, formed a backdrop of green and yellow shifting light.

He recognized no one in the cafeteria, though, as always, he had the nagging sensation he had seen one or two of the people here before, at his own University perhaps sitting on the terrace drinking coffee or somewhere along the road. An intense depression settled on him that coffee and pecan rolls could not fight alone.

"You're not very sociable," Miriam said as she sat down next to him. She was expensively even elegantly dressed in a silk dress and high heels. Again, he found her proportions overwhelming and he looked, did not look at her breasts.

"I don't know anyone," he said defensive.

"You didn't seem to have much trouble meeting people the last time I saw you." She laughed. She looked much younger than she had in the hotel, perhaps because she was wearing more rather than less make up. She looked a great deal like someone's younger sister.

"Penny for your thoughts?"

"I was thinking about you." he replied.

She gave him an indulgent smile that implied he would have to do a great deal better than that.

"I was just getting settled in. I'm looking for a room."

"Did you find one?"

He shook his head.

"Still staying at the hotel?"

"No." He waved helplessly.

"This climate's getting you down, isn't it? The rain, the humidity. It's going to rain this afternoon. You'll feel better after it starts."

"My motorcycle," He began.

"You drive a motorcycle?"

She sounded impressed, he thought. Figured she would, now his cycle was no longer reliable.

"Take me for a ride."

"Not when it's raining."

"Do you always play this hard to get?"

He smiled. "You're the one who sent me away the last time."

"Hey, I had family to take care of. Besides, maybe I won't send you away so fast this time."

"I'm open to dinner invitations."

"Good try." She laughed. "I can see the expression on my father's face now. You wearing that oversize wrestling jacket, your motorcycle parked outside the front door. It'll be a long while before I invite you to meet my family."

"Tell your Dad I'm just a student."

"That's the part that really worries me, that you're just a student."

"I am something more." He puckered his brow, trying to think of what that something was.

She noticed he stuck out his tongue while he concentrated. "Why are you here?" she asked, suddenly.

He gazed back, blankly.

"In town, in New Orleans, at the University, at 3.22 pm on a Wednesday afternoon in the early fall."

34

"I. . . I'm looking for something."

"Pete," someone called from across the cafeteria, just in time to rescue him. But who could it be? Who knew him here? Leonard. Behind Leonard, three or four others, all male, including a large fat man with a pockmarked face. "I see you found the place all the pretty girls hang out," Leonard said.

"Yeah," Wood replied, "And this is Miriam, Miriam Finestone. Miriam, I'd like you to..." But she had risen while his back was turned and he was talking to the empty air. He twisted his head 180 degrees until he located her. "You going?" he stammered.

Her books were clasped to her chest like a wall between her and the new arrivals. "Class," she replied, smiling brightly, an empty plastic smile that sealed out Leonard and his friends. The smile wasn't meant for him, was it? She had seemed so friendly only a moment ago.

Her back to the new arrivals, Miriam began to write her name and phone number on a napkin with a ballpoint, humming under her breath,
"'How come he want to kick up such a dizziness!
Nigger-business ain't white folks business.'"

She slid the napkin onto the plate in front of Wood. "Where did you meet *these* people?" she whispered.

Wood could only wave his hands helplessly, wanting to touch and afraid to touch her.

"I gave you my phone number *again*," she said, this time speaking loudly enough for Leonard and his friends to hear, "Don't loose it this time." Again she smiled brightly.

"Miriam!" Wood called. But she had slipped away along the cafeteria wall and was gone.

"Easy come, easy go," Leonard said. "Pete, this is George, Dave, Arn, and Jerry."

"Pleased to meet you." "Pleased to meet you." "Where are you from?" "Been in town long?" they said to him, and then turning to the fat man, "Heck of a story, George." "Finish the story, George."

"Let me sit down first," the fat man, George Barcus, said.

"Get you a cup of coffee, George?" Leonard said. "You too? Pete? No? You come with me anyway." Wood stood up. Leonard took his arm conspiratorially and leaned toward him speaking into his ear as if imparting a confidence. "You move out, O.K.?"

Wood nodded. No regrets then on either side.

"Good. Going to have some people over tonight. Maybe a young lady. Looks like you got yourself a young lady. Newcombe girl."

Wood tried to look modest.

"They teach them to fuck genteelly here," Leonard continued, "you know with the left pinkie raised." All this time Leonard had been speaking in a normal conversational tone, so that two girls at a nearby table looked up shocked. Before Wood could divert him, Leonard himself had changed the subject.

"I tell you it's been a crazy afternoon," he said.

"Me, too, Lennie; there's this pair of sisters, must be in their eighties..."

Leonard ignored him. "I told you I was going to a sit-in, didn't I."

Wood gave him a quizzical glance.

"Bunch of people milling around, nobody has any idea what we're supposed to do. The one girl who says she's seen a sit-in before doesn't even show up. People in Woolworths all scared giving us the eye. People behind the counter scared, think we're crazy. People with us are scared, they think we're crazy. I'm scared, only not as much because I know I'm crazy.

"Reporters are supposed to be on hand No reporters. Cops are supposed to come. They don't. No TV cameras. Manager comes out, finally, wants to know what's going on. We explain it to him. He asks, why didn't somebody tell him? He's talking like a sit-in is some kind of publicity stunt they thought up at the home office in Atlanta. Doesn't have any idea what's going on, until one of those FBI types that's been following us whispers in his ear. Even then, he still doesn't believe that black people want to eat at his lunch counter.

"Me, I don't care about eating. I just want a cup of coffee. Get my picture taken. Try it again next week.

"Now, black people are coming up saying we must be crazy. This white lady behind the counter is saying we must be crazy, only she's mad at us if you get the distinction.

"Mind you, we still haven't sat down yet, so how can it be a sit-in?"

"Wait a minute?" Wood interrupted. "I still don't understand what you're trying to do."

"We're trying to hold a sit-in," Leonard replied, "so that black people and white people can eat alongside one another."

"Black people and white people do eat alongside one another."

"They do where you come from. They don't here.

"Do you know, black persons have no place in the Quarters they can eat, no place downtown. They can't even get a drink of water. Where do you think they go to the bathroom?"

Again, one of the girls at an adjacent table, a beautiful brunette in a white ribbed sweater, looked up and frowned.

"I mean it. The nearest place for them to eat is maybe twenty blocks away. And don't talk about going to the bathroom. It's not right. We've got to change it."

They got their coffee, Wood with a single cup, Leonard a tray full of cups and saucers, and walked back to the table. Everyone else in the cafeteria seemed to be taking the sit-in calmly. At least no one else seemed to be talking about it. Until he saw a sit-in on TV some weeks later, Wood would wonder if the incident had all been in Leonard's mind.

Wood's saddlebags had been pushed out and away from the table and someone had taken his chair. In the middle of an anecdote, the fat man was making broad gestures with his hands and the others were laughing. Wood leaned forward to hear what the fat man was saying.

"Pete." Leonard speaking in his ear, interrupting. Leonard stepped between Wood and the table, and pinned him against the glass to the swimming pool. Dim misty figures swam by on the other side of the glass.

"Yeah, Len?"

"We're going to have a sit-in. We're going to keep coming back day after day until they serve us."

"Right." and Wood turned his attention back to the fat man. "Peckerheads," "champeen fools," "Earl Long," and "Gillis," he heard the fat man say, and someone called "Nixon" wore makeup and toupee.

"We weren't organized." Leonard muttered behind him, "We're just going to have to learn to do it right. This time we'll have somebody call the papers, make sure the reporters are there. Telephone the store manager and the head office first, so they know why we are there. And we're going to have signs, so the people who are just standing around will know too."

"Sounds good." Wood said placating.

"I'm going to see Zambrowski, tomorrow. Or next week, anyway. You want to come along?"

"Sure, Leonard."

"Tomorrow, first thing. Well, maybe around noon, you know." Leonard grinned. His grin said O.K. I take myself seriously but not that seriously.

The fat man left. Several of the students sitting with them left too, but their chairs were quickly taken. One of the new arrivals had brought dice and a stack of foolscap paper that he cut up into sections. He started passing out the paper saying, "Leonard, you are England, Arnie, you're France." Somebody else drew a map of Europe on the table.

A bus girl who'd been cleaning up the coffee cups nearby, shook a finger at them when she saw the drawing taking shape. Leonard shook a finger back at her.

Wood wondered where the girls were Leonard talked about all the time. They sure weren't sitting with him. They were scattered all about the cafeteria though in dresses, in sweaters, in sheer nylon stockings, in short skirts.

"Want to go one on one?" a blond boy who looked like a crane challenged him. "We see who can pick up a girl first. Or who can pick up the most girls in a thirty-minute period."

Wood thought the dare over carefully and then shook his head, "You know more people here than I do. It would have to be a girl you don't know very well. It would have to be a girl you don't know at all, one you just wanted to meet."

"Understood." the blond boy said.

Wood introduced himself.

"Parsons." the blond boy said in turn.

They shook hands.

"Dinner," Leonard said.

"I know a stripper," Wood said to Parsons between forkfuls of shepherd's pie. The pickup contest had never actually materialized.

"I slept with a Chinese girl once," Parsons said.

"How was it?" Wood asked curious.

"She came almost as much as I did. It was like lather."

"The only girls you boys slept with was yo' sisters," Leonard said in a put-on accent.

"Huh! I been married. I am married," Parsons snapped back.

"Sixteen and out of the bayou," said Leonard.

The three stood outside in the early evening. It had rained while Wood had been inside the cafeteria, how long ago — three, four hours

38

he could not be sure. Off to the side, he could see one or two raincoat-clad students, textbooks under their arms, heading toward the Center the two new friends had just abandoned.

"We still got to find you a place to stay," said Leonard.

"He stays with me," Parsons said.

"What happened to your wife?"

"Gone."

"Hmm," said Leonard as if the comings and goings of Parson's wife were a well-established occurrence. He clapped Wood on the shoulder. "Day after tomorrow, O.K. buddy. Noon my place. We go see Zambrowski."

"O.K."

Parsons and Wood walked on alone together toward the north of campus. The street lamps reflected off the pavement mirrored in the dark pools of water. The classroom buildings around them were all darkened, though the occasional solitary light could be seen burning on an upper floor. What's that?" Wood asked, pointing to one of the upper windows where a shadow peeked around a window blind.

"A professor probably, planning some mischief. Or a custodian. It could be me," Parsons said, "Except my office is back in that direction."

"I've got an office on campus in Berkeley," Wood said.

"Then the leather jacket and the motor cycle are all a facade?"

"I don't know."

Parsons signaled his approval. The two new friends walked on in the night, Wood pushing the motorcycle.

Chapter 6 (Mason)

In fact, Professor Mason was in his office on the third floor of
Dewiler Hall at the very moment Wood and Parsons walked by. As
always, he had stayed after classes, not so much to work on his
lectures as to hide from the emptiness of his household. Although he
cared for both his daughters, the present held little that was
attractive for him, the future even less. Only in the past, or in his
carefully edited memories of the past, did he find some small
measure of happiness.

For a short while, he remained leaning on the windowsill, staring
out across the darkened quadrangle. The night air, the soft
murmuring voices, the rain fresh fragrances of lilac and mimosa, cast
him deeper into reflection. Each perfume carried with it a memory,
part thought, part feeling, so that at one and the same time he was
both a watcher in the shadows and an actor on stage. He thought of
the wife who had deserted him and of the wife-to-be of fifteen years
before. He remembered a game of touch football in his first year of
college that went on and on into the late evening until it was too dark
to play. He had a brief vision of his daughter's first wobbly efforts to
ride a bicycle, then made a mental note to stop on the way home for
milk and eggs.

Behind him, on the floor next to his desk, a stack of reference
works formed the basis of the text he planned to write some day.
(And hoped to still.) His desk held a photograph of his ex-wife taken
many years before, (blurring inexplicably to reveal the face of his
youngest child,) a pen and pencil set, two crayoned portraits
inscribed "from a loving daughter," a student's senior dissertation on
army recruitment and the race problem, a fruitless exchange of letters
with a publisher who'd accepted, then rejected his book in progress,
and notes, some signed, some not, from passing colleagues who
wished to remind him they "had just looked in," "couldn't meet
him," and "would come again." In the end, he turned to his diary,
the one unvarying focal point of his evenings and, to avoid his
feelings, read again its empty phrases:

Though I was born and raised near Shamokin, Pennsylvania and
spent my early twenties at Cambridge and in New York, I have
grown to look upon myself as a Southerner. I first came to the South,
to New Orleans Louisiana, shortly after completing my doctorate at

Columbia. It was my first teaching position. Temporary at first, it was to become a permanent appointment.

Wendy was born shortly after we moved to New Orleans, and six years later Diane, a planned child, was born. The children attended schools in New Orleans and, for a short period, a private school across the lake. With the exception of the few trips we made every second summer to the girls' grandmother in Virginia and the first few months of Wendy's life, they have never been outside the South. And just as one's children tend to view the world through the eyes of their parents, so I tend to view it through theirs.

I can remember Susie and Caroline, the little girls who lived next door to our first house on Calhoun St, better than my own playmates. I can remember when Wendy broke her arm falling off her bicycle, and Diane came running in screaming that a tree had hit her.

In the spring of the year Wendy started school, it rained for two weeks in a row and the Mississippi, already swollen from the spring thaw, threatened to overflow its banks. We had to evacuate, walking for almost five miles on top of the levee.

Though I know I carried Wendy piggyback on my shoulders, and Violet held Diane, the memory I have is of someone else, a stranger, carrying me to safety. Around us, other parents scurry by with their children and their possessions. We walk more slowly. The river seems so calm, so far away beneath us. Yet when we reach Carrollton, we can see a chain of men with hip-high boots passing sandbags from one to another. Far out in the middle of the river, a log that looks not much bigger than a tree branch hits the side of a barge. We hear a crack, like the boom of a distant cannon, and all at once realize how wild and turbulent the waters are.

But can this memory really be mine? Wasn't I raised in a country of green lawns and softly falling snow?

Now, I have grown used to spending the occasional Sunday afternoon talking to Mavis' grandmother about whites and colored, and listening to her reminisce about her teenage years, the Cotillions and Balls, the members of the King's Court who danced with her the year she was chosen Queen. Didn't we always go to Mardi Gras parades and sing Dixie at every opportunity?

Violet and I often went dancing when we first moved to New Orleans, to live music, not records. A party in the smallest apartment would still have a five-or six-man jazz band. They played a sound one can hear today only on a few scattered 78's or at a colored jazzman's funeral. Violet was dancing with her shoes off in the centre of a clapping circle when I borrowed one of the colored fellow's instruments — a trumpet, and soon anyone who could improvise had taken over from the band. 'The Faculty Five' played together for two or three years after that. At our own parties and at student dances, weekend after weekend. I've always preferred to believe people just stopped giving them.

I met Violet shortly after I received my doctorate at Columbia. Almost, but not quite ready then for marriage, I was utterly lacking in self-confidence. For several years, I had served my fellow graduate students as a reliable source of information on inexpensive housing, cheap but good Italian restaurants, laundries and shoemakers willing to extend credit. Now, about to graduate and move to a different, as yet undetermined city, my hard-earned knowledge would be of value only to others.

My uncertainty betrayed itself in my lectures. I'd been asked to present my dissertation at neighboring Hunter College, the first step toward a possible faculty appointment. Violet was a freshman graduate student hiding in the back row. We had not met yet, though we would meet casually and, on my part, forgettably that afternoon. The story of our meeting is amusing. . . in retrospect.

Professor Harkness had not been on my examination committee and looked upon his omission as a deliberate slight. He used my lecture to exact retribution, bombarding me with a series of detailed questions only a few of which I was able to answer coherently. At the merciful conclusion of my talk, while still vainly attempting to give correct answers to a departed audience, an attractive young woman, Violet, appeared with cookies and tea. I can't recall accepting them, but some time later, walking with long strides through Central Park, I realized I was still carrying the teacup and threw it into the bushes.

Several bleak days later I was introduced to a very attractive young woman in a dark blue dress meant to be professional but still very feminine and seductive. She admitted to being the bearer of tea and cookies, a gift I had totally forgotten! I was confused, apologized profusely, and finally promised to take her to the theatre to make up for the slight. So confused, I never questioned a woman so attractive accepting what, after all, was an invitation to a date.

(Of course, I can't really recall the details of this anecdote, but it has been told and retold in my presence so many times it seems part of me. All my notebook says, surprisingly, is "met girl in corridor, dark hair. She knows Bob Barnes; new in the department, take to theatre." Bob Barnes is, I imagine, someone I knew in the department at that time, though the details aren't too clear now.)

I do remember everything, though not unbiasedly, of our first evening. Walking, offering her a series of compliments, her dress so different from the awkwardly fitting clothes that were then the normal anti-feminine attire. Fascinated with her face and body, her dark eyes, the pronounced hollow at her throat, her pale skin so much in contrast with the night-like blackness of her hair, I became more daring, said some things to her I might not ordinarily have said. She threatened to wear long, full skirts when I looked too long and longingly at her legs. A few short weeks later, we broke through to the state I'd dreamed of when, walking by myself, I'd seen other couples hand in hand, laughter and love moving in resonant waves between them.

(And can I tell Wendy and Diane that promises of love are never guarantees? Holding hands when you are infatuated is one of the most beautiful experiences in the world. Being truly in love, partner in hundreds of shared yet exclusive moments, can be an elusive goal. But the two—infatuation and love, are not necessarily comparable.)

I suppose I made all the mistakes one can make in a courtship. We went pretentiously to the Ballet, the Symphony, and Exhibitions. And discovered we both preferred to spend the evening watching a movie or dancing. Violet loved to dance. I loved to see her radiant with joy, feel her respond to my own movements. "I want to dance all night in a brand new dress," she would purr, "to forget above wars and love and the South."

She liked to dress up, would wear innumerable lace half-slips and formal dresses, full skirts that floated about her as she moved. I bought her bouquets of white camellias, an unflagging admirer, seeing with pride her image mirrored in a dozen other admirers' eyes.

A friend from college, Harry Chambers, visited me every so often. We had been roommates and I had suffered by contrast because of his success with women. I would be embarrassed when he brought a girl to our room, not knowing what to say to her, or whether and when to leave.

Harry came to town once while I was dating Violet and for some reason I avoided introducing him to her. The next time, I arranged for the three of us to spend an evening together at the ballet. We spent a pleasant enough evening, yet his expected roguish comments were not forthcoming. "Well, what did you think of her?" I asked afterward, stepping out of character to force a compliment from him. "She's O.K." Exactly what he'd said about every other girl I'd dated!

Harry's indifference broke the spell a little. Though my other friends, thankfully, were enthusiastic about my discovery. As our friendship grew, I became more and conscious of detail, of the tiny crinkly lines at the corner of her mouth, the slight indentation in the crook of her left elbow that broke the perfect contour of otherwise flawless skin. After we were married, her body was unexpectedly voluptuous.

That Violet chanced to be a graduate student in history, too, was I suspect the result of a series of rebellions and compromises with what she thought her mother wanted: To be married, to be among bright young men who would flatter her, to bring the young and distinguished into her mother's home.

Violet knew how to dress, how to listen, how to make a man feel wanted and admirable. "And while they are talking," she said, "underneath, I am thinking a hundred other thoughts, and putting all of history in order.

"I've planned my day before I ever get out of bed, from what I will wear to breakfast to what I will wear beside you at night. But I haven't the faintest idea what I will be doing tomorrow, or where I will be next week."

Violet's mother had never had any long-range objectives for her, nor had her father. They were not that sort of family. Her father, a minor but well-paid executive in a small company, busied himself at work. And though Violet loved to be with him, she claimed his commitment to the company and her mother's demands never gave him time to spend with her.

Similarly neglected, her mother threw herself into community activities. She led a drive for scrap iron for the Japanese one year, spearheaded war relief for the Chinese the next. (Never mind the one led to the need for the other.) Gathering the reins of their small town's leisure class, she played the queen, serving as president of one community organization, arbitrator of the next.

Like Mrs. Jellyby, that legendary practitioner of telescopic philanthropy, her own immediate family — father and daughter — were abandoned for long periods, until, like some expensive and forgotten dolls, they would be taken from storage, to be dressed and exhibited to others. Years later, Violet still complained to me that her mother treated her more as a show horse and hired companion than as a child.

But perhaps I may have misjudged Violet's mother; this same mixture of attributes, velvet and perfumed lotions on the outside, hardened steel beneath, was, in its time, exactly what the world expected of a plantation owner's wife: to remain eternally feminine while organizing and running a large household.

Her mother's prejudices spoiled my initial visits. Even when dressed in the suit I wore only for interviews, the final touches made by Violet's caressing hand, I was made to feel like an intruder, and the natural warmth with which she bathed her social equals, was kept firmly shut away.

She and Violet spoke in a code of their own, their conversation filled with oblique references to persons and events unknown to me. When I took Violet to task, she replied, bemused, "mother rambles so," as if Violet herself had been only a bystander, rather than an active participant in my discomfiture.

Violet's mother was always a threat to our relationship, but just before the marriage she appeared to change her mind about me. Out of the closet I came with my interview suit to be introduced to a steady procession of friends and business associates.

Perhaps she anticipated the great occasion the wedding would make. Or, perhaps, tired of waiting for Violet to commit herself to one of her many beaus, she made the decision to marry for her. ("I like you," she said to me once, several years after the divorce, when she was much older, and confined to bed much of the time, "always have liked you. You've got stuff.")

I was a Northerner, of course, from New York via Eastern Pennsylvania, but whatever her mother's private thoughts about having a "Yankee" in the family, she succeeded in concealing them in public. She made a point of introducing me as "Doctor" Mason, and of emphasizing my unblemished (sic) New England ancestry.

My ancestors were not from New England, of course, but Pennsylvania. Quakers, in their own quiet way they had once been as militant as Violet's Confederate forbearers. My father, a schoolteacher and an amateur cabinetmaker, taught at the high school I attended. The school was unusual for a public institution in that it prided itself upon having the same traditions as a Quaker school which had stood in the same location sixty years before, and which, as the rector was fond of reminding us at weekly assembly, had been modeled upon a 'Dissenters' school erected one hundred and twenty years before that. The rector took great pleasure in our traditions, like the coat and tie we were obliged to wear each day to the unending amusement of less-fortunate scholars (sic) who attended less-desirable schools nearby. But how could I be proud of a school where my father taught and the other students made fun of me because of it?

My father, a Latin teacher, taught history as well. Perhaps this was why I was not particularly impressed by the efforts of my own history teacher, a thoroughly conscientious man and close friend of my father who embellished his lectures with maps, models, and conjectured battle plans. My indifference was unfortunate, because, looking back, I can see this man was one of the rare exceptions, a teacher who saw the thousand ideas inherent in the material yet was sensitive enough to realize most lay beyond the grasp of the average student.

The discovery of some letters and a collection of birth records stored in our attic aroused my own interest in history as a field of study. I proceeded to fashion them into a family tree and, later, submitted my genealogy to my teacher as a term project. He was interested in my efforts as he was in all the projects his students brought to him, but he attempted to override a number of things I found (prematurely) important, disagreements in dates, discrepancies among correspondents, the details that are the life blood of history. My father, I imagine, must really have been much the same sort of man.

Violet and I were fortunate her mother's continued intervention in community affairs kept her too occupied to tamper with our relationship, though, from time to time, we were besieged with advice. Toward the end of our two-year engagement, Violet and I were still very much in love. Driving south on our honeymoon, depressed by a series of minor travel irritations, we stopped at Manassas and Bull Run, justifying our departure from her mother's planned itinerary by the area's historical interest. There, where Jackson had sat astride his horse, 'standing like a wall of stone,' we walked across the long lush grass of Manassas preserved like some great English manorial estate, a phoebe crying in the distance, the light hum of insects darting and feeding beneath the golden sun, and our hands reached instinctively for each other's once again.

Chapter 7 (Wood)

Wood was surprised to discover Parsons did not have a room, but an apartment, and in the married students' quarters at that. Children's toys and bicycles lay in the alleyway near Parsons' Quonset hut. A large child's ball sat next to the step, but Parsons merely booted the ball aside rather than picking it up.

Once inside, Parsons disappeared almost immediately, leaving Wood standing alone in the doorway wondering where to put his saddlebags. The large front room held an alcove for a kitchen on one side. At the far end stood bookshelves and a wooden study table with a box of cereal and a bowl on it. Close by the doorway, a thin, uncomfortable looking couch looked ready to repel all boarders.

Wood picked up the telephone and dialed Miriam's number. The phone rang several times. A pad by the phone, covered with doodles, revealed the name "Kelly" written over and over again.

A mature woman's voice answered, "Yes?"

"This is Peter Wood, may I speak to Miriam?"

"Peter Wood?" the voice questioned.

Wood heard the sound of an air-conditioner starting up in the next room. Parsons reappeared and clicked on a second air-conditioner over the couch. "Always get this going, the minute you get home," Parsons said, "otherwise the place begins to smell. Besides, electricity is included in the rent."

"Peter Wood? Do I know you?" the woman repeated.

Wood grinned evilly, "Yes."

After a definite pause, the woman's voice confided, "Miriam is not home."

"Can you tell me when she will return?"

"Anytime," the woman said. "Perhaps, you might try after nine-thirty, Peter." As she pronounced the name, "Peter" remained tentative, questioning.

"Thank you, I'll call back then."

He hung up. Parsons gave him a long quizzical look. "Got her mother eh. Miriam? Newcombe girl, big, Jewish." Parsons used his hands to show what part of the anatomy he meant by big.

Parsons disappeared a second time. When he reemerged, he was carrying a glass of milk for Wood and a second glass for himself. "I've got to go out," he said, "Just make yourself at home."

"Have you got a sleeping bag?" Wood asked.

"No need. You sleep on the couch.

"It folds out," Parsons added when he saw Wood's look of dismay. "I'll take the bedroom. In there." he gestured toward a door on the other side of the dining alcove. "I've got a big double bed. Large enough for three."

"Have you ever had two women at one time?" Wood asked.

"Not lately," Parsons replied. "I'm working on it."

"Wanta go looking for women tonight?"

"I've got my pots and pans to do first. I'm a Revere man," he continued in response to Wood's puzzled look, "I sell pots and pans to pay my alimony. I sell by appointment. The company sets it up. I just go in, cook them a meal, and sell them some pots."

"You selling any."

Parsons grunted.

"What about homework, stuff like that?" Wood persisted.

"I really wasn't getting anywhere on my thesis."

"Me neither," Wood said.

"Lots of single girls buy 'em, would you believe that? They don't have a husband; they buy pots and pans instead. Well, goodbye." Parsons stepped out the door, closed it, then turned back into the house. Wood hadn't moved. "If Kelly calls, you tell her I'm out, O.K.?"

Parsons gone, Wood prowled the apartment. The refrigerator was empty except for the milk, a head of lettuce, some dead carrots, and a small sack of coffee. A jar of candied figs at the back of the refrigerator opened easily and Wood ate one.

Most of the small bedroom was taken up by a big double bed, with a heap of laundry beside it on the floor. A light-colored area next to the far wall revealed where a bureau had once stood. The closet held a rack of dress shirts and dress pants, close duplicates of the ones Parson had been wearing. The pants were too long for Wood, the neckties in poor taste. A woman's nightgown lay on the floor, a hanger still inside it. Kelly's? Wood held it up before him. She was a very short girl whoever she was. Parsons' daughter? No, the embroidery showed the gown was a woman's.

Wood tried Miriam's number again. "No, I'm sorry, she hasn't come home yet. Shall I tell her you called?"

"Yes. No, I'll see her at school."

Dr. Mason was dressed in an ill-fitting suit that made him look like an athlete who has lost weight or whose muscles have atrophied. He sat alone at a corner table in the Napoleon House. Or is he with someone, Miriam wondered. I am alone, she thought, though she sat as part of a laughing foursome, two fraternity brothers and a sorority sister. Why had she joined the sorority? Or, more reasonably, why had the people who joined with her changed? Her new sisters, friends she had gone to school with since the second grade, were now such phonies. They ooed and awed over the prospect of a date and look who they went out with: Two Delta Zeebs, teeth straightened by the best orthodontist in New Orleans, muscles bulging from regular two-hour workouts in the gym, med-school bound, and the most boring, unintelligent, sophomoric, and, above all, undergraduate persons she had ever met.

She wondered what it would be like to sit at a corner table with Dr. Mason. Would they talk about politics and the role of America in world affairs? She was sure their conversation would bounce from subject to subject like that of guests on David Susskind. Perhaps, she and Dr. Mason would not talk at all as the two fraternity men insisted on doing. They just would sit together quietly and listen to the classical music coming from the hi-fi in the corner of the room. Sit and listen as Mason and his companion had been doing when Miriam first walked in. She was sure Dr. Mason had been sitting with someone else earlier, a girl with blond brown hair, short, but curvy and attractive.

The girl—where had she gone to, the rest room perhaps—had appeared to be much younger than Mason, perhaps only a year or two older than Miriam, herself, though her clothes, drab and tasteless, had been those of a much older woman. Miriam darted a quick admiring glance at her own dress, a plain dark blue skirt, and a silk shantung blouse wild with color. I'm really a tropical person she thought. I should have been born in South or Central America.

What if she were to go over now and sit with them? What would she and Mason talk about, she wondered, and how would he start the conversation?

Her own date was plucking at her sleeve trying to get her attention. Perhaps she ought to get up and go to the ladies room. Get Julie to come with her. On the way back, she would stop by Mason's table, let him lure her into conversation. They would sit together in the Napoleon House until the wee hours of the morning. Her date would have left hours before—she would have told the Delta Zeeb, oh, Professor Mason will drive me home. But what about Mason's date, she wondered?

The short, poorly dressed girl returned from the restroom. She walked slowly as if she were a bit drunk or were a much heavier person. Her sad glance, as melancholy as Mason's own, took in all of the room, Miriam and her table included, and broke into a broad smile only when it lit on Mason himself. He stood up as she returned to the table, held out a chair for her, and the two sat down together smiling. Miriam felt more alone than ever.

"Another brandy, Margaret?" her father asked.

"Why not Daddy," she replied, "The evening's young."

Chapter 8 (Barcus)

Barcus awoke as always, slowly and luxuriously. He gaped a long time at the water-stained ceiling which the bed's long Florentine posts turned into a canopy. The sounds of his mother moving in the next apartment woke him frequently. He stirred and the single coverlet slipped to the floor; the blind quivered for an instant. He itched and scratched in his sleep.

Someone knocked furiously on the front door. Barcus lay motionless until they went away. His dreams were pleasant and only turned vicious toward noon. Then, he sat up helplessly like an animal roused from estivation, slowly rotating his hips till his legs fell over the edge of the bed. He blinked. He counted his toes, rubbing them one against the other.

"George, are you up George? Do you want lunch?" A harsh woman's voice, commanding, pleading—his mother.

He did not answer.

He rocked forward off the bed and rose in an enormous yawn to which the whole room responded. For several moments he stood letting the sweat condense on his haunches. The moisture dripped in rivulets from his massive thighs. A single red bulb in the ceiling made his fat calves glow pleasantly and he rubbed them admiringly with a forefinger.

Where to go? What to do? He sat back heavily on the big double bed and the mattress began to absorb his sweat once again. He moved uneasily; the bed quivered and his gun thumped against the bedpost. (A shield on the holster testified he was or had been a deputy sheriff. For the State of Louisiana. Under the administration of Governor Earl K. Long.)

His acres of itching skin drove him finally to the shower where he would not have to listen to the noise of his mother vacuuming. When he returned, she had left for work and he spent a long time drying himself, wandering like a somnambulant, resigned to his heat soured thoughts, past the tiers of bookshelves lining the walls of the apartment. The toweling continued long after he was dry. He cleared a space with his bare foot among the piles of papers and half-open books before the mirror: "Nudist Diary," Margaret Mead, "Rise and Fall of The Third Reich," the Picayune, the Post-Dispatch, the Spectator. A scrap of paper on which was written "A clever man who imagines that fools will let themselves be taught by him, is not far from being a fool himself."

Barcus' irregular working hours were determined by his profession — politics. He did not run for office but threw his 'support' behind others. President of the New Southern Democratic Club, ward leader-fourteenth ward-for the Crescent City Regular Democrats, and one of the founders of the new Spanish-American Democratic Society, he occasionally spoke at meetings in one or the other of his official capacities, but most political professionals were aware the membership of the groups he controlled overlapped and consisted primarily of officers and friends.

Although the political support he offered was largely a fabrication, from time to time he was awarded small offices — deputy sheriff or appraiser, positions he lost in unfavorable political climates, regained with a change of views.

Barcus chortled softly to himself as he knotted a tie in front of the mirror, a wide mauve tie that clashed with his bright orange shirt; the colors emphasized his paunch but he enjoyed them; he savored the knowledge his cronies dressed that way naturally.

When the postman arrived, Barcus was sitting on the bed leafing through a gun manual. Without looking at his mail, he walked out of the house and across a series of backyards and alleys to the campus.

As he always did about noon every day, Barcus entered the campus cafeteria and held court for three or four hours. The best way to get his attention was to hold an interesting conversation within his hearing; a hesitant approach led to instant rejection; accepted protocol was the addition of an extra chair to his table and a quick diatribe before someone else interrupts. Barcus himself said little but would usually nod agreement or laugh if he had the opportunity.

When Zellner arrived, Barcus would have lunch with him. In Zellner's absence, Barcus ate alone and, over dessert, let Dr. Starr complain to him about the University administration. Barcus would talk with the faculty, with the staff, with anyone but the colored busgirls. He preferred talking with students, particularly with those who made him laugh or who had many friends. He was looking for a certain type of male student, quiet, shy, like Little Hamilton, who need advice on what to say or do, whose fingers are still sensitive and nimble. Barcus likes to have them over to his apartment alone in the evenings to see his collection of guns. Lennie likes him anyway.

The students drifted to and from Barcus' table and might visit him several times in the course of an afternoon. Each time someone went for coffee, Barcus would have them bring him another cup or a doughnut. From time to time he would leave to make a phone call or purchase a pencil, though the prolonged transaction with the mousy-haired wench in the bookstore offset the sweetness of sharpening it.

Parsons, a tall blond Mississippi boy with the stalking gait of a crane, was among the regulars at Barcus' table. Parsons peered at people and things over his beak-like nose, hypnotizing them into immobility until he passed on disdainfully. He assumed Barcus was always tuned to his wavelength, began talking a little before he sat down and picked up again each time he passed the table. Parsons was good for Barcus. The laughter comes bursting up from Barcus's belly and his fat hams moan on the seat as he listens.

"Pete Wood is a madman. Pete Wood is an anarchist. Pete Wood is an imposter. He's brash and bold and from the North. He knew me for five minutes when he moved in. And do you know what he said? He said 'Do you have space in your pad, man?' Like that, 'Do you have space in your pad, man?'"

"Who's this?" said someone, marveling at the words 'pad' and 'man' as Parsons drawled them.

"His roommate."

"I thought Parsons was married?"

"He walked into our office in motorcycle boots and a black leather jacket and asked to see the boss. While he was waiting he moved in on me and then tried to get a date with the secretary.

"When he spoke to the boss he told him he was the world's greatest living expert. Expert! He didn't have a cent in his pockets! After five minutes he had a job, after ten he'd gotten a project. Armadillos! Armadillos. Grometz walked out of the conference and had Mary the secretary order fifteen of them. They tore down an entire wall of mouse cages to make room.

"He gets on your nerves. He's bossy. Never stops talking. Keeps wanting me to buy food. When Alice slashed her wrists, he laughed and laughed because she did such a lousy job.

"Some cycle he has. It breaks down every two blocks. He's got 'Jesus saves' painted on the front fender."

"What about the armadillos?" someone interrupted.

"Hey want to hear a joke?"

"He moved right in to my apartment and keeps telling me he'll get a job. His cycle has been parked in front of my house since he got here and he hasn't been able to start it.

"Walt and his wife had a party last week out by the airport and after Wood got us both covered with grease we still had to take a bus.

"He pisses me off. Always ordering me around. Wants me to hold his damn tools. Do you know he sold all of Kelly's science fiction books; says he spent all the money on flowers."

"Why does it take three Aggies to eat an armadillo?" the joker persisted, but Parsons could not be stopped.

"Kicks me out of the house because he wants to bring home a woman. Jesus!

"You know we've got to get a car. Can anybody lend me a car?"

"Kicked you out of your apartment?" someone said.

"Two to . . ."

"I sleep down in my office anyway because of my asthma. It's air-conditioned. What I object to is his stealing my shirts and insulting my friends.

"I've known Alice a lot longer than he has. She's afraid if we get married she'll be excommunicated. I only let Wood stay at my pad in the first place to fool the private detective."

"Pad?" someone ventured as the least dangerous course.

"Damn him. We've got to get that cycle fixed; I know he's going to want me to pay for it. I'm afraid Dixie's going to stop feeding him. When he finishes cleaning the place, if Marge comes back, I'm going to move."

Parsons walked out abruptly, leaving the others gaping. He stopped between two bushes in the window facing them and for a moment looked as if he were about to spear a frog that had hopped out on the wet pavement; then he disappeared disdainfully in the dense shrubbery.

A new arrival asked what was happening. The tears were running down Barcus's cheeks and he continued to chortle spasmodically. "Nothing, you little tit," Barcus cooed and patted him on the head.

"Tell us about graft and corruption, Barcus," said the new arrivals. But he was feeling good enough to bear the addled chatter of the girl with the deliberately large breasts who sold pencils and left to get some.

Chapter 9 (Miriam)

Alice's car raced along the Jeff Davis Parkway, impatient with being confined between line and sidewalk. It rose to the dividing strip, curved down with a bump on the pavement, but not before its wheels had left their imprint on the grass.

Bumpty-bump went the Chevrolet as the driver seesawed on the gas pedal, turned right from the left lane onto Canal. Bumpty-bump.

"A girl is sitting in the car with you," Miriam thought, "be nice to her."

Wood remembered the bemused expression on the examiner's face the day he'd appeared for the driving test on Harold, a motor scooter, the predecessor of his cycle. He'd been ordered to follow a car also taking the test and had done so steering with his knees, making signals with both hands. He'd passed.

Wood turned the steering wheel gleefully; the car responded, leaping first to the right, then to the left of the road. Occasionally, Wood lost his grip on the wheel when the car hit a bump or slid along a trolley track. Wood's confidence never flagged.

His vision obscured by a dusty windshield, he poked his head out the side window: "It's the view," he said, releasing the wheel to point at the restricting window frame. "Motorcycle has four sides."

"Watch the road," Miriam whispered to herself. Frightened and polite she did not speak while Wood was looking everywhere and at everything it seemed. "The light!" she screamed to herself.

"You ran a red light," the patrolman said.

Wood looked up, surprised, from the road map between his knees at the sour-faced officer. "Where do you get your cycle repaired?" Wood asked.

"Doc's. Most of the boys take em to Doc's. You, eh, got one?"

"Yeah."

"Whaat kine?"

"Jawa."

"Ja-va, huh. Must be one of those Jap bikes."

"Thanks," Wood said. "Doc's huh," he shouted as he drove off.

The auto whipped into a side street, down black pathways, its lights slightly out of focus. Miriam was thrown against the door and then bounced up and down in her seat as the car met the cobbles and ruts of the rain-scutted street. The steering wheel spun carelessly, the car jumping from side to side; it turned furiously in a maze of corners, backing and whining where the roads ended in flats or rubble.

"Where are we going?" Miriam asked pleasantly. She tried to follow his pointing finger on the map and at the same time keep track of street signs. "Where are we going?" she asked confused.

The car was not approaching its goal, but had gone past it, for it doubled back-or circled it-for it suddenly shot left again. The map showed the river bordering the town on three sides and to the north Lake Pontchatrain. Wood's finger traced a canal to the point where it turned into a bayou adjoining the City Park. But she still did not understand.

He was looking for Basin Street. He was looking for water, for a tree that grew by the water in which to carve their initials. (Never mind the Basin was where the colored whores used to wash their clothes.)

He stopped the car behind a stand of trees. "The canal should be there," he said, pointing through the windshield.

"You want to go to the canal? It's just some sort of a big ditch. The lake is nicer," she suggested.

"All these streets seem to change direction before the canal," he continued, ignoring her. "Where does this street go? Basin Street? It even changes its name."

"Do you really want to go to the canal?"

It was just some sort of big ditch. A long, unilluminated concrete ditch. The water naked but invisible. A few concrete blocks loomed along the rubble, gravel mounds and flattened tin cans where other cars and trucks had been. (His eyes laced the cracked patterns of clay.) Strange and so unlike the other boys she dated who parked by the river or the lake. (He was looking at nothing, flattened tin cans glistening in the car's headlamps.) She remembered sitting in another car parked by the river: Hands groped beneath her sweater while two barges passed very slowly in the middle of the flow; several moments later the delayed pup-pup of the boats' passage reached the shore. "What does he remember?" she wondered, for Wood was not disappointed but absorbed and relaxed after that crazy unnecessary chase.

"I want to get out and put my hands in the water."

A few pignuts bounced off the roof of the car.

She knew that he would kiss her. Soon. "Tell me something about yourself," she said.

He thought for a moment.

56

She wondered, does he have a father, a mother, a younger sister like me? "Tell me about your family," she said.

"I have a father, a mother, a younger brother. They don't live together. My father's got his own place, an apartment. I used to go back and forth between the two of them. When I was in high school, I'd go to my father's apartment after school to study. We had a fight. I haven't seen him in a while."

"How old were you?" she prompted when he did not continue on his own.

"Sixteen," he said, "I'm waiting for him to call." He paused as if waiting for sympathy.

"You know the saddest story I ever heard?," she said. "A sorority sister of mine found out she was adopted. She kept asking her mother over and over who her parents were. 'I'm your mother,' her mother said, 'That's all you need to know.' Finally, her mother told her the truth. Her mother had been pregnant when she got married. Her stepfather, that is her mother's husband, had married her mother even though she was pregnant with someone else's child. Her sisters were really her half sisters.

"Her real father, her natural father lived in Dallas. She found that out. She took the train to Dallas, she phoned him from the station.

"'I don't have any money,' was the first thing he said to her.

"She started to cry, 'I don't want your money. I just want to see you.' And then she told him she was at the train station.

"'Send me a postcard the next time you're in town,' he said.

"She took the train back to New Orleans and she cried and cried the entire way."

They sat in silence. He did not tell her any more about himself although she'd hoped he would. He slipped an arm around her shoulder. But nothing happened. The arm fell away and he restarted the car with the abruptness with which he seemed to make all his decisions. As they drove off, however, she could sense that he was still debating, fighting something out in his mind.

"Peter?"

No answer.

A three-block stretch of Carrollton Boulevard, lined on one side by trees, gave way to a business section; he slowed the automobile, drove in a loop around the median and stopped before a lone bar on the corner.

"You've been here before?" she asked.

The only lights in the Stardust Lounge were over the bar. Darkened tables in the back room sat near a silent jukebox. A slot machine and the bar, itself, were separated from the tables by a wooden partition.

They danced in the blue phosphorescent glow of the jukebox and sat in the darkness. The bartender waited on the tables, came silently and left without payment. Pete traced her lips with his tongue, let his hands fall on her shoulder. He pressed his body against hers; she wondered why he hadn't touched her breasts.

Later, he touched her breasts and kissed her again. They remained in the lounge long past the time the car was due to be returned. Then they left abruptly. Without paying. She sat alone for a moment after he left the table not realizing he expected her to follow. She waited and when he returned for her, she reached up for his arm without a trace of embarrassment.

Outside the bar, they circled each other warily. Two-thirty, hours past her weekday deadline and Miriam was sure one of her parents would be sitting up in bed waiting for her, ears cocked to hear her footsteps. When he started to speak, she cut him off with a finger to his lips. She kissed him, reaching up on her toes to kiss him full in the mouth, both of them visible in the light from the bar to anyone driving by. After he drove her home, she kissed him again and slipped out of the car, not expecting him to follow. She guessed wherever he spent the night, whether in the front seat of his car or in that crazy apartment he'd described to her, he'd be O.K.

Chapter 10 (New Orleans, May 1961)

At the corner of Canal Street sits a tobacco shop and next to it a record store with a loudspeaker blaring Dixieland into the crowds. Pictures of all the famous jazz musicians are in its window. Next to the music store is a fruit store where a man and his son sell fruit. Squnched in a corner, an old colored woman with a gray bandana sells pralines and peanuts in little cones of newspaper.

Wood followed Lennie through the noon-hour crowds, stumbling on the inner edges of his borrowed shoes. They had an appointment with Zambroski. Although their appointment was for two, they had been wandering aimlessly shuffling in the heat since before noon. They had walked along Bourbon Street, faded and unresponsive in the sunlight, and along Carondelet among the tall buildings. They had walked several blocks on both sides of Canal Street looking in the windows. Canal was a broad street and it was not possible to see what was happening on the other side without crossing over.

Sometimes Wood would grow impatient and would dart on ahead or stop in the middle of traffic to think. Once he lost Lennie completely. Wood had stopped to watch two girls. One was a skinny blonde and both were of high school age.

The blonde said "Yeah?," her friend said "Yeah."

"Yeah!"

"Yeah."

And the story was complete.

Wood smiled at them and at each of the passersby. (Later in the afternoon they would be seeing Zambroski.) None of the secretaries on their lunch hour smiled at him. One fat old white lady walked around him staring him full in the face and not smiling at all. Lennie's arm would always reappear to guide him through the crowds.

Lennie said that Zambroski was a great man whom he very much admired. Sitting with negroes at lunch counters and handing out pamphlets, was easy compared with what Zambroski had done. Zambroski had even been shot at. Twice bombs had been thrown into his office.

Standing on the sidewalk before them in the shadow of the bank building were three older Negro men. One was a tall man with a moon like face and a clean collar. All three were handsomely dressed. The tall Negro was introducing his friend to the third, a stout individual who bobbed back and forth on his heels when he shook hands and said, "How do ya do, how do ya do," without looking into the other men's faces.

When the stout man, Dr. Cleanneth, saw Lennie, he walked over and shook his hand too. He shook Pete's hand, clasping it in both of his, but he looked off to the side so that Pete could not catch his eye.

Lennie had a number of things he wanted to ask this man and he began to talk quickly, stammering, as if afraid Dr. Cleanneth, would disappear. Dr. Cleanneth continued to clasp Wood's hand while Lennie spoke to him. He did not reply directly to what Lennie was saying but shook his head sympathetically. A little web of spit had accumulated at the corner of his lips so that his words were accompanied by a fine spray, like a man's breath in winter. Yes, he was interested. Yes, something was being done. A glorious future lay before them. He himself would be taking charge, personally. And at that time, all Lennie's help and suggestions would be appreciated. He always appreciated the help of Northern liberals.

"I was born in Georgia." Lennie replied, offended.

Dr. Cleanneth nodded and then asked Pete where he was from.

He's asking me, Pete realized with a start. "I'm from California and before that . . . ."

"Wonderful place, California." Dr. Cleanneth effused, "I think it's of tremendous importance that people like ourselves from the North, and from the South, and from the West should be getting together to discuss these problems." He released Wood's hand with a final firm clasp, gripped Lennie's in turn and bobbed a final good-bye, still looking off somewhere in the distance.

"He's not doing..." Lennie stammered after the retreating figure, "Oh, he'll not do it. Not much he will." He turned to Pete: "I've got to see him!"

"Zambroski?"

"Let's go to the hotel."

"To eat?"

"After we see Moody. Then we'll eat. Then we'll go..."

"To Zambroski's office."

The hotel unfolded in all its rich volumes above a long carpeted stairway whose base lay at the egress of the revolving doors. The foyer was divided by pillars that reduced its length and, at the same time, led the eye up to the vaulted ceiling and its glass chandeliers suspended by gold cords. Wood walked softly on the deep-piled carpet. The others in the lobby continued to move impassively around them toward the main floor coffee shop and the businessman's lunch.

The bank of elevators was recessed in a dark wood-paneled alcove. Leonard let one elevator fill and pass upwards. When the next arrived, he stepped aboard, Wood following. The operator stepped out as they entered and looked carefully about the lobby before reboarding his elevator.

"A man's trying to catch..." Wood began before the porter brought the handle down and the thick wooden doors closed on the lobby. They rode upward in silence.

On the tenth floor, the top floor, they stopped.

"What did the man have to say?" the deep baritone voice of the elevator operator broke the silence.

Zellner cleared his throat. "I just talked to Cleanneth."

"What did the good Reverend want?" The voice was bitter.

"For us to get more guys together and wait till the opportune moment came, and then, why we'd all get together. He said he was already working on it."

"And that's the plan?" The elevator operator turned around and uncorking to his full height, towered an inch or two, black, above them. "That's the plan? Shit, that's no plan at all. That's sit and wait."

"We're not going to wait. We're going to move. Tonight we're going to move. Who's chairman?"

"I am." Lennie said.

"We're going to ask for volunteers. Tonight. Tomorrow we'll be down on Canal Street. Tomorrow. Not next year. Not when Dr. Cleanneth's ready. That old fool of a Tom."

The buzzer sounded in the elevator. Lennie jumped, startled. "I didn't like him either." Wood interjected.

"I'm going to see Zambroski this afternoon." Lennie said.

"Wha fo?" The operator's entire body radiated menace.

"He's been working in the movement a long time. He might have some ideas."

"Some ideas! I'll bet he has! I'll bet he'll be just full up with i-de-as." The buzzer sounded again, Lennie nervous, the operator indifferent. "You ask him for a contribution." Moody continued, " O.K. A con-tri-bu-tion." The elevator plummeted suddenly. When its doors opened, two fat tourist ladies, several businessmen and a waiter squeezed on board. Disgust was written all over the operator's face. Without a further word to Lennie or a backward glance into the elevator, he stalked away.

Lennie and Wood followed sheepishly after. They ate lunch hurriedly. Only an hour remained before their appointment with Zambroski.

At ten past two, they left the hotel and paced briskly through the Quarters. Three blocks along Royal, three blocks along Carondelet. After an interval, they turned right. They walked up a block, doubled back, and turned left again. A half-block from where they had been originally, they entered an old brick building. Inside, a creaky freight elevator carried them up two flights and, with the suspicious eye of the elevator operator upon them, they ascended the third flight on foot.

The wooden landing on the third floor is worn as smooth as the floor of a confessional. The J.C. Tick Corporation has offices there. Whoever owns the company now, and it may still be D. R. Murphy, its most frequent visitor is the postman. The same may be said of the office of Nathan Zambroski, the executive secretary of the SRLC next door. The remaining office has no sign on it and is, it fact, just a little cupboard where the elevator man may have a smoke. Still, the evidence of twenty years' wear is on its scarred flooring.

. . . Zambroski crossed his hands, interlaced the slender liver-spotted fingers, and extended them upwards and outwards. In the last twenty years, he told them, his organization had dispensed over twenty thousand dollars in scholarships to worthy Negro children. And while this may not have sounded like much compared with, say, the efforts of the State of Mississippi during the same period (Wood moved his chair restlessly....

They waited in the outer office while Zambroski's secretary went on with her seemingly endless typing. Every few minutes she would jerk the paper free, crumple it and toss it in the basket and replace it with a fresh sheet. The girl was dark and pockmarked and really not very attractive. Her hair was drawn up in a bun from which a few loose tufts had broken free. On the desk beside her was a carton of milk and on the very edge of the desk a piece of wax paper unfolded in a tray held four lady fingers.

The summons came from the inner office. Behind a broad paper-strewn desk sat a distinguished looking haired-haired gentleman. With his salt and pepper hair and brief moustache, he reminded Wood of an uncle who had been a major in the Royal Canadian Air Force. Wood's uncle used to swing him through the air, pulling him between his legs without a tumble. When Zambroski rose to greet them, Wood saw he was crippled and wore a brace.

Zambroski's arm remained extended above the desk, pointed toward Wood until Lennie brought their hands up to meet each other. "This is Peter Wood; this is Nathan Zambroski."

"I am very pleased to meet you." Wood did not seem pleased at all; nor did Zambroski. His Uncle Michael had not liked children as a rule, not even his own.

"May we have your address," Zambroski asked, "so that we can send you our bulletin?"

"Pete. Give him your address." Lennie said, cracking his knuckles nervously.

Wood gave him Parsons' address.

"You're not from the South, though?"

Wood gave his head a little shake.

"But you're interested in our work?"

"At any rate, please let us know if you change your address. Then we can be sure to update our mailing list."

. . . In the beginning there had been many difficulties, much resistance, but now people were beginning to work together . .

A series of newspaper clippings were spread across Zambroski's desk; Wood rose and looked over Lennie's shoulder. Lennie stepped back so his friend could see them properly. After awhile, Zambroski took the clippings away from Wood and handed them back to Zellner.

"Read what they did in Baton Rouge."

"It's horrible."

"He'd only been with us three months."

"I thought George Patterson was with the SCLC."

"I meant he was part of the movement," Zambroski replied indulgently. "We identify with all groups here and, in fact, function as a sort of central clearance agency."

"Oh," Wood said aloud, for Lennie appeared very much impressed.

"We have been doing so for many years, despite interference from the outside." The resulting silence while Zambroski waited for Lennie to examine the other clippings seemed to preclude further comment and Wood, the outside influence, used the opportunity to slip away to the outer office. Lennie seemed impressed with everything Zambroski was showing him.

The secretary had added to her stack of letters, but three ladyfingers still lay on the front edge of the desk. Wood looked at the remaining ladyfingers. The girl looked at Wood in return until she was summoned from the inner office. When the girl got back, Wood was standing very close to the tray.

A collection of brochures had replaced the clippings on Zambroski's desk. The various activities in which Zambroski's organization had or intended to engage were depicted in green lettering. Despite the evident discomfort standing caused him, Zambroski's voice rose to a youthful pitch while he described his work ...

Wood stirred uneasily in his chair until Zambroski became annoyed. "Are you uncomfortable?"

Wood did not hasten to reply.

"I didn't get this brace through having a bomb thrown at me. (Lennie blushed scarlet.)

"I had polio. But bombs have been thrown at me. Here. In this office.

"I'm sorry this couldn't have happened while you were here." Zambroski halted, embarrassed for he had not meant to be sarcastic. Blame not the ignorant, he thought, when so many knowledgeable men preach hatred and intolerance. Nor hate the man who threw the bomb, but work to discredit the politician who made the speech, the editor who printed Zambroski's picture alongside his name and address in the paper.

"Integrationist," "Nigger-lover." Labels for those with whom we disagree, all-too-convenient excuses for hating other men.

Wood waited outside the door. In the inner office, Lennie waited for Zambroski to tell him what to do. And Zambroski waited for Zellner and all the others of his generation to do . . . what needed to be done.

Chapter 11. How Wood met Maggie:

While Dave Parsons went looking for an apartment, if that was his aim, Buddy Jefferson and Lennie Zellner visited a friend in jail. Their friend, Dick Diamond, a surly broad-shouldered Negro, had a talent for following in an obstinate and disruptive fashion. During a confrontation between the Governor of a Southern state and the President of a Southern Negro university in which the latter appeared to forget many of his own earlier lectures on the dignity of man, his obstinacy raised Diamond to the status of student leader. His indefinite incarceration on charges of criminal mischief followed in lieu of seven thousand dollars bail.

Diamond's enforced absence was actually a relief to the real leadership of SCNVA (Student Core for Non-Violent Action) as Diamond tended to be disruptive at meetings, his presence characterized by wild laughter, threats, and growling affirmations of motions proposed by his friend Buddy Jefferson. If Buddy's proposals were not well received, (Buddy had a certain flair for unnecessary spectacle), Diamond would attempt to bully and intimidate the other members or would suddenly turn on Buddy with savage accusations of his own.

Diamond had never fully grasped the principles of non-violence. During the training camps or workshops at which the group would attempt to simulate the conditions they would be exposed to at lunch counters and in jail, he would suddenly lash out with his fists at his tormentors; when it came his turn to play the role of a policeman, he would pound away with real gusto until his victims collapsed.

A year later, through the intervention of Dr. Starr, Diamond would be fortunate enough to receive a scholarship to a Northern university. He would last only a semester. His failure would not be attributed to his ignorance nor his lack of application, though these were important factors, but to his personality. His backers at the Northern university found him unsmiling, ungracious, unable to Twist, and devoid of rhythm. He possessed none of the attributes expected of his friendly race and tended to shoplift and sneak into movie theatres.

In jail, as later, Diamond was unable to grasp the nature of his role as leader of the movement, though he took a certain pride in the amount of his bail. He was sullen toward jailors and visitors alike, except to his mother, whose visits were of necessity limited.

Buddy Jefferson, a true leader of the Student Core for Non-Violent Action, though his diction and bearing caused him to be overlooked by Northern liberals dispensing scholarships, was all too aware of his friend's limitations, their possible consequences, and the extent of his own responsibility.

Leonard Zellner, white field secretary for SCNVA, its only white member, some say its only saint, was not aware of Dick's flaws and knowing would not have understood. The son of missionary parents, Lennie had been educated in the South and joined the movement immediately upon graduation from a small Baptist college. He had spent only twenty-four days in the succeeding six months out of court and out of jail.

The prison guards despised negroes and had an unyielding hate of integrationists (and of communists and labor organizers with whom integrationists were often confused). They had a primeval loathing for white and black that traveled together, claiming to be friends. Jefferson and Zellner were received at the jail in a silence that yielded only the reluctant information "No visiting today.

"No, no visiting prisoners tomorrow. Maybe Sunday."

Less tolerant men would have perceived this lack of enthusiasm and graciousness on the jailers' part. Not Buddy Jefferson, not Leonard Zellner. They asked if they could bring their friend food and magazines and took the blank stares of hate to signify acceptance. When they returned with half a dozen peaches and a copy of Newsweek they were arrested and charged with criminal anarchy and their friend's bail raised to twelve thousand dollars.

No immediate public outcry resulted. Diamond, it is true, blackened Buddy's eye when he learned his bail had been raised, but outside the prison the public were not and would not have been interested in the fate of two negroes and a white companion. If, that is, they had learned about them. The chance incarceration of three integrationists was not news, as any Southern editor would and did reason-not exciting and, certainly, not important.

Consider a newspaper's readers, the demanding public for whom the editors choose and shape their columns: Dave Parsons, a Mississippi boy, high-spirited, generous to a fault he admitted, cursing Wood. Less reasoned but more reasonable, Miriam's father, who observed the Passover, treated his colored help fairly, and paid them only what convention and the law demanded. Or Professor Mason, who hearing of the incident through certain informal channels, filed the information away until it should finally have achieved its true historical synthesis.

The news aroused and amused Barcus. It happened he was down at the police station at the time of the arrests, paroling a drunk and disorderly relative. He found the story of Leonard and Leonard's friends downright hilarious. But then Barcus loved to witness the exercise of raw power and is an exception.

Barcus wanted to retell the story and share the laughter with someone, anyone, immediately. The desk sergeant appreciated the tale—"Serves them niggers right," he said—but failed to discern its underlying mythic quality. Lieutenant Arnold, a man of some education, only compounded the comedy by remarking, "I believe, when we caught those two, we got the brains of the mob." It literally hurt Barcus to contain his laughter.

Barcus had to take a slow trolley home. He cursed the negroes sitting behind him because they would not have understood the hilarity of Leonard's plight nor would, in any case, have been willing to reason through a white man's telling of the story. Barcus contented himself with passing out leaflets that described his political organization and promised "Equal representation for all, the right of all men to work, improved welfare, and free education."

Uptown, Dave Parsons was out looking for an apartment, if that was his aim. Pete Wood was sprawled naked on the couch in Parson's old apartment, two big fans blowing across his back. Pete woke up intermittently, smelled the stench of roaches from the kitchen, watched a large brown roach almost three inches in length demolish a bread crumb, and slept again. The couch had a pronounced ridge running across its center. Alternatively, the bed Parsons slept in when he was home sagged in the middle and you had to be careful of a jutting spring. Neither option was attractive.

Barcus called on Parsons not really expecting to find him and found in his place another crude youngster of Parsons' generation. Barcus told the story of the three integrationists anyway, told it with his usual hearty chuckle for graft and corruption. The existence of raw power aroused his latent feelings. ("Barcus loves his mother," Parsons said once and Wood was not sure what this meant.)

Afterwards, Barcus dragged Pete to the student center for a cup of coffee and a chance to retell his anecdote in a loud voice. Pete looked at a pretty face, short curly hair. No one stopped to interrupt Barcus or ask a question. Pete saw she was talking to another pretty face with long black hair. The second girl was skinny. The first was full breasted, but short in the legs. Barcus, enraged at the lack of audience, left Pete staring.

Pete watched until the girls finished and stepped away from the table. The brown-haired girl's silhouette remained on his retina; he wanted her very badly. When he looked up, she'd returned with a second cup of coffee and was sitting alone.

He wanted to talk to her but could not think what to say or how to begin. "I am not like other people here. I am not like other people you have talked to. I am like and not like other boys you have known."

Where could he take her? Where could he invite her? She was so beautiful. What could he say to her that others had not already said?

He rose and walked unsteadily to the door of the Student Center. The damp heat gripped him as he crossed the threshold. He was already depressed; the date with Miriam, the visit to Zambrowski had led nowhere. "Even if I fail, will it matter?" he said digging his palm with his nails. "Even if she laughs... will it matter what anyone here thinks?"

He returned to the air-conditioned room. Maggie looked up abstractly, licking the crumbs from her fingertips. Wood walked over and sat down abruptly at her table. He said to her, "Why do you have a pencil behind your ear instead of a carrot?"

Chapter 12. (Barcus)

On the wall of Barcus' room is a quotation from The Awakening of the Fountain that a friend had sent him:
Kiep sau, ngyuen lan than ngua ma tra nghia sau;
and below it penciled in English is the translation:
At your next rebirth
I hope to be a water buffalo or a horse
To be of better service to you.

Lennie would stand for a long time before the placard, moving his lips as he read it over to himself. Barcus had no patience with him. He would thrust out his big belly and gradually bump Lennie along the narrow corridor between the wall and the bed, or wave a clipping before Lennie's face in an effort to distract him. Barcus, himself, would chortle spasmodically each time he spied the placard, but he was afraid Lennie would want to discuss the quotation or copy it down to discuss at one of his meetings.

Each day about noon, Barcus would leave his apartment and walk across a series of backyards and alleyways to the campus. There, he would meet Lennie in the Student Center and have lunch, seldom alone, often with newspaper men who had come to interview Lennie, or with some of Lennie's co-conspirators. When they had no guests, he would permit professors or students who enjoyed hearing him talk to sit at the table and eat with them.

After lunch they would play bridge, choosing partners from among the idlers, chiefly students. Barcus and Zellner would sit at adjacent seats, for Zellner despite constant practice was a poor player. Their game usually attracted a large number of kibitzers and whenever one of the players left he was quickly replaced. Often among the kibitzers, though he would refrain from joining the play, was Little Hamilton.

George Edmond Hamilton came from Madison, Wisconsin where his father, Robert Edmond Hamilton, owned a restaurant. He was five feet, four. Timid, reserved, he had the open blank-faced expression of someone used to being told to stay out of the kitchen, practice the piano, and get out of the way. He never said anything about himself, but would talk about his older brother Bob who had played football for Wisconsin before going to Law School. "He used to lift me over his head nine times each morning when he couldn't find his weights."

Little Hamilton, himself, was muscular and well built for his height, although he did not show off his strength. His slim hips, the Prectalorian arch to his spine, the long look of black hair that fell lovingly over his uncombed forehead attracted and bewitched Barcus. In his mind, Barcus had already determined a life, a direction for the beautifully unformed and eager Little Hamilton. And because Little Hamilton's activities, like those of so many of his generation, seemed so spastic, so without purpose, Barcus was in a constant state of near explosion.

Hamilton spent most of the day in the student center with a group of boys from his dormitory playing hearts or "The Game" or simply playing pranks — salt in the sugar bowl, scribbling on the walls, calling "fink" across the room to some tardy member of their party. "Why do you go around with those idiots?" Barcus would scream.

"Oh, I don't know, to have fun, I guess."

"What did you do last night?"

"Got drunk."

"And that's fun?"

Actually it hadn't been fun. Little Hamilton's stomach felt bad the next day and he had thrown up in his sleep. But Hamilton supposed the same was true for all the other fellows who'd got drunk with him. He started to listen more to Barcus' advice and, at the same time, Barcus endeavored to make himself more endearing to Little Hamilton.

They had seen an astronomical number of movies together. That is, as long as the whole gang went, Little Hamilton would go too, and sit next to Barcus and laugh at the picture or the comments from the audience. But he would not go to the movies with Barcus alone.

In vain would Barcus threaten, bluster, invent, embellish, depict, decry, declaim.

"I agree with you, but no I don't want to," Little Hamilton would say. "I'm just chicken," he'd agree. He would agree all the time but he would not cooperate. Barcus was compassionate, Barcus forgave. "Think for yourself," Barcus would say. But Hamilton was content to ride with the group. "If the group does it, O.K."

"I'm not about to hold an orgy." Barcus would reply gruffly.

It is a shame Barcus was never able to feel the same compassion for Parson's problems with women. Perhaps because Barcus felt women were of a lower order. In truth, Parson's problems were of a lower order: Girls who didn't bother to take precautions.

"Why don't you take precautions, then?" Lennie would holler at him.

"What good would that do?" Parsons would reply. Or Parsons would have two girls lined up for the same night. "Alice won't lend me her car," he'd complain, "How can I get from Mary's to Barbara's house in time?" A problem in logistics with which Barcus felt no sympathy whatever.

Once Barcus had ventured to ask Parsons, "Do you have any trouble, getting the girl to go out with you. I mean the first time." To which Parsons had answered, "Hell, no! These broads'll go out with anything in pants." This answer confirmed Barcus' suspicions but did not aid him in his quest.

An affinity exited between him and Little Hamilton, Barcus was sure of it. Hamilton had a fertile mind and a supple body. He appreciated what Barcus had to show him. And yet, when Barcus would invite him over to see the latest additions to Barcus' collection of African relics, Hamilton would ask, "Is there going to be a party?"

The day after Lennie's latest escapade — excessive visitation or criminal anarchy depending on one's point of view, he was again released on bail and shortly after noon, but a little later than usual, he joined Barcus in the student cafeteria. His black colleagues, Buddy Jefferson and Dick Diamond, were not released at that time.

SCNVA (Student Core for NonViolent Action) had intervened on Leonard's behalf. They provided an attorney and arranged to post Lennie's bond. The colored members of the movement, as always, were left to depend on their own resources and those of their families. Lennie's constant evasion of punitive bail had a marked positive effect on morale. But less abstract motives dictated his quick release.

Louisiana prisons are segregated. At the start of their detention, Leonard would be separated from his black comrades and placed among the other white prisoners. But vagrants, drunks, and purse-snatchers are no less Southerners for having been imprisoned. They are capable of feeling and expressing righteous indignation. (They may even be encouraged in this respect by civilian authorities.) Unless bail were posted immediately, Leonard was safe only in solitary confinement. Perhaps not even then.

"They left the cell door open all night," Leonard remarked once. Barcus quavered and turned ashen. The same day, Barcus went to see

Sergeant Gremlin who owed his position to him. "Why was the door left open?" Barcus demanded.

"I've done too much for your friend already," Gremlin replied.

Following each of Leonard's far from inevitable releases, he returned immediately to joking, bridge playing, and cutting classes. Barcus could not hope to teach Lennie where experience had failed; Barcus merely did his best each time Lennie was on the outside to show him how enjoyable life — a meal in the cafeteria or an afternoon spent playing bridge — could be.

That afternoon, their opponents at the bridge table were two of the most inept swindlers Barcus had ever encountered. Their careless and unavailing chicanery was in marked contrast to the form of advanced gamesmanship at which Barcus himself excelled. Alas, few alternatives existed. Better the devil we know. And he took Lennie as his partner for much the same reason.

His fears were confirmed immediately. A finesse that was guaranteed success met a blank in their opponent's hand (?) and a trump in place of the missing king. The return was the king of spades, which won, and the king was followed by a lead in the suit which had been void a moment before! Barcus was enraged. (Lennie, too, showed poor taste in turning over the previous tricks and frowning.) Neither the spirit of the renege nor the slim possibility of its succeeding had aroused Barcus' ire, but the colossal stupidity of such a risky (and highly illicit) maneuver without a covering delay of at least six to seven tricks!

Barcus found himself reaching across the table and pounding his opponents' fingers each time they dealt out of turn. He roared to cover his opponents' cross talk. Still, their winks, gestures and moans went on unaffected. Desperate, Barcus called out to Little Hamilton and asked him to play in Leonard's place. Little Hamilton refused-he was a spectator at a game of hearts across the way-but Barcus found himself calmed for a few moments simply by his presence. Now, looking up for consolation, Barcus saw Hamilton had left to join a pack of young idiots tormenting a busgirl. Barcus' fury redoubled almost to the bursting point, but a hand remained to complete the rubber.

In the play that followed, he could only marvel at a fate that made him participant rather than spectator. Leonard failed to bid game in his hand while their opponents established a pre-emptive three. Then, without a card being played, opponent number one who was named Parsons turned to opponent number two who was named Brownlee and asked him why he had not raised the bid from three to four seeing he had a rebiddable suit. Barcus rose as abruptly as his bulk would permit and, signaling for Lennie to follow, stalked across the cafeteria after Little Hamilton.

"Not bad," said Parsons to Brownlee who had been keeping score because he was a statistician, "but I think you added a few points here and there."

"We needed them. Look at the way you underbid the last contract."

"Oh, I don't know about that. You had a seven card suit; why didn't you bid your spades a second time?"

"Say Parsons!" called a stranger, threading his way toward them through the maze of tables; the stranger let his hand drop idly on the shoulder of a seated girl as he passed; the girl looked up indignantly above her Peter-Pan collar and blushed. "Say Parsons, do you have the key?" The stranger, Parson's roommate, wore a black leather jacket, unlaced ski boots, a rumpled shirt, and a pair of food-spattered dress pants. His conversation belied his appearance for he seemed to hale from the same rarefied academic atmosphere as Parsons who still wore the white shirt and blue striped bow tie he had used to teach in that day.

The balance of the conversation was a mystery to Brownlee. Parsons and the stranger discussed girls, although Brownlee supposed Parsons to be married, and innumerable semi-illicit ways of making money. They kept up a barrage of jests and one-upmanship that only a thin line separated from outright hostility. Brownlee tried to participate but sensed the two were both ignoring and making fun of him. He tried to think of what he should do next but, shamefaced, was unable to think of anything at all.

"I've got this idea, Wood," Parsons said: "We're going to dress you like an old man, put you in shabby clothes, gray your hair, get you a false beard, and then, and then you're going down to the Bourbon House and play the violin."

Brownlee giggled and sat up abruptly to find the other two glaring at him; he folded himself up immediately in a pretence of sleep and was not even conscious of Wood and Parsons' later departure.

"I saw Maggie, today." said Parsons to Wood. "She likes you. I had a long talk with her. She took practically a three-hour coffee break to talk to me. She thinks you're the greatest. You've really got her hypnotized. I think you can have her anytime you want."

A self-confident smile, a kind of lustful smirk, crossed Wood's face.

"Do you know she used to work as a barmaid?" said Parsons, changing topics abruptly. "Yes. Down at the end of that long street.

"She's been working in the student store for three or four years, now. She doesn't like working there. She told me she was having coffee with me because she didn't want to sit with all the gossipy old women that work in the supply room. She doesn't like them. They don't talk about anything, just gossip. They remind her of her father.

"That's why she likes you. You're so completely different from her old man. You know, free. He's a professor here in school. Not in my department, thank God! She says he's all right though, unless you have to live with him.

"He's divorced apparently and Maggie's been living with him alone in their house for five years. I think that's why she went off with all those boys. But she says that wasn't the reason. She said she was in love with them."

(Wood could not understand how she could have been in love with other boys or have gone to bed with others. But of course she would have had to have gone to bed with them. To be ... for it to be as easy as it had been. He had not had to struggle taking off her dress in the darkness, kissing her breasts as he pushed her dress up and away from her body.)

"You weren't her first lover," Parsons continued as if arguing with him, "she's had many lovers. Many. She says she can't even count them all."

Wood looked at him through a sharply narrowed focus, an orange pane of light set in an irregular green iris, at Parsons' arm and gesticulating hand too close to the camera. Parsons' gestures seemed to be made between and independent of his words. Wood tried to answer toughly, "What difference does that make?," but his mouth never opened; one could only read the reply in the tenseness of his throat. Parsons paused; Wood still did not speak; his silence did not betray him because Parsons was not the sort to listen to others.

("Are you going to marry her?" Brownlee had asked. Brownlee did not understand what women were for. And why he was in New Orleans. Of course Maggie was something different. Maggie had made him happier than any girl had before. And they made love because they were in love. But then she was foolish too, for letting him. He was proud he could control her. And that he made her happy while Parsons slept uptown in his office.)

74

."..I think you've struck yourself a gold mine." Parsons said.

"As long as you stay out of the apartment," Wood bantered.

"Oh, I will, I like sleeping in the office; the air-conditioner is good for my asthma. Besides, I've borrowed an air-mattress from Morgan."

Across the room, Barcus stood over Little Hamilton watching them play "The Game." The Game made no sense to Barcus. Territories carved with a knife and inked in carefully on the Formica tabletop. Little notes scrawled on napkins and passed from hand to hand. Would it go on forever? Little Hamilton watched with what amounted to fascination and seemed unable to hear what Barcus was saying. The game ended abruptly while Barcus was talking and the players and kibitzers walked off to their dormitories to eat. Barcus, of course, was left behind.

Chapter 13. (Wood)

There was no place he could take her.
Down a poorly lit street lined by trees, their long,
Horizontal branches hiding the sky.
Houses, set well back from the street,
Whose gardens had ripened in tropic profusion
Through and over
The torn remains of unpainted fences.
"I want to walk this way," she said.
Grasses,
In some cases even the bare roots,
Stretched across the cracked pavement.
The scent of mint, mimosa,
Rich undefinable spices,
was overpowering.
She walked against the fence;
He walked outside;
The honeysuckle crept out along the thick overhead branches.
"Why?
Why do you want to walk this way?"
"It has certain memories."
While he struggled to keep his thoughts outside
Himself,
She begged, "Please don't ask me about them."
He said some silly unnecessary things,
About how cute she was. Her dimples. The fall of her curls
Along her slender white neck.
Her neck, her breasts, her shoulders,
Fell just within the narrow limits
Assigned to perfect beauty.
"You shouldn't walk down these streets after dark."
Why?
(The why of the stranger. Observations never to be used.
I have come across the burning desert.
Did you mean to run your hand across my chest,
And press your face
Against my shoulder?
Why is a challenge to unseen figures.)
"Niggers. Niggers'll knock you over the head

76

For a quarter." She swirled on her toes and looked at
Him, through the scent of jasmine.
"Svengali."
"My beloved."
"I am weak. My knees and ... hold me?"
(What's that noise you make?
"It's hard to breathe with you on top of me."
Rest. Rest, I'll place my weight on my elbows.)
He braced her moist back with his warm arm,
His shoulder protectively behind her head.
She danced a few steps forward and he danced after.
They walked side by side, her hips brushing against him.
(When they walk together beside the oak tree
There won't be room enough for both to pass.)
They halt in the middle of the sidewalk.
He lifts her across the roots of the oak.
Teeth against teeth; she opens; against him
Her cotton dress, her body warm in the warm evening,
Her breasts full.
He kisses her mouth and traces her lips with his tongue.
Her lips are moist and burning.
How long they stood in the fuchsia-hung doorway
(Nobody counts in the shadows)
Exploring, arousing. Someone passes on the other side.
Her street led to a lighted area, laundromats and hardware.
"Let's go in here."
As if we had been walking toward a tavern all along;
As if she were used to walking into taverns.
"Tell me about yourself?
"Do you like New Orleans?
"Order Eastern beer for both of us.
(Someone played Nina Simone on the jukebox.)
"I used to come into this place a lot;
"It's changed.
"We can dance here. (Do you kiss like this always?)
"Please be careful."
A wet cloth moved along the bar
Moistening it and capturing the spillings.
He danced with Maggie.
The man drinking whiskey knew the barmaid's daughter
When she was just a little girl.

A dark street, a bright street.
A light wind
That lifts the clothes from their bodies.
Her hair lifts slightly. She sees
Him watching her movements. She has
A slightly hunted look, as if she were
Afraid, reluctant
To forget who she is.
"I want to love."
I love you, Maggie
"Where are you staying?"
In there. In those apartments.
I stay in the one on the left toward the back.
"Then you are married."
No.
(The fear inside of him, too.
All the things he has been saying are the right things
As in his dreams,
And all her answers, his.)
They kissed on the doorstep while Parsons' bell was ringing,
Hating to break their lips apart.
Parsons answered the door in a bath towel
Left to pull on a pair of slacks.
He had been drinking beer
And was very Enthusiastic without making them feel comfortable.
He began to pull on his clothes,
Poking and probing at the mess on the floor, Apologizing.
Pete wiped the lipstick smudges from his cheek
While Maggie tidied automatically, sweeping the strewn papers into
piles.
Forgive the garbage in the kitchen, the roaches and the stink;
Wood and Parsons sleep naked on the springs.
"Is this your bed?"
"I'm going to the office because of my asthma." Parsons said,
Taking his books, his books and his beer, with him.
Svengali was uncertain.
She undid the buttons at the front of her dress, and
Slipped it over her head.
He locked the door. Rushed to the back of the house and checked
The curtains. Where books or child's toys lay barricading the floor,
He pushed them out of the way.

He mounted her breasts with his hands
(A dream of flight)
Brought them from under her slip and kissed them while
She waited to finish undressing.
They kissed, her lips wide and wet.
She stroked his forehead.
(I am not afraid. I am foolish.)
"How long has it been since you had a woman," Maggie asked him.
She showed him where to put his hands a second time.
He lay behind the swell of her hip and probed. She moved
Bringing her live breasts against his chest.
He did not protest—
Tired lips pressed to a withdrawn nipple—
Daddy summoned her home in a cab.
She left. He listened to the window fan awhile
Then went to sleep uninterrupted.
To Maggie,
One thing only is important:
Whether she loves the man she sleeps with;
And the second thing,
Some people go directly to their work and do not see around them,
Wood drank in life and never felt experience.

Chapter 14. (Mason's diary)

Although Maggie had been remarkably self reliant as a child, by the time she was ready to enter high school her pendulum had swung the other way. While her classmates had a new interest—boys, Maggie was still a gawky tomboy, much as Diane is today. The social pressures made her understandably anxious. Of course, one cannot explain to a child that people mature at different times and in different ways.

We tried Cotillions. This was a social group run by the parents to which all the parents contributed. On Wednesdays, the children took dance lessons. On Fridays, they were supposed to have fun and practice what they had learned. Each of the girls had a dance card. The boys had to sign up for the dances and they weren't allowed to keep signing one girl's card over and over, so, eventually, each of the girls would have her card filled out completely.

At first, the Cotillions seemed to demand as much from the parents as from the children. We would have to walk or drive them to the dance, and then stay through the first few numbers until everything had been settled. And we would have to pick them up again and bring them home afterwards. Once the children all knew one another, Maggie was able to go to the Cotillions with a group of friends she had met there. They would travel in a flock down to the trolley chattering and laughing as young girls do. After awhile we stopped paying very much attention, so it was several weeks before I realized she had stopped going. "They were such snobs," she said.

Toward the end of her first year in high school, we began to hear a great deal of a young man named Bill Green. Precise details seemed to be lacking. I never met the boy and what I learned came from overhearing snatches of telephone conversations. He owned his own car and drove "dreadfully" fast. He did not own his own car but was in danger of coming under the influence of a girl who did. Nothing was certain.

Except that it was love, it was Bill Green. Or as Maggie put it in her earnest conversations over the phone: "Can it be love? Can I love him?" In the summertime, one could overhear her on the lawn confiding inadvisably with the neighbors and the postman: "Can it be love? Bill Green!" Much later, I learned she'd never met the boy for whom she sighed so romantically.

Maggie's lack of self confidence, her feelings that she was plain and unlovable were only confirmed when we moved and she had to change schools. She lost many of her old friends and had to begin again to make new ones. Perhaps this was why when she finally began to bloom, the boys she brought home were still the outcasts — pimply, adenoidal, non-athletic. Even when she attained an almost precocious beauty, to a degree that Diane despite her dark hair and fine features will never attain, the pattern continued. Her dates stepped on her feet and theirs, kissed other girls — girls they didn't like, and walked at a distance from Maggie. They picked her up in cars borrowed from their parents, or (and perhaps I should have been grateful for this) their parents picked them up and deposited them back at our door.

Robert was the first college boy she dated. They met she said by accident. She and her friend Joyce had been sitting at an outside table in the French Market pretending to be debutantes. Robert and his friend told the girls they were businessmen from out of town or were with their fathers on business or something. Red faces all around when Robert and his friend met the girls again one morning on their way to school.

Robert liked to sit with her and buy her cigarettes. He would take her any place he thought she wanted to go, even if he couldn't enjoy being there himself. He took her to Pontchatrain Park-"He got sick on the roller coaster, Daddy."-and to the zoo. He took her to the Comus ball and sat for hours in the upper deck next to Maggie while she gazed enthralled at the dancers and the debutantes, the costumes and the speechmakers.

At the end of their first three months together, Robert took her to his fraternity formal. He couldn't dance very well and arranged for his fraternity brothers to dance with her so she would be happy. And she was only happy when they went to the wrong restaurant afterward and she munched at a flavorless fried pecan pie, listening to him as he watched her, watching him eat it for her.

(Maggie has always had this marvelous quality of being a friend. She can sit for hours with someone she likes; it doesn't matter what they're doing; if the friend has something he or she must do alone, Maggie will sit with them still; she doesn't have to have a book or magazine to pass the time, she is happy just being with her friends. She was a big help to me after her mother left. A companion in the evenings and whenever I felt alone. We would go out in the evenings together and have one or two beers and listen to the music. And not talk. Just listen.)

Robert was a polite boy. In fact, I doubt . . . but my view is so distant. After their first few dates, she wished out loud he could be more lively and more affectionate. He came over often after supper to sit, perhaps help her or Diane with their homework, and would still be sitting with her in the living room when I got back, neither of them talking, he sucking on the pipe he had bought when all the other fellows in his group bought one, and she would be dozing. This happened not merely on one or two occasions, but continued for a period of five to six months. It ended, finally, when at the conclusion of a party in his fraternity, slightly drunk and acting on a dare, he grabbed Maggie and tried to kiss her. She slapped him in front of everyone and wouldn't have anything more to do with him after that.

Maggie matured unevenly. She was in braces long after the other girls her age had shed theirs. She filled out suddenly, waking one morning to discover she was big bosomed, like her mother. Like her mother, she was taught to dress with restraint. "So that I might still be flat chested for all anybody knows about it."

Mike was about her best prospect; like Robert he was a college boy, but he had a more solid notion of his future career. He was studying to be an engineer. For a long while, I thought Mike and Maggie would get married. He was perhaps the most intelligent of the boys she dated, likeable enough, and of course Maggie worshipped him.

On top of that he was more than ordinarily attractive, tall and strong, with sandy hair and a clean masculine face. Maggie said he gave up all sorts of girls to go steady with her. She even took up typing in night school for a while because she wanted to help Mike send in job applications.

Maggie used to attend night school off and on; I always tried to encourage her but she never really completed a course. She'd sit down the way one should and plan the courses she'd be taking, and then she'd change her mind at the last minute and take something else entirely. With the encouragement of her girl friends, most of whom were mature steady individuals, I hoped she'd ultimately get her teaching credential, something she could fall back on if she were married and lost her husband, but she never did. Sometimes Maggie would pick up a textbook she had purchased years earlier and read for an entire evening (I often do much the same thing) but she might or might not go back to finish it.

I once thought of getting her a tutor, though I know this sounds like a ridiculous idea. Once, when she accompanied me for a few months on my sabbatical in England, a rather bluff and too hearty English boy offered to tutor her. He was so involved already in debating clubs and rowing that I don't think he ever got around to it. I don't believe he ever went out with her either.

Mike was a good student and she used to sit with him at the library, or at our house or his apartment, studying. She'd catnap and wake up when he wanted to go out for coffee, sitting at the table listening while he and his friends were talking. They talked about their courses and their professors-"They never mention you, Daddy."-(they were of course in the engineering school)-about their future jobs and, surprisingly for men of their age group, about marriage. Most of Mike's friends were engaged and perhaps Maggie felt she was, too. They never made any formal commitment, however, and Mike married another girl after he graduated.

Maggie was pregnant by that time and Mike offered to do what he could to help. I told him I could take care of the whole thing, but after he found employment in Baton Rouge, he sent me a check for medical expenses and a polite note saying he felt responsible. I felt a certain measure of guilt, even of repugnance at the time, but I do not feel I should discuss this here.

Chapter 15

At 8:20 A.M., the recreation room of the Dryades Street YMCA was deserted except for a pimply yellow-faced youth who was playing ping-pong with himself against the wall. He had pushed the table against the wall and was hitting shots against it and then hitting them again as they ricocheted from the table. By 8:30, the youth had been displaced by two very busy sign painters. He had tried to stay and even continued to play ping-pong, but they had taken the table away from him and spread their painted cardboards on the table to dry.

When the youth snorted something silly after he recognized the words "Do Not Shop," and "Kresses" the two had begun to block in with paint between the penciled letters, they made him leave the room entirely.

At 8:40, Lennie arrived but he did not stay. He had been up all night playing cards and there were circles under his eyes. He told the sign painters he was going to bed and to awaken him at noon. At nine A.M., Tom Moody, a tall lanky negro who seemed to unfold and grow taller the closer he came, arrived and cursed them for letting Leonard get away. But Moody had too many other things to do to worry about Lennie as other workers arrived and had to be given their assignments.

By 9:30 A.M. everyone had been assigned something to do and was either doing it, or rehearsing what he or she would be doing later. No one was allowed to kibitz the painters, and two boys who lived in the Y and had wandered in but did not seem eager to participate were hustled out almost immediately.

At ten minutes of ten, Dick Diamond arrived all hair lotion and big toothy smile. Startled black faces greeted him the way you'd greet the ghost of a long dead but revered relative, partly awe and partly dismay, and much was made of his unexpected release from jail. So pleased were they to see him, so cordial was the reception, with so much ooing and awing and hey-hey, that almost ten minutes passed before anyone, even Moody, remembered how much work remained to be done. Even when they all did go back to work, Dick lingered to exchange greetings, and to wander around and offer encouragement and get in everyone's way.

Finally, Moody asked Dick where Buddie Jefferies was.

"Oh, Buddie's still in jail. He like it dere." Diamond confided.

And Moody cursed the maleficent fate that imprisoned one like Buddie who could do the work of a hundred and gave him worthless Dick Diamond instead. No explaining it. No way of undoing it. Here was Dick Diamond, black and useless. There was Buddie Jefferies, his hardest worker, in jail indefinitely, bail set at seventeen thousand dollars.

"You want to go with us this afternoon?" Moody asked, mostly because the others were listening, and hoping Diamond would say "no."

"Why not, man."

So be it. Well, Diamond would be back in jail and out from underfoot soon enough.

"When's the meeting?" Dick asked.

"Jesus," Moody said; he looked at his watch and cursed; then he sent Martha out to the payphone to call Leonard.

"He says he's asleep, call back later," Martha reported.

Moody's voice thundered through the room-a convent girl from Sisters of Charity looked up startled-"There is no later. We need Lennie now!" But he didn't do anything about getting Lennie himself.

About 10:45, Bill Williams brought down some film clip that included shots of the crowds, white and black, milling around a Woolworths in Atlanta where a demonstration similar to the one planned for the afternoon had just taken place. In one of the pictures, they could see a young white woman with a child in her arms kicking at one of the picketers.

"What I don't understand," someone interjected almost as soon as the meeting began at eleven, still without Lennie, "is just who is sponsoring this demonstration?"

"Does it matter?" said Martha.

"What she's trying to say," Moody amplified, "is that all groups goin' to have to work together if ... if we are goin' to have a movement."

"Does that include the Urban League?"

"That includes everybody. We're going to have to work together." (It seemed so simple, so fundamental a principle, yet he always had to repeat it over and over, to white and black alike.)

"Where's our white man?"

"He'll be here."

"Too many people. We got to-o many. The po-lice will use dogs."

"We're not scared," Martha said.

"We ain't scared of shit," Dick Diamond interjected.

"Of course, we don't want trouble," Moody said soothingly, "but we do want to make a showing, solidarity. Together."

They tried Lennie on the phone again just before they left. Though he was still in bed when they called, Leonard got up immediately. He walked to Barcus' place where he borrowed a dollar for cab fare. At one on the dot, he met the picketers outside of Kresses, grabbing a sign with one hand and tipping the cab driver with the other. By three, both he and Dick Diamond were back in jail.

Chapter 16 (Mason)

My name is Durwood Mason. While I was on sabbatical in England my wife went off with another man, not one of my good friends, but one whom we had both known for some time. I have two daughters whose names are Margaret and Diane.

(Wood is brash and bold. He is a mad man and an impostor, a communist and a fool. Barcus rubs his hands together briskly, the fingers not touching. He thinks of Little Hamilton whom he will meet that evening in the center. He hopes to entice Little Hamilton to his apartment where he will turn on the circle of dull red lights above the chandelier of shrunken heads and phallic symbols.)

After we stopped going to parties and I became accustomed to the janitor, a Basque whose English education had begun and ended while he herded sheep in Montana, leaving little notes to himself on the pad in my office:

> 1 dust pan T-7
> 1 hand broom
> 1 12" ladder,

I settled down to the realization that certain letters would never be uncovered, and that the controversy between Delbert and the eminent historian Walsh was settled solely because Walsh was alive and publishing. My students (the few that did not go, the many that came back from the Korean War) learned soon to develop critical attitudes and an excessive scorn for the predicated fact, attitudes the department chairman warned would do them injustice in later life.

Diane, whose birth was deferred until six years after that of her sister, was an unhealthy baby. Violet spent her evenings tending Diane and devising ways to amuse Maggie and plans for getting her to bed on time. I usually worked late at the office and rose during the night to give Diane her medicine. Maggie might wake up then too, and I would tell her stories about the English kings and lull her to sleep with Alfred, Alfred, John, Edward, William, John.

When Violet left, I was away in England and Maggie was with me. One of Violet's friends wrote me at her request, a long letter that only blurted out the truth at the end. I wrote Violet for details; she answered briefly, told me who he was, apologized, and said she would be leaving soon and moving to Rhode Island to live.

Maggie went back to New Orleans by herself and without my knowledge spent her first few days in New Orleans without a place to stay. She spent the time driving around the city in a sports car with a boy she knew from high school. One night—they even drove all night, "because I didn't live anyplace and there wasn't much point in going to his house because his parents would only have yelled at him"—the boy who owned the car cracked them both up against a wall. I rushed home immediately—I had to terminate my sabbatical early—when I learned she was in the hospital. They had grafted the flesh from her thigh onto her cheek and had given her an artificial dimple.

I had hoped to see Violet before she left but with Maggie's problems so immediate there was just no opportunity. I barely managed to contact the boy involved. Of course, he had no insurance. (Not that it was a question of money. It never has been where the welfare of my children is involved. But surely, he would feel some responsibility.)

After the convalescence, Maggie lived with someone, a fisherman, for two days and nights and then came home. Sometimes she brought one of her boy friends to her room in the evening while I was away and there would be an angry confrontation at the breakfast table. The quarrels never went on for long, but they were fierce and unsettling while they lasted.

Both of us understood the important thing was to provide a stable home for Diane. I would try to explain why it was best we look at things from Diane's point of view and, at the same time, my hapless oldest child would stand before me, arms folded, barring the way as if she were protecting her younger sister. Finally I'd holler, "Put some clothes on! Get up or go back to bed for heavens sake." And then Diane would appear, sleepy-eyed, in time to gobble her breakfast and have me wait five minutes in the car while she got her things together for school.

(In her alternation of total dependence and self-reliance, Maggie is very much like her mother's mother, but the oscillations are more frequent, the peaks more extreme. Maggie seemed totally lost after her mother left. She'd been planning on getting a job. She got a whole series of them but was unable to keep any one job for long. She's not a bad girl. With the money she earns she often buys things for her sister and her friends.)

I still went to the office in the evenings, though the term did not start for several months, dividing all the papers into two piles between which I shifted endlessly. The children seemed adjusted, to my presence or my absence. Often I would arrange to have Maggie meet me at school while Diane ate at a friend's house. Usually Maggie and I would sit alone and talk. I think in some ways she is more settled than I. Once we toured the Quarter and got half-drunk together.

She's been planning on getting a job. She's had a whole series of them since her mother left, always returning to her job at the University where her co-workers are her friends.

Chapter 17 (Wood)

White skulls piled around the town
Where groups of families lay;
Crumpled blackbirds in the square
Who could not fly away

An arm, a leg, an eye, a tooth,
All once parts of men
Whose twisted mouths and angry scowls
Betray their final pain.

Alone in the elm-shaded streets
I feel them rushing by
Hear shuffling feet, whispers, moans,
A single plaintive cry
But when I turn, eyes open, look
Here, only corpses lie.

Leave now, leave now
Whimpers the wind
You're safe, my mother says
Would I sooner killed than killer be?
Leave now or join ...

His sleep had not been an easy one. The air in the room was hot, much hotter than he was used to. He could not understand how it could be September, almost October, and still be this warm, this early in the morning. As always, his dreams were near paralyzing, the images startling, unrecognizable, as if he had been dreaming someone else's dream.

That morning, Wood set out for the Quarters, a guidebook in his hand. He started at the Absinthe House (a bar has been here since 1861; the original absinthe, made from wormwood, was outlawed in 1925), and ended at the Ursuline Convent (built in 1734 and featuring high chimneys and a double sloping mansard roof).

From Bourbon, he cut down to Royal where the tourists thronged the antique stores, and then down a second half block to Chartre. He saw the outside of Broussard's, Brennan's, Antoine's and pressed his nose to the latter dreaming of the food. On Chartre, in the Napoleon House, he read, "Here Mayor Girod and others gathered to rescue Napoleon from his exile on St Helena."

He learned the architecture of the French Quarter was as often Spanish as French, that its cast iron railings had been brought by steamer from Philadelphia. He tasted pralines, fingered antique armor, and sucked on sugar cane purchased in the market.

He studied each home in the guidebook, the grillwork on the windows, the molding and cornices and sloping roofs, but he was as taken with the contents of the Central Grocery — tall jars of olives, fragrant herbs and spices, and cheeses stacked on barrel heads and shelves, swinging from the rafters overhead, as with the architecture of the two-hundred year old building.

He saw Madame John's Legacy, the Cornstalk Fence, the Pontalba buildings in Jackson Square. He cut down back alleys where the black dishwashers and porters take time for a smoke, and the black cooks can be seen hard at work at their ovens and ranges. He ate a muffuletta — cold cuts and cheese on French bread bathed in a green and black olive salad.

He peeked in to the Court of the Palm, craning his neck to see through the iron railings, past the lush green vegetation. He was tempted to ring the bell, to hide inside the entrance when the gate clicked open, then roam the courtyard and the long internal balconies, looking just looking.

At last, he stared up at the sloping roofs of the Ursuline Convent. Here where the guidebook ended, he ate spumoni in an Italian ice cream parlor and watched the Skipper, Ginger and Mary-Anne try to escape from Gilligan's Isle. A first and then a second Dr. Pepper left him still hot and thirsty. He thought of visiting Dixie, the stripper he had met the first night he was in New Orleans. They had talked once on the phone since then and she had invited him to visit her. Hadn't she? A payphone sat just inside the door of the ice cream parlor.

"Sure I want you to come over."

"You sound asleep," he said.

"I was asleep."

"It's almost noon."

"Oh!" she groaned. "But you can come over anyway."

The route to Dixie's place took him outside the Quarters, past the mournful cries of slaves buried alive within the LaLaurie House, through the mean streets of the Fabourg Mariguey. The buildings went from worn to shabby, from rough brick to rotten wood and a general sense of decay.

A few of the houses had tiny lawns; Dixie's had a single palm tree set in concrete and a bougainvillea that grew down from one of the windows on the east side of the building.

He galloped up the outside stairway two steps at a time and knocked. "Dixie?" No response. Perhaps she had gone back to sleep after he called. "Dixie?" Wood pushed the door open and stepped inside the apartment.

Dixie's apartment had been decorated by several different personalities: One who collected children's books she never owned as a child; one who succumbed to an encyclopedia salesman—"I could have got them for you at half price," said Barcus, later; one who picked up used paper backs at the club, brought them home, read them once, and put them away forever in the best book case behind glass; one who had a painter for a boy friend—she looked like a boy in the sketch he'd made of her, taken from the rear; and a final personality, carefully hidden in her bedroom, who hung a bleeding Jesus and framed mottos knitted by the Sisters of the Sacred Heart next to a photograph of a small boy standing with his grandparents.

The living room was a collection of shelves and shelving, most of them empty except for the glass-fronted paperback collection in the corner. In the hallway, between another portrait of Dixie and some prints that Dixie's painter friend had left behind, was a retouched black and white photograph of a Belle-Isle swamp with the mosses carefully tinted green and yellow.

"Hi," Dixie said and touched his arm.

"Hi," he said back and kissed her on the forehead.

"You seem quieter," she said thoughtfully, "More mature." She held him at arms length and examined him closely as a woman

92

might examine a dress she had just taken from the rack. "You have a girlfriend now, don't you?"

She stepped forward and gave him a little hug leaving him conscious of her small breasts pressing against him through the opening in her housecoat. She turned her back to him then and walked off down the hall. Her aroma, a not unpleasant mixture of body odor and stale perfume, aroused him further and he followed her down the hall and into the bedroom.

Dixie scooped a glass from a chair, took a sip from it, and then sat own heavily on the bed. She patted the space beside her and indicated she wanted him to sit down too.

"What have you been doing, Peter?" she asked as he sat down on the bed next to her. He told her about his tour of the Quarters.

"I was educated by the nuns," she said when he described the Ursuline Convent. "You can't trust those Italians," she added, when he mentioned the spumoni ice cream. "My boss is an Itie. They're like this about money." She squeezed an imaginary penny between her fingers.

She hiccupped and then fell against him, her head on his shoulder. Her fingers fumbled with his shirt collar and then undid the top button of his short. "Hey," he said. She slid her fingers under his waistband, causing him to squirm and almost slip away. "It's all right," she said.

She moved her head so she could look at him face to face once more, examining each detail as if determined to buy the dress despite its flaws. "Do you want to?" she began bravely, but she had to look down at her hands before she finished speaking.

"Want to what?" he said hoarsely.

"Make love to me," she said. She looked him in the eyes again, then she reached up, pulled his head down to hers and kissed him full on the lips.

Her breath tasted almost medicinal, her lips warm and dry. He struggled a little but it was only after they had been kissing for several minutes and had kissed twice.

"I've sort of got someone," he said.

Without replying, she took his hand and brought it to her breast. The breast itself was soft but the nipple was rigid and alive. He kissed it softly and she pushed him back on the bed. She took off her housecoat. She unzipped him using both her hands and kissed him again as he sprang into life.

Afterwards, as he was standing, slipping into his pants again, he said, "I need your help."

She watched him without speaking, her eyes as big and round and childlike as they had been before they made love.

"I need somewhere to stay," he said.

"You can't stay here," she replied, "Because of my kid. But you can come back anytime. I want you to come back."

"I don't understand," he said.

"It's complicated. But it's what the lawyers arranged. You just can't leave your clothes here."

"But you'll be working at night." he pleaded. She looked off in the distance, not meeting his eye. "I need someplace to stay." he repeated.

"You'll find someplace."

But he needed much more than that.

Chapter 19 (Dick Diamond)

Dere is no excuse fo mah being heah.

Dere is no excuse fo coming heah. Jus another scuse fo de showoffs t'get all de glo'y. Mah mother treatn me lak a kid, allus yammering bout gitting better grades, n studyin hard. But these peoples treats me no bettah than a slave. And they ain't my momma! Whatevah they do, Dick gotta do it. They'se afraid to do it alone. We can't do it without you, Dick. Sure dey can't. But dat don mean I'm goin t'do it fo' m.

Dere's no point in my comin heah. Fust thing, I got be inroduced to all these white people. An dey is so glad to meet me. Dey slap Lennie on de back and say "what a great guy," and dey shake my han and say mo of de same. What make em think I wanna shake deah han? I don't wan no friends talks like dem. If dey so brave why ain't dem sitting wit us, stead of sending theah regards. Lennie says, these ar de good peoples. Looks jus lak de bad ones to me.

Heah's dat youn fart Heller. He's brung a gal. Well, ain't he de hero. An he know Dick Diamond. Ain't he de big man. He gonna inroduce me to his girl. Ain't dat nice. S'pose I tell how much black pussy I'se introduced him to.

I don' want meet no white girls; I don't want no white boy messin around no black ones. What's de difference, Lennie say. Dey's my girls is what I mean. I don't wan no young white fart chasing after my girls. I knock him down. Make no difference if he in the movement. What's de use of dese people? Dey wants to lead parades. Dey wants to shack up wi a black gir. Wha's de mattah, no white woman want anything do wid em?

An heah come de bastards. Dey's goin t' be a quarrel. Lennie, he sit down and look nonviolent, and de crowd of friends yell back and fo. Now wheah is young Heller? Oh, he goin to take his girl away now deah is trouble. He come back, he say. I bet he come back in time fo de pictures. Gonna git yo picture in de newspaper, Lennie. Git you a job up No'th that way; some boss see yo picture. Momma don't want to move No'th, though. Like it heah. Don't get no good food up North, she say. Dat okay wi me; but wheah I git me a job so I can be boss? Work fo yo uncle. I don't want t'work for my uncle. Dat ain't no practical business he got. I got an education mamma. That O.K., she say, you study real hard and get good grades. What am I gonna do wi dem grades? Take em to Mr. Perez. He gon say you sure a smart nigger you got good grades, I gon make you gov'nor of Lou'siana.

Hey, heah a photographer. I don't want my picture took photographer, I want a hamburger. Gonna put this picture in yoah scrapbook, Lennie. What! Dey want me turn my head, photograph mah right side. Dat's good. Momma likes mah right side. She say de lef make me look too solemn. Dat my Solomen profile... Ain't gonna be no piture? Dat wern't a photographer. Hell, ah knew dat weren't no photographer. Dats one of dose States Rights fucks wit da cammera. Dey probably got mah piture up in de po-lice station in half an hour. You gon likes dat, mama. Ain't nobody in Lous'sianna not know what Dick look like. . . He took Lennie's piture, stead. What about mah piture? Day ain't worried bout me? Well I ain't worried bout dem. What we heah fo anyway? Ain't gonna hep de black man what happen heah.

Wait and see, Lennie say. Hell, I'm waitin, ain't I? Waitin fo a hamburger. Been waiting a long time. If ah was to eat in a place like dis evry night, git mighty hungry . . . When I gits home Mamma gonna fix me some sausage; course she gonna moan and groan a liddle furst, but she fix me somethin fo shuh. Hey Lennie, don you think we could git a little sumpin. Heah dat crowd growling, man. Dat ain no crowd, dat's ma stomach. Jus me, Dick Diamond.

Wait and see. He wrong. We got no reason t'come heah, no reason atall. Lennie get his name sent to de Dean's office. I git in trouble. What fo? What fo? Who cares if dey serve a coloured person a hamburger or not? No coloured man gon come heah to get a hamburger.

And all dem coloured gals dat work heah. Dey embarrassed; ain't gon do no good go up to 'm and say, I's heah to 'stablish precedent.

"A what!" they say.

A precedent, don't you go to school like me?
"No, I don't but I got sense enough not to eat no hamburgers heah. 'Sides how you gonna pay fo it. You don look like you could ford a nickel coke wid you lunch bag. You spects to go to school heah? How you gonna pay de fees? I heah it cost dese chillen mo to go to school den I makes in a yeah."

Wait, I tell em, soon you gon get better salaries. "Yeah? What is you a politician? Go run fo King Zulu, I vote for you." Listen, I say. List-en. You stick wi dese white fren of mine, they get you fed.

"What kind of fren?" dey say. White, I tell em. A white boh wid a preacher daddy. Dat en de conversation.

No chance to make de speech. Lennie, we got no business to come heah. Go downtown and march, I say. Why dem stoahs would go out of business in a week if it weren't fo de coloured folk. Now, that makes good sense. Don't treat us right an we don buy. That's what my mamma says. "If a mulatta clerk don treat me right, why honey I jus don't stop theah."

Now, why didn't Buddy go long with me. "I want to visit the school," he say. Some visit. Dey don like us heah man; I don like dem. I heah what yo yelling white boy. I ain't afraid. Takes mo guts sit heah 'en it does to come out swinging, and believe me white boy, when I comes in swinging I hits hard. Yo football team don't play ouahs, you know. Dey fraid of getting hurt.

Lennie arguing wi dem; he know he not s'pposed t'do that. They's a plan Moody made. Eight-thirty, we supposed to go up and order coffee and a hamburger. Give me plenty tomatoes and onions. I gonna smile at de fry-cook but dat won' do me no good, she gon burn it on me.

Now dey bringing in signs. Yes white-folk, I see de signs and I kin read. "Go home coon ass." Yeah. See me latah white folk when youse alone. Dey's no point in dis Lennie. Dey gon 'sult us ev'r time. We stronger den dey is. Teacher say get the vote. O.K., two months I go register. But dat won't do no good, dey don't register us. Teacher don say nothing. Teacher nevah has. You evah vote Teach? No, he don't say nothing. Who you gon' vote foh? Mr. Perez for governor.

Heah's dat new friend of Lennie's. He walks tru de mob like it ain't theah. He talks strange. He bring his girl ovah, too, see what a big hero he is. She don't like negroes. He talk a mile a minute. She don't say nothin. She look at me like I'm crazy. She so right.

Who dat man, I say to Lennie when dey leave, he try talk cool. Lennie don't answer. Now he standing up. Heah come Mr. Two-faced Barcus, de peoples fren. Ho-ho, he knocks de camera out of de young squirt's arms. Lennie 'n him an nother guy talking, leave me and t'others staring at ouah hands.

"O.K., Lennie say we got to go." Moody finally opens his mouth.

"So soon, it ain't eight-thirty yet. I's hungry."

"Some other time."

"What Mr. Barcus da peoples fren say?" I ask.

"Oh he broke up the lynching party."

"The bastards," Calhoun say, and turn gray.

Man, you been in worse trouble; this bunch weren't nevah gone do nothin but yell; an we weren' nevah gon do nothin but sit and look foolish.

I received a letter from Violet today. She does not write often and this is the very first time she has asked for money. Not for a great deal and she was very apologetic about asking. I think I will send her a check for the whole amount. I've never had to pay her anything; legally, she's made no demands upon me.

There is no hesitation in my giving. It's just that her letter raised all the old questions. Of course, there is nothing to forgive her for; it's a matter of withdrawing barriers, erasing the lines.

At first I hated her for leaving. Her going made me realize so many things about myself. We're just not the same people we were when we married. Her present husband, too, turned out to be completely different from the way she expected. But the money is for something else.

Peggy, Peggy. Stop rushing forward two steps ahead of your ability to cope. Talk with me. If only your mother had thought things through. (Or would she have married me in the first place?)

"You leave your wash cloths in the bathtub.

"You never clean your hairbrush."

I wonder if I still have those old habits.

I used to detest the way Violet picked at the hair on her legs. Today, the thought of a girl with hairy legs is richly attractive.

Five years ago, deferring the issue might have made all the difference. It just doesn't matter now. Undoubtedly, Violet is older than I remember her. Peggy has shown me photographs and Violet looks grayer, more like her mother. She is too heavy in the bust, her cheekbones puffy.

Someone knocked on my office door. I hollered, "Come in." It was Henry Starr.

"Oh it's you, Henry. It's a little early for coffee. There's some mail and a few things I wanted to clear up this evening.

"In time for what? The Centre stays open till eleven.

"A girl? One of your students. Well, why not. But take her somewhere else as soon as you can. The Dean is a bit of a gossip. We've all a bit of the gossip.

"No, I can't agree with you on that. A gossip but not a fool. You're far too extreme. In fact, it's wishful thinking on your part that all your enemies should be bad very bad and all your friends good very good. Too much Superman comics and abridged Classic tales.

"I am your friend and I'm not all that good. The Dean, perhaps, is not your friend, though he tried to be at first, but he's not all that bad and he's represented us very well for someone who, after all, was appointed by the administration. The salaries are not high by Eastern standards perhaps, but they're considerably higher than they were when the Dean took office. I can't complain. Most of us can't complain. This is why so many of your little campaigns just aren't going any place.

"Couldn't you just be quiet for awhile and sit? I've only a few papers to be graded. About nine o'clock, we'll go and have a cup just before the Center closes. Or say, why don't we go down to the Quarters and have a brandy at the Napoleon house?

"She must be quite a girl. But surely you don't need me. You're free, white, and twenty-one, fully capable of coping with the opposite sex on your own.

"Not want to appear too forward. Yes, I can understand. But she's a student, Henry. You already bathe in awe. I remember, Violet. . . it seemed impossible to me then, you've no idea how attractive she was by comparison to other girls I'd dated, and I, well I was just starting out.

"Yes, I heard from her. This letter I was reading. She. . . she did ask after Maggie and Diane. But they stay with her every summer anyway, at least Diane does. No, just family business.

"You're sure you want to go and that I'm an essential component. Honestly, Henry I wish someone had told me what I'm telling you now when I was your age.

"Since you were thirteen. No, I can't match that story. Standing at the foot of a ladder. Oh I can match it now, but you see I didn't know or understand what it meant then. When I was twelve and thirteen, all the girls suddenly seemed to change their behavior, wanting to have parties and dancing. I found the changes embarrassing.

"You know, we'd always played together. The boys and girls who lived on our street. We'd played softball, and tag, and Ring-a-levio. But I wasn't ready for the parties, just one or two couples, and once just Carole, the girl on my ladder, she was twelve, and anybody, any boy, who wanted to come. I know Bill and I didn't particularly want to go to Carole's party. We were into magic tricks. But John went. I don't think they did anything. She took off her panties and he looked.

"Carole started going with older boys then, and you didn't see her on the block. The other girls started to disappear into their houses, too. You saw them occasionally in the spring and the fall but it wasn't the same.

"You know, my first year in college, I came back and looked for her, Carole, and Marline too, but they had moved away. . . ."

It had rained briefly while we sat in my office. The trees dripped water along the edges of the path. The students waded delightedly down the middle of the road, shouting, but the sounds of their laughter were absorbed in the darkness.

The cafeteria was remarkably crowded for a weekday evening. The crowd was thickest in the far corner of the room, away from the windows where I usually sat, but I found myself guided by Henry in that direction. Surprisingly, all the tables in that corner, with one exception, were unoccupied.

Coffee cups in hand, the students stood in clumps, talking animatedly or not talking at all, occasionally tossing glances over their shoulders toward that one table in the corner. I noticed that I was noticed by several of my students.

A cluster of girls who had been standing motionless in front of our table, paddled away noisily and I could see Zellner, Leonard Zellner, sitting in the corner. Two colored boys sat with him sipping coffee. They wore neckties and seemed quite well behaved.

Zellner was another matter. He wore an open-neck white polo shirt and a pair of dark, tight pants. Where the two colored boys were hunched in on themselves, he was laughing and waving to people in the crowd. His hair was loose and untidy and he kept running his fingers though the strands making them look wilder still.

A constant ebb and flow as the crowd around us jockeyed for position. Everyone wanted to see, but few actually wanted to be participants. Those at the front of the crowd were silent for the most part, but an occasional chorus of jeers sounded from somewhere in back. Someone in the crowd called to Zellner and he yelled back "No trouble, no trouble." He meant, I imagine, they'd had no difficulty in ordering food.

A studious young man with horn-rimmed glasses, vest, and pants too tight for his ample rump, stopped by our table uninvited and began quarreling with Henry. The student's end of the conversation seemed more that of a district attorney than of someone who wanted to learn, while Henry, in turn, was lecturing rather than listening, studiously avoiding addressing the boy as an individual. "Don't you think it was a mistake bringing these people here, Mr. Starr?"

"No, I don't."

"Would you care to make a statement?"

"I think you know my position."

"I do, but perhaps these others would like to know more about your rather liberal political beliefs."

"My beliefs have nothing...it's a simple matter of..."

"And perhaps, they ought to know who you represent."

"The law is fairly clear."

The student simpered, cocked thumbs expressing disapproval.

"Yes, these people have every legal right to eat here." Henry continued.

"And don't those of us who pay to come here also have rights."

Oh come now, my young debating club member or whatever you are, let us have some concern for the facts. Despite my distaste for the situation Henry had drawn me into, I found myself interrupting their father-son monologue to point out the majority of the students did not seem too unfriendly.

"Oh, hello Professor Mason; I didn't expected to see you involved in this?"

"I'm not exactly involved."

"It's good to see you anyway, Sir." The boy shook my hand, a little too firmly considering the remote nature of our relationship. "I hadn't expected to see you here."

Looking up at his sincere grin and close-cropped head, I began to regret having had my own hair cut short.

"No," the boy said, no longer addressing me or Henry but haranguing the crowd, "We are not behaving erratically nor is this gathering likely to degenerate into a street brawl, though of course I can't speak for everyone. Most of us are mature individuals, whatever Dr. Starr may believe, and I'm sure I express a general opinion when I say we resent outsiders coming in and stirring up trouble."

"Tell him. Tell him." cried a half dozen young voices, the last warning before the invasion of Austria. The boy and Henry crossed glances and I'm afraid Henry looked away first.

"In a moment," the boy continued, "I will go over to their table and ask them to leave. Altogether, I think it would be preferable if you were to ask them."

"They have a right to be here," Henry replied sullenly.

"Perhaps you would like to talk to all of us then about your views?" The boy cupped his hand as if to embrace the crowd of students massed behind him.

I interrupted, "I think I'll have some more coffee. How about you, Henry?" and got up, assuming he would follow me.

The line for coffee stretched almost to the door of the building. The door to the hallway opened suddenly and Maggie appeared in front of me. We stood face to face for a moment until a tousled young man in a ill-fitting motorcycle jacket two sizes too large for him appeared beside her. She saw me, once could not mistake her look of recognition, but she did not say hello before her young man pulled her away across the room toward where the negroes were sitting. I thought I would mention having seen them the next morning, if she woke up before I left for work.

The crowd had formed a tight ring about Zellner's table, and Henry and the student in the green suit were trapped together in the middle of the ring. There wasn't much I could do other than to ask a boy ahead of me, one of my students in fact, to pass Henry's coffee forward.

"I'm going to have to ask you to leave," green vest said to the two colored men.

"G'won get out of here," someone shouted and the group took it up as a chant.

"Get out you black bastards before we ram that doughnut where they belong," snarled a ripe-lipped young man with a head like a crane and little gift for human language.

"Who's that white guy with them?" "Who's that old guy?" "Throw them out."

The cafeteria manager, Murrow I think his name is, spoke to green vest and then to Henry. A large man, almost elephantine in bulk, whom I thought I recognized from almost a decade before, pressed forward through the crowd escorted by a group of youths. He stood beside the manager and momentarily the crowd was silent.

"Barcus'll throw them out," someone said.

Barcus, if that was his name, spoke briefly to green vest, then summoned Zellner, who came running forward, giggling and still playing the fool. Green vest started to say something else and Barcus thrust him back into the crowd.

Under the fat man's direction, a path was cleared, and Zellner led his group out of the restaurant. It took only a few minutes. A momentary chorus of boos followed them. The two colored boys walked stiffly, their eyes on the ground.

I'm sure that only the minority of the students had actually contemplated violence. Most were mere onlookers. One of my freshman students later confided this had been about the most exciting date he'd had all semester. And back amongst their own, the two colored boys were probably turning the whole incident into a lighthearted prank.

The crowd began to thin out; the restaurant manager calmed down sufficiently to organize the cafeteria employees behind the counter and start alleviating the pent-up demand for coffee. Only Barcus and his group remained on their feet talking for fifteen or twenty additional minutes. I rejoined Henry.

"The Dean was here," he said "he didn't do anything."

"Well, what can you expect," I began.

"Why didn't he do anything?"

I waved my hands helplessly; it seemed to me either one understood the Dean's position or one didn't.

"I... I'll tell you. He was afraid. They're all afraid. Deep down inside most of them are dead. And who's the exception? That snot-nosed little bastard who was stirring up the crowd a moment ago."

"Henry, give them their due."

A buxom Jewish girl with a plump face and a blank, almost bovine expression passed by our table. Henry called to her. The girl looked unmasked, embarrassed as anyone would be that had been hailed by Henry that evening. She finally decided it would cause less commotion to join us than to flee and eased her heavy sensual body into the chair held out by Henry.

"We're only two harmless professors . . ." he began.

Seeing the girl up close, I recognized her as the butt of many jokes Henry and I had made while sitting together in the cafeteria. As expected, a sorority pin reposed on her sweater above one remarkably large breast. While Henry went after more coffee for the two of them, I gave her the standard set of questions. Do you enjoy school? What are you studying? She seemed less interested than I in the answers.

Eventually, we did manage a fairly spirited conversation. She was a history major and had actually taken one of my classes in her sophomore year. Our shared enthusiasm seemed to annoy Henry, and he sat stiffly, sullenly in his chair as if pretending he were part of some other group. Despite Henry, I enjoyed talking with the girl and

104

was both ashamed and intrigued by some of the thoughts about her that crept into my mind. When she left, excusing herself politely, I felt I had correctly appraised Henry's problem and, annoyed by the lack of sociability he had demonstrated, told him, "Henry, you ought to be married."

Chapter 21 (Miriam)

Miriam held her cup tightly, her fingers coiled around the handle and base away from the heat of the liquid. Between sips, she held the cup only a few inches from her face beneath the visor of her sun glasses. She had taken to wearing sunglasses all the time now, indoors and out, even to the movies. "It's Miriam's blue period," her sister who painted said.

The remaining hand was used to push back the stray wisps of hair that unwound from the thick coil piled high at the back of her head. The hair had been sprayed repeatedly with lacquer to keep it in place but still it broke free. It's coarse and dirty, she thought. Why can't it always be the first day after my permanent?

Looking around at the other girls in the cafeteria, she could see no one whose hair she really admired. Ann Tolman was talking to Cathy, but Ann's hair was attractive merely because it was long and for no other reason.

She was glad Cathy had found another girl to talk to, someone else willing to listen while Cathy rambled on, not paying attention when you tried to say something in return. It had been nice for a while having someone to sit with even if it had been Cathy. Cathy was kidding herself if she thought Ann would be her friend for long. Ann had a new friend, a new project every week.

She remembered the week Cathy had given up smoking, the two of them sitting together, Miriam talking, trying to take Cathy's mind off tobacco—she'd never learned to smoke herself, had tried often enough, but the paper always stuck to her lip and the cigarette left little flecks of tobacco at the corner of her mouth and a damp ugly stub in the ashtray when she was through—and then someone would sit down who was smoking, a boy usually, and Cathy would bum a cigarette from him and start smoking all over again. She talked Miriam into buying a pack of cigarettes—"my emergency supply," — and then, one after the other, she borrowed the cigarettes from Miriam and smoked them.

Cathy smiled at her from across the room and then turned and spoke to Ann. Ann looked up and smiled also. Miriam wondered if they were talking about her. She wondered if she'd ever really been Cathy's friend or just a conversation piece Cathy could tell all her real friends about.

"You're Jewish aren't you?" had been one of the first things Cathy had said to Miriam. Next she said, "It's so difficult to make friends here," which wasn't true at all, it wasn't difficult to meet people at the college, it was difficult to avoid people you had already met. "I'm joining the choir," Cathy said next, "they say it is one of the best ways to meet people. And I'm glad I have a Jewish friend."

Miriam shrugged irritably as if to push the whole weight of Cathy from her shoulders, along with boys who wouldn't date her because she was Jewish, and boys who thought she was easy because she was Jewish, and a Jewish mother who watched every move she made. Well, Ann seemed to be enjoying Cathy's company, although Ann herself was too self-centered to tolerate anyone else's peculiarities for long.

Miriam's cup was empty and she let it dangle from her fingers. The last drops spilled on her paisley blouse. Damn, she thought, blushing rose on olive, and tried to dab at the stain with a napkin. She really ought to go to the bathroom and work on it with cold water. But she didn't want anyone staring at her while she walked to the woman's room. Damn Wood anyway for being late.

"Time means nothing in the South," he'd say if she berated him.

That's crackers, she'd reply, I'm a student, I've got to study, time is very important to me. She slipped the end of her blouse out of her skirt before standing up to de-emphasize the lines of her bust when she walked. People will think I'm wearing maternity clothes. A second thought intruded on the first, "What will Peter say, if I tell him I am pregnant?"

The stain had to go. She just hoped no one was watching her walk across the room. "Nothing to be ashamed of," said her mother. "Lots of goodies," said her sister. "A fine pair," said Peter and Henry and every boy she'd been with, but still she didn't want them staring, not even in the bedroom.

The sound of bubbling laughter. Was someone laughing at her? Ann Tolman? No one else was laughing; Ann always laughed at strange things. Not at me, she hoped. But she saw that Cathy and Ann were huddled together, talking a mile a minute and laughing and not caring how anyone else felt.

Cathy listens to Ann, Miriam thought; now Miriam knew she had never been more than a curiosity to her. Cathy never listens to anyone, another part of Miriam's mind spoke up. Cathy must want something from Ann. Miriam knew this wasn't true either.

Why can't I say what I feel? Cathy is just the opposite: she does what she wants, she says what she wants to. (Cathy hasn't got your body, another happier thought intruded, but Miriam shoved the thought aside, determined to feel the woman scorned.) Cathy was the only girl on campus with a motorbike. And the only girl on campus to wreck a motorbike. She was one of the few people Miriam knew who were willing to come out openly and say they favored integration. In fact, for a few days, Cathy has been the most active integrationist on campus, going to meetings, berating the Dean, doing almost everything an integrationist should do, except, of course, actually sitting or talking with a black person.

Two colored men were sitting at a corner table! Why hadn't she noticed them before? So occupied with her own thoughts, she hadn't noticed anyone coming in to the cafeteria that evening and yet it was almost full, despite the hour. She recognized classmates, her cousin, two sorority sisters, and almost half the members of her cousin's fraternity. Almost everyone is here tonight except Wood, she though bitterly.

Even Professor Webb was there, though she couldn't imagine he'd come to look at the colored students. The professor's head was buried in a book as always, shoulders slumped and head thrust forward close to the pages. There was a dribble of coffee on his chin. (He's as bad as me, she thought.) The professor had horrible habits. He would pick his nose while he was lecturing. If she didn't think he was a brilliant man, she wouldn't enroll in any of his classes, none of the students would. And he wasn't a particularly good lecturer. Once he'd delivered the same lecture twice in a row, almost word for word.

And you couldn't get him to pay attention to you. Oh, he'd answer your questions, maybe. But more likely he would talk about something else that interested him, some other question that your question reminded him of. "Take the course twice," someone had suggested, "He's sure to answer this year's questions next year."

Professor Webb looked up at her abstractly, his rheumy eyes almost but not quite focusing and gave a rhythmic nod of recognition. Was he really nodding to her? (He doesn't even know my name and I have taken his courses twice, and talked with him after class. I am going to major in his subject.)

Two other professors in the history department were standing immediately behind her, hiding their coffee in their hands, and looking for a place to sit. Professor Mason, she thought, and Dr.

Starr. At the synagogue, they'd tried to pair her a couple of times with Starr, but nothing doing. He was old, even if he was young, and boring. Mason, by contrast, was interesting and distinguished looking, very virile; he looked like Wood without the motorcycle jacket.

Starr nodded at her abstractly, Mason looked her up and down. It's the coffee stain she thought or he breasts.

From what she could overhear of the professors' conversation, Starr and a graduate student in the history department named Zellner were responsible for the colored men being there. Other colored people were in the restaurant too, she saw for an instant, the bus girls and the cooks in their starched white uniforms, but they were huddled together behind the counter and out of the way.

She knew who Zellner was, of course, everyone did, at least by reputation. She'd seen him around the Den playing cards and kibitzing "The Game" and, once, Wood had actually tried to introduce her. Zellner's head, blond and curly, could be glimpsed between those of two of the colored boys. He sat back relaxed in jersey and dress pants, while the colored boys wore suit coats and ties. A third colored boy with a broad chest sat by himself at an adjacent table glaring. What could he be so mad about?

A group of freshman from New York or someplace else up North walked over to Zellner's table and took turns shaking Zellner's hand. She'd tutored one of the freshmen — she couldn't remember his name, and he'd spent most of his time with her staring at the table.

Michael Godfrey — wasn't he always in to everything? — walked up to Zellner's table still dragging Laurie by the hand. Laurie wasn't the brightest member of this year's pledge class, but surely she could do better than Michael. No, they went everywhere together. They'd been going steady since the beginning of the year. Why had the sorority pledged Laurie anyway? Oh yes, she was Shelia's cousin. Laurie wasn't bad looking in a skimpy sort of way. Surprising to see Godfrey paired with her considering his reputation as a grabber. She'd been surprised too when he'd gone with Cathy for a while.

"Isn't he a little egotistical?" she'd asked Cathy.

"You'd better believe it," Cathy replied. "I don't know why they ever let him into the movement. All he wants is the publicity. He doesn't really care about the negro."

And Michael's Jewish, too, Miriam thought. Maybe you collect Jews, Cathy, first me, then Michael, and now Ann.

Arnie Schwartz, the editor of the school paper, stood leaning against the wall with half a dozen of his cronies. Sandra Cohen, who'd gone dramatic this year, was with her drama teacher and he was with his wife.

Tyler Caldwell, the campus' best dressed male – he thinks – President of the Tulane YAFers, hovered over Cathy's table. Tyler and Ann had gotten into a shouting match, and she looked about ready to scratch his eyes out. The unflappable Tyler just turned his back on her and began to cuss out Cathy instead. Well, she deserved it. "Go back to Montana and take your nigger friends with you." (Or had he said "nigger-loving friends"?) Another five minutes and Miriam would know all the details of the quarrel that Ann was retailing in her high-pitched voice to anyone who would listen.

Time to go to the ladies room. Nobody would notice her if she got up to leave now, but she was not sure she could get out. She could no longer see Godfrey or Cathy through the solid wall of students formed around Zellner's table. They were booing and hissing. Tyler was ranting still but not everyone was listening to him. A line of fraternity men carried freshly painted signs, "Go home Niggah," and "Tigers 5, Niggers 2;" they were laughing and cracking jokes at the back and making fun of Tyler and Ann.

Now Godfrey had stood up and was barring his fangs at Tyler. Good for Mick. Of course, Mick was acting as if he were personally responsible for bringing the colored boys to the cafeteria. And If she knew anything about Mick, he'd only found out about the negroes by accident. Laurie had released Mick's hand, finally, Miriam was glad to see, and moved to a table some distance away from him.

The gold sleeve of a blue and gold wrestling jacket caught her eye. Wood stood in the entrance to the Den. Damn him. He was heading directly for her, stopping to slap backs and to shake hands along the way. Incredible how every man always thought he and he alone was the center of attention.

A girl clung to Wood's arm. She was short with mousy brown hair and barely came up to his shoulder. Damn him. Absolutely the last straw, bringing his girl friend to meet her. He probably expected to leave the two of them together – "have a nice talk, girls" – while he pushed his way into the center of the crowd. Miriam got up first instead, walked proudly past where Ann and Cathy were sitting together and headed for the side door to the cafeteria.

Chapter 22

The jukebox was playing something blue and funky. "I know that tune," the old man cackled.

"Oh yeah, what? What is it?" Blackie said sourly.

"I know that tune. But can you name the band?"

"Of course, I can name the band."

"Can you name the singer?"

"Of course, I can name the singer."

"Can you name the singer and the band?"

"Of course, I can."

"Then name them!" and the old man's cackles rang out over the bar.

"I like him, Daddy"

"I'm glad."

"There's something about him. He's different."

"Different may not be enough."

"I need someone different Daddy. My life isn't going anywhere."

"You have your job in the bookstore."

"Oh, Daddy!"

"God, will you look at the tits on her."

"They're not so big."

"She's got a beautiful face."

"Who cares about the face."

"She plays pool like a man. I like that."

"Leonard?"

Leonard who was bent over the bar arranging three nickels and a dime on a napkin didn't look up at Wood. "Yeah?" he said abstractly.

"Why do you do it?"

"It's a trick."

"Not the pennies."

"They're nickels. A dime and three nickels. You're supposed to show me how to move the dime without moving the nickels."

Someone hit the lantern over the bar with his cue and it began to oscillate to and fro creating strange patterns on the walls. "Why do you do it?" Wood persisted.

"It's a trick."

"Go around. Get involved in sit-ins. Risk your life."

Zellner drew back from the bar and the coins that lay there. The famous Zellner grin split his face. You could see why people admired him, hated him, followed him. "It beats studying," he said.

"Emil called," Professor Mason said.
"Emil called! Whatever for? He's not supposed to call me."
"Well, he called."
"Is he still in the hospital?"
"He didn't say."
"God, I hope he's still there. He's not supposed to call. They're not supposed to let him call."
"He used to be your closest friend." Emil was different too, Professor Mason wanted to remind her.
"Used to be, Daddy. Used to be."

"I want a 'nother one. A 'nother one," Blackie said.
"You've had too much already," snapped the bartender.
"Hey," said the old man, "He lost the bet. Let him buy me a drink, will ya."

A click as the cue ball struck the object. Nina Simone and all the murmuring voices, at the bar and at the tables, sang of loneliness, sang of want. A thud, as the object ball dropped into the pocket. The tall blond laughed. She threw her shoulders back and her breasts moved up and taut against her sweater. Parsons writhed as if in actual pain.

"Daddy?"
"Yes?"
"I think I'm going to go away."
"Think it over, O.K.?"
"O.K."
Maggie sipped her brandy. After a pause, she said, "You know, he's a lot like you."
Mason tried to look attentive.
"He's going to be a professor."
"Do you want to marry a professor?"
"If he turns out like you, Daddy."
He smiled but inside he was thinking of all he'd wanted to do and hadn't, of Violet, of his book, and that he'd once wanted to be Dean. "I'm not sure you'd want that."

112

"You turned out O.K., Daddy, honestly."

Dr. Mason smiled and this time felt the smile grow inside him. "Thanks." It was hard not to believe you were O.K., when the person you loved best in all the world said so.

"They were a great band," said Blackie.

"Used to know'm all. They used to all come into the bar after the show. Sampson'd sit over there. Washington here. They weren't s'pposed to let Washington drink in the bar him being colored and all, so they drew a line on the bar here and said this is the colored section. Then he'd take out his trumpet when he'd had enough to drink and he'd play. God what notes he would play."

"Better n'Armstrong."

"Much better. Better n'anybody."

"And that singer, Anita somebody?"

"Anna...

"Anna, Anita, 'member her?"

"They were a great band."

"I'll bet, I could just go up and ask her, ask her if she would go out with me."

"Why don't you, then," cried half a dozen young voices.

"She's awfully tough," Little Hamilton offered.

"You want me to ask her?"

"I can ask her, I think. You think, I should Lennie?"

"You do it or I'll do it. You decide," Leonard said.

"Wait Lennie," Wood interrupted, "You told me we were going to..."

"Do it Lennie." the chorus said.

"She's got a boyfriend," the boy who wanted to ask but couldn't decide said hesitantly.

"Fat, sloppy, and three inches shorter," said the chorus.

"Shit," said Zellner and he walked over to the girl, a tall blond in a blue wool sweater and skirt combination that emphasized her breasts and her buttocks. They could see Zellner talking to the girl though they could not hear him. The girl laughed. Her boyfriend scurried around the table, lining up his shots, pretending to be indifferent to Zellner's presence.

Zellner and the girl left the bar. The chorus broke into applause while the boyfriend stared open mouthed. "Shit," said the boy who had wanted to ask the girl but couldn't decide.

Peter wondered if Maggie would be waiting outside Parsons' place when he got there or whether she would come over to Parsons' later.

Chapter 23

At 9 A.M., the thumping of children's heads against the wall and the raucous cries of "Hey Stella," and "I'm not going to make your dammed breakfast," woke him to a new day.

During the preceding night, a series of strange dreams had drained Wood of all energy:

He had been traveling along the road at night stretched out on a sort of flatcar, like a kitchen door tilted and placed on wheels. At first, he just lay back and watched the stars. Then the sky clouded over and the car began to go faster and faster in the darkness. Soon it was pitch black, like the time he had walked along an isolated stretch of country road after a long rain. No light at all in the sky, not even a reflection from the lights in the towns ahead.

The flat car continued to accelerate. Was the road narrowing? Was that a bridge or a tunnel ahead? Men-at-work signs and some kind of construction loomed out of the darkness around him. He had to stop, must stop, but the flat car had no brakes. No way to stop the car except by reaching a hand or a foot over the side searing his flesh against the moving pavement.

He woke the first time with his arm dangling over the side of the bed rubbing against the wooden floor, the next to find himself standing by the window with its broken Venetian blind pushing uselessly against the wall.

When the noise and the half-light of dawn shielded him from further dreams, he rolled up his sleeping bag and packed his saddlebags. He walked down the long gray hallway in the semidarkness to Parson's apartment. It was early, so he knocked softly, rubbing his motorcycle key over the door in a circular scratching motion. A key to the apartment should have been above the doorsill, but he couldn't find it. He knocked harder. "Parsons? Parsons!" He was pounding furiously when a door opened behind him in the adjacent apartment and someone stepped out in the hallway with a bag full of garbage. Wood stalked by them to the outside, his nose elevated in the air.

His motorcycle wouldn't start, of course. He kicked it furiously, took off the saddlebags, then wheeled the cycle around to the side of the building and parked it underneath the archway. He called once more outside Parsons' window and threw a handful of pebbles to be sure. Then he walked away, still carrying the saddlebags.

Chapter 24

Dixie did not live in the Quarters where Parsons had expected to find her apartment but on its edge and several blocks beyond that. The houses and apartments were worn and faded, not by the centuries, but as the result of faulty wartime construction and subsequent neglect. Here were the homes of poor whites and poor coloreds; in those cases where some attempt had been made at improvement, a bit of iron railing or fresh paint on the lintels, it meant only that a house had recently been converted into apartments, and that it, too, would soon fade into the decay around it.

Parsons could recognize Dixie's window by the air conditioning unit that protruded from it and was turned on now even though the day was cool, but when he stepped onto the porch he could not see inside, and the curtains on the other windows of her apartment were unmoving.

He knocked. "Dixie?" No response. No signs either of the party he expected to find going on inside.

"Dixie?" Parsons pushed the door open and stepped inside the apartment.

The door opened directly into the living room with several other rooms and a short hallway opening off it. The living room was given over to culture, books, mostly paperbacks, and tinted photographs, though she did possess one painting, a nude, taken from behind.

The kitchen, long and bare, held a table and three chairs, a clean counter, no sign of pots and pans, an oven that was used mainly as a toaster, and an old-fashioned refrigerator with coils massed at its top.

The room smelled slightly musty as if it had not been opened in days. He was conscious of the smell of roaches and the sprays that had been used in a vain attempt to kill them.

The refrigerator contained none of the lush food of the Quarters — shrimp, olive oil, quarter-pounders, raw oysters in a jar — but only a single mold-topped container of cottage cheese. The usual bag of coffee was missing. No milk, no beer, nothing to drink, not even a can of tomato juice. The first set of cupboards he examined were empty, the second contained only two or three mismatched dishes and a serving platter. "She's a hell of a cook," Parsons thought.

"I'm a hell of a cook," Dixie said from the doorway, startling him. "Come on over in the evening with Wood some time and let me fix a meal for you."

"Sure thing," he said and moved toward her.

Moving out of his reach, she asked if he'd like a drink.

"Sure. Milk? Coke? Got a beer?"

"Something harder than that."

"Boilermakers. I like boilermakers."

"It's a little early for those. Let's see what I've got." She opened the third cupboard, the one farthest from the refrigerator. "I've got Canadian. You like Canadian? Not much in this bottle though. You like gin?"

"Milk Punch?" Parsons had tasted Milk Punches once, two of them he remembered, when he'd gone to breakfast at Brennans shortly after he was married.

"Oh, let's just drink it straight." She extracted two fruit glasses from the cupboard where the bottles were kept and filled each from the gin bottle with perhaps just a little more gin in her glass than in his. Then she topped off each of the glasses from the tap. "Cheers," she said.

"Cheers...."

They stared at each other. He sipped slowly, had to, his drink tasted like something a nurse would rub on his chest. Dixie held her drink at the back of her throat, her cheeks puffed out slowly, her lips protruding, then swallowed it abruptly in a gulp of passion. She smiled, her housecoat falling away to reveal the tops of her breasts and then her nipples. She was quite sexy, Parsons thought. She took another gulp from the glass and moved closer to him. He leaned down to kiss her. She stuck her gin-coated tongue inside his mouth and pushed some of the gin from her throat into his, but when he reached for her she just moved to the other end of the counter and stared at him.

He stared back. The hem of her housecoat was frayed and dirty. Bits of food clung to the coat front; and its armpits were stained with sweat. He should have been repulsed but was not.

She saw him admiring her and pivoted on one shapely foot. Again, the housecoat fell away, revealing a long length of shapely calf and the same small breast, a long drooping nipple falling against the fabric. The food stains forgotten, he imagined her pressed against him, undoing his belt, unbuttoning him, then kneeling, her lips warm around his cock.

The doorbell rang and someone, male judging by the fragrance of Old Spice, pushed open the kitchen door behind him. Henry Starr, swinging a bottle in one hand, announced his arrival. "I've brought some people," Henry said. The kitchen door swung open again. Leonard Zellner came into the room and Miriam Finestone and behind Miriam someone Parsons didn't recognize but who had to be a professor, too. Wood's friends he thought. Noises came from the living room where someone had turned on a record player.

"We were just talking," Parsons said.

"I've got to get dressed," Dixie sang out, "Help yourself to everything."

"We brought a bottle," Starr said.

Parsons put his gin glass down on the counter and turned to follow Dixie from the room. "Dixie?" he called.

Without answering, Dixie walked into her bedroom, stumbling for an instant on the doorsill. She removed the housecoat and lay back heavily on the bed.

A small radio on one of the chairs was just loud enough to be heard above the roar of the air conditioner. She raised one firmly muscled calf toward the ceiling and waved her foot to and fro in time to the music. Parson's came toward her, unbuttoning his shirt. She looked up and smiled.

He imagined she had wrapped her ankles around his head and pulled him toward her. She kept up the pressure until finally his tongue was inside her and he lapped at her juices unable to control the movements of his own pelvis.

He sat down beside her on the bed to act on his fantasy, but when he lunged for her, she got up and walked to the window.

Outside the bedroom, the party was in full swing. It seemed as if everyone Wood had ever met in New Orleans, even to speak to briefly, had come and brought their own friends with them. The only one absent was Wood himself.

Mason danced with Miriam while Starr, the center as always of a fierce debate, argued for lifting the embargo on trade with socialist countries. Miriam was remarkably light on her feet, Mason thought. Parsons cut in on Mason and then Mason cut back in on Parsons.

Dixie came out of the bedroom once, startling a small group holding a discussion in the kitchen. She poured herself another glass of gin, took a quick peek out at the party and then went back to the bedroom. Parsons entered the kitchen only to see her door closing on him once again.

In the living room, Mason suggested to Miriam they have a quiet drink at the Napoleon House together and Miriam agreed. On their way out, Henry waylaid Mason and insisted he contribute to the discussion. Mason could think of nothing he could or wanted to contribute, but by the time he had explained this, Miriam had disappeared into the kitchen.

Parsons was talking to Miriam. They were both drinking scotch from the bottle Henry had brought though they had to make do with paper cups. Parsons had his hand on Miriam's ass and though she didn't particularly care for his hand being there she didn't feel it was worth the trouble of telling him to remove it. The hand on the ass was all Mason saw when he looked into the room and then quickly stepped out again.

In the bedroom, Dixie was having a dream. In the dream, Wood was with her, lying next to her on the bed. She had lifted one leg for them both to admire, pointed toward the ceiling, dancing in time with the music. Wood's eyes following her long trailing fingers down her calves, to the dimple behind the knee, the white firm thighs, and the thick mat of dark hair and rosy lips where his head had rested a moment before.

"Where's Wood?" someone asked.

"Where's Professor Mason?" Miriam asked Starr.

Miriam strolled disconsolately from room to room. Why had Mason left? Had he gone alone or has someone else gone with him?

Miriam had been sitting quietly in Dixie's bedroom for several minutes before she realized someone else was there.

"You like Wood?" Dixie asked her from the bed.

"Yes," Miriam replied; yes, she realized, she liked him very much.

"He didn't come to the party."

"Someone said he's gone away. His roommate Parsons told me that."

"Parsons." Dixie almost spat the name out, "Parsons is a liar."

After a long while, Dixie got out of bed and wandered about the apartment. The party had ended almost an hour before, the guests drifting away one by one or in small groups. Someone had gone to a great deal of effort to pick up and put things away. Several bags of trash remained in the living room, but she could carry these down in the morning.

A half-full paper cup on a bookshelf was revealed hidden between two books. Scotch, Dixie thought, taking a first tentative sip.. She drank it slowly, though she would have preferred to have gin.

"I need your help," Wood had said, and started to slip on his pants.

She remembered whispering crazy things to his retreating back and asking him to come back, soon, please.

The rising sun shining through the half-open curtain made her eyes wince; she turned her head away and for an instant Dixie looked like a small sleepy-eyed child.

Returning to the bedroom, she turned up the dance music. A top-40 tune and Dixie knew many of the words. She took a gulp from her cup, set it down on the bookshelf and, raising her hands high above her head, began to dance slowly about the room.

Chapter 25 (Wood)

No longer floundering in uncertainty, but exploiting it, I slipped into someone else's dream where terror, lies, confusion, sweet deceptive argument held me because I did not want to leave; I love you Maggie.

In the dream, a man is chasing us. His name is Emil. He has a gun. First, he is said to be a cripple, later a TB patient. Emil has a terrible temper; once he went to where Maggie worked and threatened her. He would kill me, kill us both.

Is he chasing us from the hospital? The hazy noon New Orleans sky is ignited, blazing. The road I take cannot bear to leave the city but twists and turns through the suburbs. Every ten blocks or so a heavily patrolled school zone slows us to fifteen miles an hour.

We met behind the married students village at eleven a.m. We had to hide from Dr. Mason, meet in secret. Maggie slipped out on her coffee break. I gave a false name at the auto-transport agency. Only her best friend, Carole, knows we are leaving.

When she arrives, Maggie is carrying her clothing in a bushel basket instead of a suitcase. A sweater spills over the heaped edge of the basket.

"You're going to carry your clothes in that? Where are your suitcases?" The basket looks ridiculous and proves to be so later as we drag it in and out of hotel lobbies, across parking lots, across the Canadian border through customs.

"You're not my master," she shouts back. And all at once we are yelling like a married couple outside the other married couples' windows.

I drive as fast as I am able, the city doing everything it can to slow me down until we cross the Canal and push through the curtain of hot moist air that surrounds it. The air is fresh, invigorating. The road winds away from the River across a series of bridges through the bayous and down toward the Gulf. We can see only glimpses of the houses down among the trees. We drive through pampas grass almost as tall as the car itself.

At Gulfport (Biloxi?) we reach the coast. On one side of the highway, long green lawns and imposing homes are set well back from the roadway in the shade of tall moss-covered oak and banyan trees. The water is on the other side, separated from the highway only by a narrow strip of grass and beach. The water is still; the air above it shimmers in the heat reflected from the white sand. Boats lie at anchor, ships sail south and west and disappear into the horizon.

We park and walk down to the water, up close, a disappointing muddy brown; the sewer lines empty beneath the piers and across the highway, the oaks and banyans feast.

We walk hand in hand along the beach. A shrill cry and a rush of wings as a patrolling sea gull dives to the attack. I raise my arm; I want to control the gull's flight, like a carnival roustabout I'd seen once in a movie who controlled the movements of the ponies with his hands. The gull snaps at my pointing fingers. Maggie laughs.

We take shelter in a palm-thatched hut. It is open to the winds, and the pursuing gull soon follows us inside. We flee before it, the shrill cries and buffeting wings of the gull and his mate only a step or two behind until we cross their unseen boundary and slip to safety beneath an uneven wooden pier.

We eat in a cheap restaurant, see part of a carnival. We drive for hours following the road that travels between the stately homes and the beach. After Mobile, the road heads inland and up into the hills, amid red clay and pine forest fleeing from the glaciers. I tell her about the glaciers that four million years before had carved the rocks from the Canadian Shield to mid-Alabama.
She looks at me as if I am crazy, laughs, "If there are glaciers here, we could make a fortune selling ice."

And all the while we talk, the pine forest and the ginkgo, the banyans and the Spanish bayonet stay just outside the glacier's reach.

Later, Dr. Mason told me Emil did have a terrible temper. And in New Orleans, people of Emil's sort often did carry guns. What is fantasy and what is reality may depend on the culture. I'd studied the Chinese philosopher who dreamt he was a butterfly, then woke to wonder if he were a butterfly dreaming he was a man. "But," said Dr. Mason wryly, "his lack of certitude didn't affect the luxury in which the sage lived at court, or the power and influence he wielded."

We drive on long after we've grown tired of driving. Up a rise looking into the moon, then down into a mist-filled hollow, a pool of molten silver created by a passing car. When we rise again, each shape, each stunted pine tree outlined against the moon is an attacker.

Maggie doesn't drive; she was in a car crash when she was seventeen (this would account for the scar above her upper lip). I am

122

too tired to drive. What if two approaching cars meet in the blinding glare of a mist-filled hollow?

"Dim your lights!" she cries as we dive over the crest. I am asleep; she lies beside me; I can feel her buttock against my buttock, a hand thrown back limply so it rests against my thigh.

We reach a town finally, long after I'd ceased to put a conscious effort in my driving, stop at an old rooming house kept by two sisters. They congratulate us on our recent marriage. And we do not disappoint them in the creakings from our bed, though one partner is still half asleep, the other beyond sleep, exhausted, searching for relief. We sleep though, my head between her breasts, her hand thrown back limply against my shoulder.

The road to North Carolina takes us through Alabama, across a corner of Georgia, and into Tennessee. Moving always toward the East, upon this last adventure, the sun strikes at our bones and warms them, the heat of a log so long in the fire, that long ago the brightness ate its heart.

We stop to explore caverns, stalagmites and stalactites hidden in absolute darkness. We drive through the Smokies (walk along a nature trail, eat an apple, watch a waterfall), along the Blue Ridge Trail, to Ashville, Winston-Salem, Raleigh, not forgetting a small corner of the state, where a chain gang labors on a strip of broken road. The white guard perspires in the sun, his uniform sweaty and caked with dirt. The twelve men in the gang work with shovels and a vat of hot tar. Two of them, Maggie says, are trustees. They supervise the work under the white guard's direction. Several of the men look up when we pass but only for an instant from the corners of their eyes.

We have stopped for coffee down the road when we see the guard again. A few country people and two commercial travelers are sitting at the counter and we are off by ourselves at a table. The proprietor is fussing down at our end of the room; he's asked us twice about the score of the William and Mary game and I've lied and said we are ahead. The proprietor says he has a son who played for William and Mary and a daughter who married an engineer. The proprietor is nervous — "about us," Maggie whispers — and he is talking in an attempt to draw the two ends of the room, counter and tables, South and North, together. When the guard comes in and sits at the counter, the proprietor yells to him that William and Mary are ahead.

"Maggie, are you going to phone your father?" I ask.

Her reply is inaudible. The proprietor is perched near our table trying to shield us from the others in the room. The guard orders coffee that he sips from a spoon and a piece of pie. A moment later, one of the colored trustees walks in.

The Negro enters quietly and walks slowly a step a time; no one notices him until he is halfway to the middle of room where he stops a few feet from the guard. He starts to walk closer, thinks better of it and stops again. This slow approach continues, step, pause, step for over a minute while the guard sips his coffee and finishes his pie. We are all watching the man, but no one, including the proprietor, has anything to say. Finally, one of the locals at the counter asks, "What the hell's that nigger doing in heah?" The guard repeats the question in a loud voice as if it were his own, still without moving or looking up at the man in back of him. The colored trustee approaches closer. The guard waves him back. Maggie's hand nestles in mine and she whispers that the colored boy might have a gun. As if thinking the same thing, the guard draws his own gun on the man.

The two walk out of the restaurant, the trustee in front, the guard behind still with his gun out and pointing at the man in front of him.

The screen slams to on the guard's heel, where it stays propped open while the guard talks in low whispers to the colored man. A moment later, the guard returns to the counter and drops a quarter by his plate; it rolls halfway down the counter before the waitress snatches it up. The guard reholsters his gun, gestures helplessly toward the rest of us, and walks away. One or two of the group at the counter walk after him. The remainder begin to talk among themselves.

The proprietor turns to us apologetically. He motions to the waitress to bring refills to the other customers before they can get up from their chairs.

Maggie says she doesn't want to stay there anymore and we leave. One of the commercial travelers steps out on the porch with us and says it is the first time he's ever seen a coon come in to that restaurant. Maggie says she saw it happen once where she was working and she didn't like it. The salesman says it happens all the time up north.

In the car, Maggie whispers that prisoners who escape from the chain gang will hide in the brush by the narrower parts of the road and try to hijack an automobile. We lock the doors, roll up the windows, leaving only a thin opening between each window and the car roof, and drive at high speed for an hour until we get to higher country.

Green rolling hills, far off purple ridges masked by the haze of dozens of burning forest fires. We travel the back roads, make love in the morning, sometimes just a few feet from the pavement. I take her weight on me if there are brambles.

After Winston-Salem, a turnpike carries us north through the hills to Richmond, past the battlefields at Shiloh and Manassas, past the green, enormous lawns, round and round the traffic circle in sight of the Capitol, across the longest suspension bridge, ending in a wait to take the ferry between Delaware and New Jersey.

We don't think about Emil chasing us. Once, while we are parked by a desolate stretch of dune, an old Chevrolet with Louisiana plates stops behind us, but the driver doesn't get out of the car. I persuade Maggie to phone her father, but he isn't home. She calls Parsons and asks him to pass the news of our departure along. In New York, I drive the wrong way on one of the Avenues. When I get to a friend's place—a friend of a friend—a handwritten card with an address someone had passed to me in San Francisco—

it is three in the morning. I go to sleep immediately in a back room, but Maggie stays up to talk. "I've never talked to New Yorkers," she says.

Chapter 26. (Wood)

He lay in his sleeping bag on the floor of Simon's living room listening to Simon and Maggie discuss him. He made no effort to get up and get dressed and join in the conversation, but basked in the repeated mention of his name, snorting whenever they touched upon one of his weak points. They ignored his interruptions and pretended he was still asleep. ("He will be after awhile," Simon said to Maggie, "you'll see.")

"Tell me about yourself," she said to Simon.

"I'm an engineer. I've lived in South Africa and I've lived here. I specialize in building apartment and office complexes and in meeting strange people."

"Like Pete."

"Exactly."

Maggie and Peter had walked up the hill from the train station, still toting the saddlebags and the bushel basket they had been carrying since they left their drive-away car at its destination. Pete raced ahead, Maggie puffing along behind, till he turned, saw her, and ran back to walk with her again. "This is where I went to high school," he told her. "The guys would stand around the corner here and smoke where the teachers couldn't see them."

"We did the same thing."

The houses downtown sat flush, one against the other, without intervening lawns or alleyways. Each had three stories and a basement and a long curving staircase that went up to the second story. The exception was a tall featureless apartment building with a sign in front that read, "Efficiencies still available." "This building wasn't here when I went to school," Pete said.

Simon's old window still had the big red curtains that closed out the light and Simon still lived there. Pete woke him up with loud knocks and a stone tossed at the window. A thick tousled head of curly hair came from between the curtains, hollered "Who's there," and a hand slipped the latch from the door without waiting for an answer. "You can put your sleeping bag here," Simon said, first offering Pete a choice of the mattress or the box springs from his bed and then, in the same breath, "three days is the limit."

Simon had gone back to sleep without once asking where Wood had been or what he'd been up to for the past three years. Nor did it seem to surprise him when Wood let Maggie in the door the next evening. "No," he said when Wood offered to borrow his car. Simon spent an hour talking with Maggie and then, about a half an hour before his usual bedtime, announced to her, "If you're going to stay here. And you might as well. I'm going to have Moira spend the night." And the four of them had spent the next two nights in Simon's two-room apartment, male and female on the mattress, male and female on the box springs.

"I think you'll like Montreal," Simon said to Maggie. "It has a certain flavor. It takes getting used to, though."

"I don't know about that." Maggie replied. "I don't know how long we'll be here." She looked expectantly at the sleeping bag, which yielded only a series of artificial snores in return.

"How was your trip?" Simon asked politely.

"We saw a lot of interesting things," she said, inadequately Wood thought.

"Tell him about the bears," came a sleepy voice from the floor.

"The What?" Simon asked.

"Oh, we saw some bears," Maggie replied.

"No, no. Tell him the whole thing." the voice from the floor persisted

"You do it."

"Will somebody please tell me about the bears before I die of curiosity."

But then he fell asleep before he heard what she had to say.

"Simon...?," he called after he was sure both Maggie and Moira were asleep. "Simon...?" Was he awake? Finally, Wood heard Simon grunt.

"Did you ever build any important buildings?"

A grunt that might have been "yes" or "no," but more likely "What?"

"I mean the buildings you built, are any of them the sort that people would go to and say 'Oh, look here's one of Simon's buildings.'"

"I'm not an architect if that's what you mean. I'm a construction engineer. I go around and make sure the contractor is following the plans. I check the specifications so when the city engineer comes around there won't be any variances."

"But then you ..."

"Never get my name on any of the buildings. But I worked on a Miles Van der Rohe once."

"Mihles...?"

128

"Van der Rohe. He's quite a famous architect. His buildings are all over the world, Paris, Stockholm, Amsterdam. The one I built is on Sherbrooke Street. It's the one with the apartments on top, offices underneath."

"I've seen it," Wood said, "It's all flat. No...no ornamentation, no windowsills. Just concrete and glass."

"I disagree completely. But I'm not sure I've time to give you a complete lesson in architecture. What time is it, anyway? I might as well just go to work."

"I don't like them." Wood persisted. "Those boring buildings."

"Oh, God. As if we designed them to your specifications.

"You don't have to like them. They're very functional. They make a very efficient use of materials. And they conserve energy."

"They're not what I remember."

"Of course not. They're twentieth century architecture. What you remember is eighteenth and nineteenth. If you want to see old buildings, just walk three blocks east."

A pause while Wood mustered his next argument; late at night, his thoughts always came slowly. "What about this building we're in now?"

"It's a shack they threw up during the First World War. Good God, I need my sleep."

The next night when Simon got home to his apartment, Maggie and Moira were in the kitchen fixing dinner, but Wood was missing.

"He's off talking to his mother."

"Good. Usually, she calls here looking for him and I end up being in the middle."

"How often does he come here?" Maggie asked.

"Every couple of years. Pops in for a few days. Phones his mother to say he's here but he's not coming home. Then they talk back and forth. Then he goes away again. Good God, here he is now. I'd thought surely he'd have supper with his mom and leave some for us."

Supper was a contest between Simon who wanted to tell Maggie all about Montreal and Wood who wanted to tell Simon all about New Orleans. From time to time Moira also proposed "that with all the talk about eating here and eating there, someone might like to thank the cooks who prepared the meal they were eating at that instant."

Eventually, for Wood and Maggie were guests after all, New Orleans won.

"Like an enormous woman, green and fertile..." he began.

"Green!" Maggie exclaimed.

"Her every cranny fragrant with the smell of perique and ripe fruit."

"Green?"

"You wake in the morning, her scent fragrant in your nostrils, as renewed and fresh as if she'd just dabbed perfume behind each ear. After dark, her scent changes again, she becomes sultry, sensual."

"With roaches crawling along her belly."

"There's so much to do, so much to see," Wood continued his travelogue, ignoring Maggie's interruptions, "Every street has a new surprise. They have plants I'd never seen before, growing next to the most decrepit houses. The houses. The houses. They've got rooming houses with a century of tradition.

"So have we," Simon interrupted.

"All along St Charles Avenue and in the Garden District where once there were the homes of the rich."

"The Garden District? You never lived in the Garden District! You lived in Parsons' apartment." Maggie interjected.

"Before I came to Parsons' apartment, I had a room in the Garden District. Or close to it." Wood paused and looked around the room as if defying any further challenge. ("But I love him," Maggie said to Simon later.)

"And the bars never close."

"I didn't know you went to bars?" A speculative look on Simon's face foretold a further series of questions.

"I taught him," Maggie said proudly.

"And what about school? Your mother said you were doing graduate work of some sort?"

"Oh, the school will still be there when I get back."

"My father teaches school," Maggie interjected, "He teaches at the college."

"And Pete goes to the college?"

"No, Pete goes to school in California." And then Maggie recited her story beginning and ending with her first meeting with Peter.

." ... asked me 'Why do you have a pencil behind your ear instead of a carrot?'"

Eventually, two separate conversations persisted, Simon talked to Maggie, and Wood talked to the room at large and occasionally to Moira.

130

"It's a life. My daddy loves me and I got to live in New Orleans so I guess I should be grateful."

"There's just so much to do there," Wood said, and he was off again on his monolog.

Their evenings together went on like this for almost a week, well beyond Simon's three-day limit. But the calls from Wood's mother began to come with greater frequency and more and more often, Maggie felt, Wood would leave her alone, while he went off on some mysterious errand. For a while, she stayed in the apartment and then, as a young child in a new neighborhood will do as it gains confidence, she began to go off on walks of her own.

Wood saw it differently: "Mornings were spent looking for Maggie; she left our rooms early and alone and was always afraid when I found her that I wasn't going to look."

Maggie told Simon, "He's so interested in what he's doing as long as he's the one who's doing it, but he doesn't really care what someone else does unless it involves him. He doesn't even notice me unless he needs me for sex. He talks to you the minute you come back from work, not me; how often does he say, 'Hi Maggie, I love you.' He sits staring out the window at the rain as if he'd never seen rain before, but he forgets that I am sitting there too waiting for him to notice me."

"So you're disappearing to get attention." Simon said.

"Yes and no." Maggie smiled, a broad impish grin lighting up her whole face and the room as well. "Maybe, I'm looking for adventure too."

"Did you see the cathedral?" Simon asked her after one of her morning disappearances. A 17th century Catholic cathedral complete with gargoyles and possibly a hunchback occupied the corner of a nearby square. The Chateau de Ramzy and two of the many iron cannons that had been protecting the city for almost three hundred years stood alongside. Less than two blocks away were the big department stores — Morgan's, Eaton's, Simpson-Sears, Holt Renfrew, and a hundred other shops and restaurants.

"I think so," she said. "It's nice here. If we're going to stay... I'm thinking of getting a job as a waitress."

"Think twice. Montreal is a nice place to visit, but you may not want to live here. We've got long winters. Even the construction stops, thank heavens, so I can work indoors. The snow, lots of it, fills the streets, covers the sidewalks. Sometimes the whole city just settles down, crunch. It's four in the afternoon snowing and if you live in the suburbs you're lucky if you're home by seven. That's why I live downtown."

"I've never seen snow. But it gets cold in New Orleans, too, sometimes."

It will be winter soon, Pete thought. After each rain, it is just a little colder. He chases Maggie through the winding streets that enfilade the university. Schoolboys lurk in doorways, cigarettes cupped hidden in their hands, give him hard stares or turn away hoping this makes them invisible. He catches up with her finally, running up the hill ahead of him, raincoat flapping in the wind. He is sure she heard him, long before he caught up with her, galumphing along behind.

"I was so frightened," she said. But she was angry. "A man spoke to me. He called me a nice piece of pussy.

"He's gone now. He came up to me while I was walking to meet you, he came up behind me.

"Why didn't you take a taxi?" he said.

She shrugged her shoulders, pursed her lips. (He wants to kiss her; he knows a crowd is watching them, but he wants to show them all he loves her and will take care of her.)

"He followed me and I kept looking for a cop. Do you have policemen anywhere? He said, 'Can I carry your shopping bag.' He grabbed at me. I wouldn't let him near me. I talked to him for a few minutes over my shoulder and he kept saying these horrible things."

"Who was he?" His voice was harsher than he intended.

"Just a nobody."

"Why'd you talk to him? You should have just walked away."
"Maybe, I'm a nobody, too." She smiled with her whole face and crinkled her nose and then looked away as if she were going to cry. "You're going to be somebody some day. Like my father. Maybe you don't want a nobody."

I love you Maggie, he thought. Do you want me to love you? But he said, "That's not true."

"I just wish you wouldn't leave me in the mornings."

"But you left me," he said, nonplussed, "you walked out while I was talking with Simon."

"You're always talking with Simon. But you won't talk with me. You don't respect my opinions. You don't want to hear what I have to say."

"We talked in the car."

"Not the way you talk with Simon."

132

"Have you introduced her to your mother yet," Simon asked almost as soon as Wood marched through the front door and had a glass of wine in front of him.

"Sorta."

"Sorta? You've been in the States too long. Talk Canadian."

"Yes. Yes, we took a streetcar out to where my mother is living...

"Your home."

."..and I had Maggie wait in the coffee shop up the street, while I coaxed my mother over to meet her."

"But your mother invited you both to your home for dinner."

"No. She didn't. She was very clear about that. She was just inviting me. Not Maggie. And when she met Maggie, she was...curt, not rude, curt...as if we were an upper crust family and Maggie was a...

"Tramp."

"In a way she is you know. Maggie's the girl you see at the roller rink with her hair all puffed up and frizzy at the ends. She hangs out with the dropouts. She thinks working at the drive-in is a big deal."

"What are you talking about!"

"The woman I love, I guess. I fell in love with her a certain way. I always want her to be that way."

"He doesn't love me, he doesn't love anybody," was what Maggie said to Simon later that evening, and Moira listening in the kitchen said, "I can believe it."

"I though he was like your father." Simon replied.

"That's what he'd like to think. But my father's ten times the man he is."

"I've got to meet her father," Wood said.

"Haven't you met him yet?"

"No, I've been avoiding him."

"Embarrassing for Maggie, perhaps. Is it that you think you'll just argue? Because he's a Southerner. They have many of the same attitudes the Dutch have in South Africa. I never could understand them and I was born there."

"Oh, not that. Her father's a University professor. He ought to like me. All Maggie's other boy friends have been lower class, longshoremen, house painters. I mean, I'm somebody her father can approve of and, at the same time, I guess, I'm still alive enough for her."

"Do you love her?"

"Of course." A smile played on Wood's lips. "At certain moments a woman can't lie to a man."

They lay together again that night, Peter and Maggie on the box springs, Simon and Moira on the mattress, both couples vowing eternal love.

Maggie did not come back. I went out to look for her, stomping in slippers through the gutters, walking by instinct to the Greek's at the corner. The Greek's was where everyone hung out three years ago. I had to go inside to look for her. The glass in front was already opaque, the hot steam from the breakfast trays condensing on the cold October glass. But Maggie was not there.

I walked through the University grounds waving to and being waved at by people I'm sure I didn't know. I took the right paths and came out by the main gate twenty minutes later. Along the way, I stopped to look at a few of the things I remembered as an undergraduate, the leaves of the Ginkgo, a plaque in the grass commemorating a first kiss, a place on the library steps where lions should rest.

I walked downtown and by one of those crazy coincidences met Maggie walking along window-shopping, moving in little darts and jerks between the displays.

She was wearing a light summer dress and an old raincoat of Simon's. She was cold and rubbed her bare arms shivering while we talked. What an idiot, I thought, not to have brought warmer clothing.

"You didn't come back," I said.

"I wanted to go for a walk." She looked everywhere except at me.

"I'd have gone with you."

"I wanted to go by myself."

I started to speak, to admonish her, but stopped in midsentence and put my arm around her waist. She put her arm about mine and let me walk with her. We looked at things in store windows, a display of maps, one of men's overcoats, and at a five and dime. She laughed at the reflection of my slippers in the window.

I said what had to be said: "We've got two kinds of friendship. In my kind, if you are with somebody, you try to be with them. If you want to be alone, if you won't talk with the other person, you stay by yourself.

"What's the use of our being together if you won't say anything. That's why I want to be married so I'll have someone to talk with. Otherwise, I could be by myself all the time."

Maggie looked at me strangely. "I just felt like going for a walk by myself this morning."

"But we were walking together just now and you didn't talk to me. When we're with Simon and Ann, you'll talk to them and not to me. In New York..."

"Maybe, I like to talk to Simon. Maybe in my kind of friendship, the two people respect each other. Maybe you learn to leave the other person alone." She released my waist and pushed my arm away.

We walked for a block side by side but not touching. "Maybe, I'm not happy being here," Maggie said, but she looked all around her with wonder as the sun came out of the clouds and shone on the faded blue-green copper dome of the old cathedral. The caryatids too looked everywhere about them, looked down at me and her, tiny doll-like figures on the pavement.

"Very well," I said, theatrically, "no conversation. I can do without friendship. Sex will be sufficient. If this is all you want to give me, O.K., I'll take it because I love you."

Maggie drew back her tiny foot as if to kick me. "Sure you'll take it. You'll take anything you can get, like a niggah. And if you get it then you'll want more. That's why we've got to build fences with big signs saying keep away, keep away, when we didn't want to build them in the first place."

Pete smiled, satisfied he'd gotten through her shell, and kissed her tears away. Afterwards he bought her flowers and everything was all right again.

Chapter 27

The emergency meeting of the White Citizen's Council had been
called to protest the integration of New Orleans Public Schools, like
some cancerous growth, 'a grade at a time.' When Barcus and Starr
arrived, the first thirty rows of the auditorium were filled and only a
scattering of seats was available elsewhere. Starr had used Grecian
Formula on his hair to give it a grayish tinge; a patently false
moustache and the motorcycle jacket Wood had left at Parsons'
apartment completed his costume.

Judge Leander Perez of neighboring Plaquemines Parish was the
featured speaker at the meeting and after a very few preliminaries —
saluting the flag, the singing of Dixie, and a revivalist preacher who
talked a great deal about God's will — he was brought on to give the
invocation.

"This emergency meetin'" the Judge said, "is called in honor of
the parents of the chillin of McDonogh 19 and the William Franz
School for the way they responded." Five minutes of enthusiastic
applause followed of the sort seen and heard on television following
a presidential nomination. The Judge went on: "They stood up for
the welfare of their chillen the way mothers and fathers should." His
listeners' ears rang with wild applause. As the crowd of fiercely flag-
waving (and flag-poking, Barcus warned) white males settled back in
their seats, one could hear a lone woman's voice from the far rear of
the auditorium hollering, "Give it to the niggers."

But the Judge had other ideas. "In order to give you protection
from your own heartless double-crossing mayor and city officials. . .
who have refused to repeal the law that requires public school
attendance. . . we have developed a second, alternative plan."

The crowd, silent, expectant, waited for the details, but the Judge
again digressed, this time to describe an incident that had occurred
earlier that day ("At eight in the morning when decent people are
still sleeping," Barcus whispered to Henry under his breath). "It was
a degrading and true-to-form performance," the Judge said, "A few
misdirected New Orleans po-lice under orders from the mayor got
rough and brutalized a few of your fine boys and girls ('who were
throwing rocks through the school windows,' Barcus reminded
Starr)."

"That weasel snake-headed mayor of yours," said the Judge,
then paused, seemingly to take a gulp of water from the glass on the

136

stand beside him, "That weasel snake-head wants to amend your city charter so he can be elected mayor again. Are you goin t' let him?"

Their answer was unequivocal. ("The mayor's gone," said Barcus. "But don't worry, Henry, the Feds still got the atom bomb.")

Finally, and to the great relief of the pregnant woman in the back row, the Judge gave it to the niggers including a smart-aleck mulatto lawyer from New York, "one Thurgood Marshall." He gave it to the Kennedys, and he gave it to the Communists, and he gave it to the Jews, not, he said, because he was anti-Semitic, "I am not anti-Semitic whatever you may read in the papers tomorrow, I am anti-communist... I am anti-communist and so damn many of those Jews are members of the communist party."

Again the crowd was on its feet and again only a lapse of time and some good-natured horseplay could bring them back to their seats again. This time the Judge, seeing he'd found the "spirit of the meeting," settled into some "very serious business," that involved a long series of unrelated and remarkably boring (Barcus thought) statistics involving federal monies, state monies, and the relative proportions of black and white in each of the parishes in south-eastern Louisiana.

Dr. Starr shifted restlessly in his chair. "You like my moustache?" he asked Barcus. Barcus did not answer. Starr looked around slowly at the people seated near him. Their expressions were fierce, intent on the stage as if the litany of numbers the Judge recited had some secret Cabbalistic significance for them. A short blond woman in her early thirties but dressed as if she were only a year or two out of high school scowled at Henry. Starr grinned back at her and the woman looked away. Starr's moustache had slipped down on one side and it gave his grin an almost degenerate cast.

Meanwhile, the Judge had begun reciting a long list of communist-inspired and communist-dominated organizations that he'd uncovered in the Congressional record. Despite the rather prosaic nature of the list, the audience grew more spirited ("boredom setting in," Barcus thought) and much good-natured give and take occurred between the audience and the speaker.

"..read it in the papers," hollered somebody from the audience.

"No, you're not going to read it in the papers," said the Judge and the crowd roared.

"Communist. Communist and subversive. Just plain communist," said the Judge consulting his notes.

Barcus found he was gradually drifting off to sleep. Even the occasional roar from the crowd barely permeated the edges of his consciousness. By the time Barcus became aware of what Starr was doing, it was too late. A tall young student who had seemed to be merely looking for a seat in front whipped around abruptly and took their picture and that of the crowd sitting near them. The people nearby began shifting away and within a few moments an island of empty seats had formed around them.

On stage, the Judge shifted from the Jews to the Catholics. He had discovered a plot, "a most reverend plot," to force racial integration in the Catholic schools. "But we aren't going to let them are we?" he proclaimed to the presumably Protestant heavens. The crowd roared its approval.

"I think we had better go," Barcus said. A small group of ill wishers stood at the back of the auditorium watching Barcus and Starr progress slowly up the aisle. Renfrew, the tall young student who had taken their picture, and Caldwell, the young States-Righter in the three-piece suit who'd led the demonstration in the student cafeteria the week before, stood next to a large man with an open neck-shirt and a bolo tie. Barcus recognized Kent Courtney, editor of the anti-Semitic Thunderbolt, and an arm's length distant two other 'distinguished' conservatives who traveled with him. The combination could only spell trouble. Meanwhile Starr was mugging at the crowd and pulling at his moustache, openly removing and reapplying it to his upper lip as if at some kind of goddamn costume party. (Is there intelligent life on earth, Barcus wondered?) Barcus grabbed Henry by the arm and hauled him down the aisle as if indeed he were some kind of mental defective.

Their progress halted abruptly just inside the lobby. Barcus' rapid wheeling maneuver had outflanked the students but not the plainclothes police officer who had shifted quickly to stop them. "Hello, Lieutenant," Barcus said.

"You are Leonard Starr?" the Lieutenant addressed Starr referring to a Polaroid snapshot he held in his hand.

Henry's only reply was to turn slowly revealing the words "University" and "Berkeley, California" emblazoned on the back of Wood's jacket.

"You from out West, then?"

"No, Suh. I'm from right here in Peachtree Mississippi."

"Peachtree! Yoh family is from New York?"

"No, Sir. My daddy's from Mississippi, too."

"You a communist?"

"No Sir."

"Just some kind of racial agitator?

"NO Sir."

A subordinate came up and pulled at the Lieutenant's arm. The noise level rose rapidly as the lobby filled with concerned citizens determined to do Starr and Barcus ill, though the Judge could still be heard inside the auditorium perorating on the Communist-Catholic conspiracy. The students and Kent Courtney had disappeared, an ominous sign.

The Lieutenant looked up. "Mr. Starr would you please stand over to the side with this other officer?"

The Lieutenant took Barcus by the arm. "Not so funny," he said. "Lot of folk think this a serious business. Lot of folk. And theah are laws again cawmmunists.

"But I don't want to see no violence. Not that I much care whether you and you' friend gets hurt or not. I just don't want a bunch of pictures in the papers. Folks up No'th already think we all crazy. You and your friend best go straight to yo' car, get in an' driv' away."

A burly individual who might have been a stevedore, but who, equally, might have been one of those vendors who push a hot dog through the Quarters, came up and plucked at the Lieutenant's arm. "Is that Leonard Zellner?" he said pointing to Barcus.

"God's teeth," the Lieutenant said. The detective who'd been assigned to guard Starr came and pulled the man away. Then the Lieutenant and two more of his men cleared a path for Barcus and Starr and led them to the outer door.

Rain had blackened the streets while they were inside the Auditorium and it was not as warm as it had been. Barcus could see some kind of a crowd waiting on the pavement below.

The Lieutenant turned to reenter the building.

"Our car's two blocks up the street." Dr. Starr said, motioning toward the waiting group.

"Best run then," replied the Lieutenant and he stepped back inside motioning to the patrolmen to follow him within.

They ran.

Inside, the Judge told the near-capacity crowd, "My friends, good people of the City of New Orleans and the surrounding areas, your destiny is in your hands. Strike back against yo' mayor and his do-nothing legislators. Strike back against this communist conspiracy. And put an end to forced racial integration." No one dissented.

Chapter 28 (Mason)

I was attending under protest. The young States-Righter, Tyler Caldwell, had kept up a steady stream of invitations since discovering me with Henry at the cafeteria demonstration the week before. Wary of his intentions, I had declined repeatedly, but Tyler was persistent. In the end, I had yielded, the victim of his persistence and, indirectly, of Henry's friendship.

The elements seemed opposed to the venture, too. A steady all-day rain had turned into a downpour. The streets swelled with rain and before I had reached my destination, the floodwaters had lifted the chassis of my small car and I was barely able to float to the curb to park.

I walked the last block, hauling up on my pant legs as if they were skirts. Soaked through by the time I reached the front porch of the great old house on Prytania Street, I pushed by its wrought iron gate. In an hour or two, I could probably slip away again, but until then I would be trapped inside waiting for the streets to clear. Well, drinks and food would be plentiful as well as, hopefully, one or two congenial souls of my generation with whom I might pass the hour drying out by the fireplace.

The house far exceeded my expectations, even for a Garden District home: Polished hardwood floors, wood paneling, paintings on the wall (not prints), even a few small sculptures. I could glimpse Persian carpets through the openings off the hallway and antiques everywhere. In the hallway, a carved wooden coat rack accepted my drenched London Fog and an elephant's head jar collected my umbrella. The house had belonged to the Judge's family for more than one hundred years. He had inherited much of what I saw, presumably, and then had gone out and gathered more.

A negro took my wet coat and before I could ask after it, a second servant had handed me a choice of drinks from a tray. I chose a scotch served in an Old Fashioned glass. The scotch had a smoothness I'd tasted only once before, in a drink I'd been given by the Dean, himself. The drinks on offer had been limited to gin and sherry; the scotch had been a final toast alone in the Dean's study. "From a hidden bottle, I've saved for occasions like this." Yet here, the golden liquor was given away almost casually to strangers at the door.

I passed along hypnotically from the foyer to a small sitting room off to one side. Several men stood here in a ring, all strangers to me and apparently to one another, for they stood unspeaking mostly. Several men of the cloth were among them, but they seemed no more eager than the others to get the conversational ball rolling.

After a period of time, one or two of the men introduced themselves to me, although in a very perfunctory manner so that I failed to get many of the names and I'm sure they did not get mine. They were Midwestern in appearance, from the small towns and parishes up-River, and may have felt uncomfortable in the elegant surroundings. Curiously, I was the only one present with a drink in his hand.

The room opened through an archway to what might have been a dining room; a tray with three decanters and glasses was placed in the middle of the table and an impassioned if quiet discussion was in progress among the three gentlemen seated around it. Like the men in the room I'd vacated, they were not quick to greet me, continuing with their discussion just as if I had not entered the room. Educated, seemingly urbane, they referred disconcertingly often to "kikes" and "burrheads" in their well-modulated voices.

On my return to the first room with a fresh glass of scotch I'd poured for myself, I again stood among the silent circle. Occasionally, I would make eye contact with one or the other of the men, receive a nervous smile in reply and then he or I would look away again. One asked me, a simple icebreaker, I suppose, how I felt about "the problem." When I said I didn't know how I felt about it, I instantly became a center of attention. One of the clergymen, a Methodist, took great pains to familiarize me with "the colored problem" in his parish, as if I were a well-meaning but ignorant arrival from the North, and to provide me with certain solutions in great favor with his own congregation. His was a strange racist catechism echoed in his listeners' voices and it too seemed out of place with the surroundings.

I used my damp clothing as an excuse to bow out of their circle and away from their voices. Across the hall, in a second small sitting room, a fire was burning brightly and I stood quietly before it for a few moments, toasting my wet clothes and sipping my drink.

Two others were in the room with me, an older man and an attractive young woman. The man stood up the instant we made eye contact and shook my hand, though I did not get his name. "My daughter," he said, indicating the young lady in the chair, "she teaches at the new school."

"And were you at Newcombe?" I asked politely.

"Sweet Briar. She was at Sweet Briar for three years," her father replied for her. "And now she's going to teach. I think teaching is important don't you?"

"Why yes, I'm a teacher myself, that is I teach at the University."

"I hope you're not one of the new breed." replied the older man.

"Why, uh, no. That is, if I can trust my students, I'm probably one of the oldest breed there is."

I smiled at the daughter. She did not return my smile but continued to stare fixedly at an object six feet in front of her, an object none of the rest of us could see. She had something of the air of a figure in a painting, perhaps the Madonna herself, with the pale skin I admire and delicate features, a pair of full cupid's bow lips being the only and welcome exception. I cast about for some way of attracting her attention or at least garnering the beginnings of a smile. But her father, alas, was not to be gainsaid.

"Not a joking matter. The teacher is a major influence on the child. The days when we could trust our children to just anyone are over. That goes for the children of the poor as well."

"But father, perhaps the professor isn't interested in your theories." The Madonna spoke at last. She smiled too, a perfectly delightful smile that lit up the whole room. But she was not smiling for me. Tyler Caldwell, the young man whose importunities I'd been unable to resist, and another young man perhaps one or two years his senior had come into the room behind me and were standing in the entrance.

She took the second young man's hand so that the three young people stood facing the old man and I. Or did they think they were facing two old men. I was hardly as old as that.

"I'm glad you are here, Professor." Tyler said. "I've told the Judge you might be coming and he is looking forward to meeting you."

At the words "Judge," and "looking forward," both the girl and her father looked at me with a new respect, though I could detect that underneath the father's glance a small measure of misgiving persisted. The girl started out the door with her young man. "You were going to tell me about your school," I called to her.

She stopped and gave me a smile at least three-quarters as radiant as that she had given to my rival. She didn't, then, link me completely with her father's generation. "It's the new Council school," she said.

Behind me the old man cleared his throat, but he was preempted by the girl's escort who said, "Council One. It will be the first of a series of conservative Christian schools Doctor Peterson will be setting up around the country."

"For white's only," Tyler said.

"I should think so," said another man, a stranger, who had entered while we were talking.

"You see," said the old man from behind me, "the public schools have failed in their traditional mission..."

"The traditional values we have as a nation founded primarily by those of Western European extraction ...," the second voice interrupted.

."..and it is the new school's responsibility to fulfill them." the girl's escort concluded.

"What we do here would not be necessary, if it hadn't been for half a century of liberalism," Tyler interjected, sounding as always as if he were about to launch into a speech before the Constitutional Convention.

"Communism," intoned the old man solemnly

"Looks like the party is here all right," said a hale and hearty voice from the doorway, and, indeed, it now appeared that a great many if not the majority of the guests had jammed themselves into that small room with us. The fire, coupled with the wet clothes of many gave the room something of the atmosphere of a steam bath or the ninth circle of Hell. And did I imagine it or had I somehow inadvertently become the center of attention once more?

The pressure of Tyler's hand on my elbow was unsettling and a disturbing harbinger of things to come. He led (read pushed) me from the room determined (he said) I should meet Doctor Peterson and understand what was going on. Yet the more I saw of the house and the people there, the more determined I was to leave as soon as an opportune moment should arise. We paused in the hallway outside a second, larger room crowded to capacity; I could hear the sound of deep masculine voices, with a somewhat harsher and shriller tone occasionally overriding the others; I was sure I had heard the latter voice before, on the radio, perhaps, or the television.

"Tyler," I began...

"It's the Judge," he said. "You'll meet him now."

144

A young student whom I recognized from the mob scene in the cafeteria the week before, Renfrew? Merton? emerged from the room, looking like a kind of house photographer because of the camera slung around his neck, and began to talk excitedly with Tyler. "Everybody's here," he exclaimed, as if he had discovered the Constitutional Convention in progress, "The Judge, Kent and Phoebe Courtney, Dr. Overton, Guy Bannister."

Tyler smiled back as if he were personally responsible. To me, it was a disturbing litany: Bannister a cashiered FBI agent and ex-New Orleans police officer, had been discharged after brandishing a gun off-duty in a bar; Overton, head of the Overton Clinic, was an arch foe of fluoridation and socialized medicine (a category in which he included most publicly supported hospitals). To Overton at first remove, Orleanean's owed the characterization of their two major medical centers: "No mercy at Charity, no charity at Mercy." I couldn't quite place the Courtneys, when a large, florid individual, overweight as if from endless feedings on gumbo and jambalaya, came up and shook Tyler's hand and my hand too. "Pleased to meet you, Professor, I'm Kent Courtney."

"Your being here means so much to us," his wife Phoebe called from a foot behind him.

I tried to explain my presence as that of a mere onlooker, but she already had turned away and was talking to someone else. When I turned back to talk with her husband, he too had walked away, rather rudely, I felt.

"Who are the Courtneys?" I asked Tyler, though I had already placed them by their manners.

"He edits the Thunderbolt."

A thunderbolt indeed! To the disturbing roster of ex FBI-agents and distraught dentists, one could now add the editor of an anti-Semitic journal that flourished a thinly disguised swastika on each front-page. This the new conservatism? What was going on in Tyler's mind to bring me here?

"You need a drink, Professor," Courtney said pointing to my empty glass.

Yes I did. Give this middle-of-the-roader credit for some measure of perception. Tyler, where's your hospitality? Get your professor a drink. He needs it to see him through this evening.

"I'll go see if the Judge can talk with you now," Tyler said pushing past and ignoring my need.

"You're going to talk with the Judge," Phoebe Courtney wondered aloud and her words and the respect in her voice were echoed in the other voices around me. In a few moments, I had space in which to breath and a fresh drink in my hand.

It was doubtful though if Tyler would succeed in his quest. Merely reaching Dr. Peterson (Dr.?) through the press would be challenge enough and as for persuading him to alter his schedule for a university professor, well, however important I might loom in the eyes of an undergraduate, I knew my place in the larger society. Besides, I was not altogether certain I wanted to meet the man who could keep such company, despite the taste shown in his house and its furnishings.

The room at the far end of the hall contained in addition to a small tray of sandwiches, eight young ladies (the Muses?) each perched on the edge of her straight chair as if waiting to be asked to dance. Having erred socially several times already this evening, I remained aloof and apart from them sipping my drink and watching carefully. The young women at first seemed equally indifferent to my presence, yet if I focused on one or the other of them individually, immediately she would return my gaze with a look so bold and direct, I would find myself drawn closer to her chair, as if she were a member of one of those plant families that lure insects with their scent and bright petals; here, bright feminine faces lightly highlighted with rouge, touch of mascara on the eyelids, brought me closer and closer, a once mobile creature drawn into the plant's center and stripped of its protective shell.

Women like these can be found nowhere else but in the South. Though these eight were completely different in their physical appearance, from the rail-like Modigliani at the far end of the room to the plump Rubinesque enticer close by my hand, they were alike in the almost inexplicable fascination of their smiles. Choose. All you our worthy male admirer must do is choose, these smiles seemed to say.

The girl third from the end with the full-bosomed figure could rivet the attention simply by stretching, edging forward slightly in her chair; those with slighter bodies compensated with more expressive faces, more expansive gestures. A few fingers on my wrist could turn me back, a sultry voice could lead me forward, like that same hapless insect of my thoughts, and though I'd resolved to sip my drink, then run as fast as I could from everything this house and the people within it represented, I found on looking down sometime later at my watch, hearing at last the pressure of others and the sound of masculine voices behind me, that over an hour had passed among the sirens.

By that time, I knew names—they all knew my name and my profession in return—even developed a few favorites and, despite the ever present feeling I was being used as a surrogate for absent beaus, resolved to pursue one or two of them through and beyond the evening. One of these was the Modigliani, all angles in the face and body—not to my taste I would have thought, yet her pure southern voice, her delicate touch kept me circling endlessly around her chair. "I have done nothing to encourage you," her soft accent would say and I was all the more encouraged. The second was cast from a more familiar mold, a fuller-fleshed Violet; she spoke of an unseen God and of an almost nun-like dedication to his second coming. "To be born again," she sighed in a mere whisper of a voice I had to stretch out over her scented breasts to hear.

"Dr. Peterson is an unparalleled human being." came the Madonna's voice from behind me and next to it the father's voice repeating, "How can you help but be convinced by what he showed with his studies in Africa."

I turned and confronted the pair. Even in this sultry company of hothouse blossoms, my Madonna was an outstanding addition. I was equally certain she was aware of the attraction she held for me. "Tell me Dr. Mason," she began (she knew my name, then, a positive sign) "are you also convinced by Professor Peterson's studies?"

"He's a professor, then. I wasn't sure..."

"Doctor, Judge, Lawyer, sometimes even a Professor like you," her father said pontifically, "This is why he is our leader."

The pair gave way before a presence in the doorway. The Judge himself, Daniel Lloyd Peterson. Up close, the dominant imperial features that were the Judge's hallmark were somewhat disappointing. Beady eyes, a somewhat bulbous nose, and broken veins that gave his cheeks a bright red cast. His paunch was not quite hidden in a well-tailored dinner jacket. But these are only details. Disappointing as a man, the Judge was almost mythic in his proportions, even a little awe-inspiring.

The Judge's first words were calculated to put me at my ease, and I liked him after only a short interval of conversation. I find it hard to resist a man who has taken the time and trouble to research my interests, more, to respond to and approve of them. Really a nice man, I thought, intelligent and perceptive. Off the podium, when he can dispense with the theatrics, he listens as much as he talks. A well-intentioned man. Still, the people around him scare me.

But I had misjudged him once more. A short while later, when I felt the pressure of his hand escorting me to yet another dreaded meeting, I knew it was the Judge himself who must be feared as well as respected.

Only a few of us were left in the room. The sirens had all fled or did I still see my Modigliani perched against the wall waiting for my renewed attentions. The Madonna was next to her; the Madonna's father had gradually been pushed out the door by the pressure of other more imposing male dignitaries, who had come to see me I realized, come to see me and the Judge.

"Surely, Dr. Mason, something in my speeches might not be entirely to your liking. Professor to professor, aren't we always just a little critical of our colleagues?"

"Why yes, I suppose." I stammered as I tried to say something pleasing without entirely giving way. After all, I would have to face Tyler and his friends as students in the days to come.

"Go on then, tell me something you may disagree with. Something in my lecturing manner perhaps."

I searched for the right words, striving for conviviality, wanting to retain his friendship. "Yours isn't at all the kind of audience we have at the University."

"But they're good people all the same." the Judge riposted, unfairly I thought. Not the same sort of audience, indeed. He was a rabble-rouser. I knew it and he knew it.

"Of course, they're not as educated as you folks uptown. As a result, you have to talk with them a little differently."

"Give them a little fire and brimstone," I continued lightly, and over-committing myself by doing so. No room for lightness here.

"The fear of God, yes. There are definite biblical precedents for the work we do." The "sons of Ham," came an amen behind us. Urbane though the Judge might be, rich and white and upper class his present audience, I couldn't see that much difference between him and his friends and some sweating black evangelical preacher with a holy-roller congregation going a'men behind him.

"You a religious man then professor?"

I gave a rather limp wave of my hand in reply.

"Don't mind the occasional reference to the bible?"

(Was he also a clergyman then? This pompous self-annointed doctor, lawyer, judge, and clergyman.)

"Then, that wasn't the part of my speech you disliked?"

"Why, I didn't dislike any of it." (The Judge was making me eat my own words now and he knew it. Meanwhile, young Renfrew, Merton, whatever his name, was taking notes. What on earth was going on?)

"You just may have disagreed with a few parts of it." (Oh this Judge was slick as a cat waiting by a mouse hole.)

"With parts of it, I may have yes."

"Parts that disagreed with your philosophy."

"No, I wouldn't say that. I'm sure our philosophies are ... are similar. No, it's more a question..."

"A question of style." the Judge finished for me. "You wouldn't have shouted so much on the podium. Egged them on with a few waker-uppers. (I waved my hands helplessly, haplessly.) Well, professor, I'm an attorney by profession. Had the training talking to juries. Sometimes, it takes a heap of waking up before you can start convincing.

(Our audience smiled. I smiled too. For a moment, it looked as if we were all comrades again.)

"And I'm not entirely sure you're convinced.

(I stammered something in reply.)

"Sometimes I go overboard. Maybe, I speak without having all the facts."

"Oh, no, you have all the facts."

(Was my humiliation never to be complete. The women who had given me my fortitude a moment before had either slipped from the room or were staring at me in silent contempt.)

"What about communism? You don't think I went overboard on communism?"

"Well there are different kinds of communist." My voice, even to me, sounded estranged, artificial.

"Are there?"

"Most certainly. We have the original Russian communists, the syndico-anarchists, the . . ." And all of my words, pure, meaningless bullshit.

"I think there's only one kind of communist," interrupted the Judge in a voice like thunder, "the anti-American kind. This fellow Henry, Henry Starr. He a friend of yours?"

I shrugged. "A colleague." (Still, I had not grasped the significance of the Judge's change in tone, of his transition from the general to the particular.)

"Not a friend? The two of you go to coffee together."

(How would he know? Who had been spying on me? Renfrew? Tyler? Some other student or one of my colleagues?) "I must be more famous than I thought," I countered, "Having my life probed at as if I were some kind of movie star."

"Hah," laughed the Judge and slapped his thigh. But I saw his good humor was not shared by the others in the room. "No we're not watching you, Professor. It's this fellow, Henry Starr, we're watching, we think he's a communist."

"I really don't think..." I began, trying to be fair, trying to see all sides.

"You think a little too much professor. You think there's all different kinds of communists, but we know there's only one kind, the anti-American kind. Ain't that right?"

Reduced to a frozen smile, I would like to have backed away, to have left that room and that antique-filled house, but, as in the metaphor, a wall lay in the path of retreat. The rain beat against the far window. The streets still flooded, I might just as well forget my car and walk home. Frankly, I would just as soon walk, I wanted to walk.

The Judge himself escorted me from the room, away from the others who had been standing around staring, took me to his study, gave me a drink from the bottle he kept tucked away in his desk for special occasions and special guests, and we drank and talked about Henry and I must have promised half a dozen different things before he let me go out the front door into the rain again.

Chapter 29. Rain in New Orleans. Four Poems.

i We sat in the gazebo
    Listening to the rain;
    Heard the rustle
    of a thousand tiny scales,
    Saw it moving,
    Like a boa constrictor,
    Though the trees.

ii They said we couldn't get out.
And no one would drive us
But that was stupid;
Because you could get out,
And Violet led while I carried Peggy
Three miles to safety on the levee.

iii They've always had a problem
With the burial grounds
Being below sea level.
They tell the story
Of one cantankerous river man,
A riverboat gambler, retired,
Who set out for sea three times
After they'd laid him to rest.
They had to put him in a lead casket,
Finally, with silver handles.
He fancied that, I imagine,
Being the sort of dude he was.

iv In the first days of the City
The rain brought the plague's corpses to the surface
Carved swamps for mosquitoes,
Brought death and the smell of death.

Just for a joke,
My friend left a lump of sugar
On his balcony.
He watched the rain eat it away;
Day after day he watched it.

After awhile, you'd have thought
His spirit was in that sugar

The remarkable thing
(They tell me)
Is that persons of a certain stripe
Will
After a long, dreary spell of rain
(But not until the sun has come out
The earth bright green holds
A rainbow in each gutter drop)
Die by their own hand.

Durwood Mason, New Orleans, 1952.

Wood found the poems in Mason's bureau drawer while looking for
a necktie.

"It ain't fair. It ain't fair." Blackie said.

"You'll have to speak to the manager." Cybil answered from her place behind the bar. "Ain't nothing Ann or I can do for you."

"That's what I'm to do," said Blackie. "Speak to the mana, speak to, speak to the manana-nager." Blackie stepped back stiffly from the bar and looked over his shoulder as if about to turn and address the room. Lennie caught him under the arm as he fell and eased him back into position.

"You're okay." Lennie said.

"Shu .. sure I'm okay." Blackie replied, "I ain't drunk, I jus want my monn, my monn-ney, that's all."

"If you ain't drunk, whatchadoin here?" Cybil hollered.

At a table at the back of the room, Maria hummed quietly to herself. Sometimes she sang with or against the jukebox, but now she was only humming, keeping time with the music in her head.

It was the end of a long hard weekend, for her, for everyone. On Friday, despite the apprehension of his early morning callers, Lennie had made it downtown in time to be arrested. But the movement's lawyer was been tied up in court and Lennie had to spend most of the afternoon in jail. "No point in our being efficient if we're just going to waste our time in a cell," Lennie said to Dick Diamond, but he got nothing but a sneer from Diamond in return.

Lennie missed his four o'clock class, but Dick's mother fixed them all a supper of catfish and greens that made up for it. After supper, Lennie made a round of the colored bars with the others (except Moody who went to night school, regardless) and then, slowly, inevitably, a beer here and a beer there, never quite enough beer at one place to get drunk, Leonard made his way to La Siete Marina.

This was the third day Blackie had been on shore. On the first day, he gave all his money to the manager of La Siete, rented a room over the bar, and started his drinking. He spent the first and second day alternating beers and Southern Comfort—the bar was open 24 hours—so he hadn't got the use of his room yet. Now, on the third day, he was crying and beginning to get in the way of the weekend crowd, so on the fourth day they'd pack him upstairs, and a day or two later, depending on whether his was a one-or two-week leave, he'd be back in the bar or down in the Union Hall looking for work.

Lennie had lived through this cycle several times. Not Cybil apparently. She leapt on each random word of Blackie's as a pretext to berate him and to sound off to the room at large. When Lennie would defend Blackie, she would threaten to throw them both out. For almost an hour now, the three had stood declaiming at the bar, like protagonist and chorus in some ancient comedy, much to the annoyance of the other customers, much to the annoyance of Maria who was trying to sing a song a sailor had whispered in her ear while they danced, bodies close together, years before.

The truth was Cybil was more than a little drunk herself, drunker than Blackie, drunker than any of them. In an instant, she would go from belligerent to maudlin. "I got a house. I got a house." she would confide over and over. And Cybil did own a house and in this way was distinguished from the others in the bar, except the owner, who also had a house, a big one, in Jefferson Parish.

"She cheats me," Cybil confided. "She takes out social security and income tax but you think the government ever sees it? No, no." She shook a finger in Leonard's face.

Leonard didn't know what to believe about Cybil, but he knew that Blackie at least was getting a square deal. When Blackie was at his drunkest, he would buy everyone with whom he talked a drink, a bottle, or even a case till he became a magnet for every bum on Bourbon Street. As long as the owner of La Siete held the purse, Blackie's money was safe, even from him. And on the final day of his leave, Blackie would always admit, "If she hadn't kept my money, I'd a give it all away."

Lennie, thirsty and short on cash, wondered how he might promote another beer. Blackie, of course, was not going to be able to come through for him. Cybil might but, no. "Where's Dixie?" he asked.

"They took her away," Blackie said.

"Yeah, was she drunk," Cybil hollered. Cybil always hollered with a voice like the Cape May lighthouse. "Gotta go to the can," Cybil would holler, "Anyone want anything afore I come back?"

"Where is she?" Lennie asked Blackie. "What happened to her? Who took her away?"

Maria came staggering out of the darkness toward the counter. Although the rest of the bar was deserted, except for the silent man, weeping at the end of the counter, she interposed herself in the thin space between Blackie and Lennie. Elfin in profile, she possessed a broad pair of hips that eased the two men up and out of their seats.

"Put sompin in the jukebox," Maria said.

"The house can't buy'm all the time," Cybil hollered, "Put some money in yourself once in a while."

"I play it the last time," Maria shouted back, an obvious untruth.

"Where'd they take Dixie?" Lennie asked Blackie, but Blackie was hunched over his drink, complaining bitterly to no one in particular .

Dr. Starr escorted a well-fed Miriam from Rufino's restaurant and carefully considered his next move. He'd been forced to under tip at Rufino's because, as usual, he hadn't checked his wallet before leaving his apartment. He knew Miriam expected to be taken to a bar for a drink or three, but he hadn't the money. Nor did he keep a tab anywhere, but Lennie, he recalled, had a tab at the Seven Seas. If he could just see the owner of La Siete or one of the barmaids and persuade them to put his drinks on Leonard's tab. . . .

Miriam recoiled from the rich mixture of odors, some fresh, some a month or two old, which assailed her at the Seven Seas' front entrance. An ill omen, Starr thought, leading Miriam to the rear of the dimly lit barroom. "Should we go out on the patio?" she asked. But he left her in an alcove at the rear near where Maria had been sitting and scuttled to the front.

"Scuse me," Starr said quietly to the barmaid who it seemed to him, falsely, had come out obsequiously to serve him. "Excuse me. I don't seem to have my wallet with me. Would it be possible for me to get credit?"

"We don't give no credit," Cybil hollered.

You might have said so quietly, Starr thought, and turned to see if Miriam had heard. "I understand," he said. "But you see I come here quite often and I. . . I wonder if by any chance you know Leonard Zellner."

"Who?"

"Well you see, he's a friend of mine and he's got a tab here and I thought perhaps you could put our drinks on his credit."

Cybil looked at him openmouthed. "Our drinks?"

"Yes, yes, I've got a girl back there," Starr said.

Cybil leaned forward as if eager to see the girl, her enormous breasts flopping out over the bar, her breath poisoning the atmosphere around her.

Starr turned quickly and peered toward the rear where Miriam had been sitting. Too dark, particularly in the alcove where he had left her; he couldn't really see to be sure. When he turned back to Cybil, she had restored herself to an upright position.

"Leonard has credit here." Starr reasoned aloud, "You could check it. We don't need to make a fuss. I mean if you'd worked here before you'd know what I mean."

"I been here six months," Cybil lied.

"Oh, I see." Starr walked back to Miriam. Nothing for it but to confess: It appears that I left all my money at home and I thought since Lennie had a tab here. . .

Lennie was sitting at the table with Miriam. "They've taken Dixie away," Miriam said.

"Dixie, the barmaid, the one who used to buy me drinks all the time," Lennie interjected.

"What a pity," Starr murmured.

"They took her away," Blackie sobbed from behind them.

"Do you know where she is?" Lennie hollered to no one in particular.

"Who is this Dixie?" Starr asked, feeling left out.

"She's just a barmaid." Leonard replied.

"Actually, she's much more than that," Miriam lectured, "She's a stripper. She's got one child, a boy that lives with his grandmother in Gentilly. And she wants to get an education."

"Are you the one looking for Dixie?" A short hard-looking Italian had come up to their table. He looked like a man who broke arms for a living when he wasn't kicking dogs and small children. Starr wanted to say "who's asking?" but the words died on his lips.

"I'm a friend of hers." Lennie said.

"Well they took her to the hospital, see. She'd been drinking steady for three days and then her in-laws walk in on her, she gives a whoop and keels over."

"Shock," Starr suggested.

"Nah, she ain't been eating nothing."

"Malnutrition." Starr put in unnecessarily.

"Who's your friend?" the Italian asked Lennie.

"He's O.K.," Lennie said. "He teaches school. What hospital is she in?"

"They didn't have no teachers like that in my day. Mercy, I think."

"Thanks."

"Pleasure."

"Did you hear what he said about his teachers?" Starr began when the man had departed, but the others ignored him. Lennie took several deep gulps from his glass. Lennie's guzzling only emphasized Starr's own moneyless plight. And Miriam chose this moment to announce she would like a scotch and soda.

"Just a moment," Starr said, patting Miriam's arm as if she were a small, impatient child. "Well, aren't you going to go see her?" he asked Lennie.

"Maybe later."

"We could go now." Somehow, he had to get Leonard alone and talk him into loaning a dollar or two.

"Later," Lennie said, "I'm going to play some ping-pong."

"Ping-pong!" Starr exclaimed, waving an imaginary paddle.

"They've a table out on the patio," Miriam said, "But we'd better go."

"I used to be pretty good at ping-pong," Starr continued, thoughtfully.

"Now." Miriam stood up. Plenty to see as always. Her dress, an expensive one, showed off every contour and yet you could tell its wearer had class. (Like I used to be, Maria dreamed and Cybil too.) Whatever, its wearer didn't belong in La Siete Marina. Leonard smiled at her, and gave the thumbs up sign, with the fingers and the thumb coming together in a circle.

"Would you like a flower, Miriam?" Starr asked when they were outside the bar again. "That little boy is selling flowers." (And a few coins and the gift of gab should cover the cost, he thought crudely.)

"Flowers? Flowers mister for the lady?"

"Uh, how much?"

"Why he's stolen them from Jackson Square." Miriam laughed.

"Dance for you mister, tell your fortune?"

"How much are your flowers?"

"Fifty cents."

"Fifty cents!"

"I'm not going to wear any stolen flowers." Miriam said, indignantly.

"Quarter?"

"O.K., I'll take two of them."

"Henry, you are so cheap."

"Here you are mister. Flowers for your wife."

"But I'm not..." Starr began.

Inside the bar, Blackie had backed Lennie up against the bar and was demanding to be told a story. "You know a funny story, the kind you always tell. A joke. Tell me a funny story about colored people."

Lennie looked bemused. Cybil gave them both a hate-filled stare. "Well..." Lennie began. "They caught this colored fellow, one of them integrationists, you know, sitting in a booth at Woolworths. They took him up to the LSU Stadium and they buried him in sand, right there in the middle of the stadium, with only his head showing.

"Good for them!"

"Then they rented out the stadium, sold tickets and popcorn and all that, so people could come and see the colored with just his head sticking out. When the stadium was filled and everybody was waving flags and singing Dixie, they stuck a lion in the stadium with the nigger."

"A lion!" Leonard had captured Blackie's imagination and Cybil's too.

"The lion walks up and down and paws the ground and looks at the nigger, hungrily. All the people are hollering, 'Go Lion' just like at the football game.

"Lion looks mean. Nigger looks scared. The sweat is pouring off his fuzzy curls in buckets. The lion takes a few steps toward the nigger, then leaps. . . right over the Negro's head. He's playing cat and mouse with him. The crowd roars. Nigger's going crazy. He's tugging every which way trying to get loose and he can't get free. They've buried him so deep in the sand.

"The crowd is on their feet, hollering for the lion. The lion is walking up and down, licking his chops. And the nigger is wiggling every which way trying to get loose. Finally, the colored gets one arm above the sand. Just then, the lion lets out a roar and gallops across the stadium. The lion leaps. . . (Lennie's hand went soaring into the air) . . . just missing the Negro's head, when the colored guy reaches up with his free arm and grabs the lion by his balls."

"Grabs him by the balls!" Blackie wept with laughter. He rocked back and forth on his bar stool and Cybil dashed toward him trying to forestall the inevitable crash.

"The lion gives out such a mighty howl, somewhere between a screech and a roar, you could hear him all the way to New Orleans. He was hurt the lion was. And this little old man with a red neck who's been sitting in the topmost row quietly waving his flag stands up and hollers down indignantly, "Fight fair, nigger.""

158

"Grabs him by the balls." It was all too much for Blackie. His head sank down on the bar and he snored gently.

"Damn right," said one of the other patrons, a little old man with a red neck, "Fight fair." And all the bystanders in La Siete Marina who had moved in close to Lennie during the telling of the story returned to their separate corners.

Chapter 31 (Barcus)

Barcus awoke in a darkened house. The room was colder than he could understand and, covered by sweat as always, he felt chilled. He couldn't understand why the single red bulb in the ceiling was out. Then he remembered he had turned it out just before he went to sleep.

"George, George!" his mother called, banging furiously on his door.

"What the shit can she want?" Barcus mumbled to himself.

"George, will you answer the telephone? I know you're in there. Wake up George." Then silence. "George, I don't believe you care whether you answer or not. I don't have to let you use the telephone you know. I've told you to get your own telephone. Just tell your friends not to phone me."

What on earth was she mumbling about? "Ugh!" he bellowed in reply.

"George are you awake?"

He slipped from under the bed sheets, spilling a copy of *What is to be Done* onto the floor, and pawed in the darkness through a pile of dirty clothing. Adjusting his maroon bathrobe around his nude body, he tied the wide sash carefully about his middle.   "Yes what is it?" he said coldly blocking the doorway.

"George, there's a call for you."

"Fine, I'll take it."

"You know your friends aren't supposed to call all the time."

Barcus nodded indulgently.

"If they're going to call all the time, you could get your own phone you know."

He nodded again like some Dickie-bird dipping into its glass of water.

"It's not fair to ask your friends to wait all the time, while I have to go and wake you."

"I'll talk to him right away mother."

"You could at least help with the phone bill."

"All right. Now get the christ out of the way so I can answer the phone. What time is it?"

"You ought to be ashamed of yourself talking to your mother that way. It's because of all the beatnik friends you bring home. Six-

160

thirty. It's the evening, George. Not the morning. I swear, I'm not going to put up with this any longer."

But by this time she was talking to her son's retreating back. Barcus had disappeared into the adjoining apartment, trying to figure out where his mother might have left the phone. Seeing him gone, she leaned over the railing and addressed the colored man sweeping the walk next door. "That boy's no good," she said.

"No, Maam."

"I swear I'm going to put him out in the street."

"I wish he wouldn't use my garbage pail."

"That's not your garbage pail."

"Oh yes, it is Maam."

George picked up the receiver that his mother had somehow managed to hide beneath an unreachably low table. "Hello," George said after quite calmly hurling the table across the room, scattering his mother's yarn with the pieces.

"Oh hello," George repeated warmly recognizing Little Hamilton's breathless tones.

"Guess where I am?" Little Hamilton said.

George cringed inwardly but cooed his reply, "The University Centre?"

"No, jail."

"What the Christ are you doing in jail!" George bellowed.

"I was arrested."

"Oh shut up," George said to his mother who was hovering in the background. "What for?"

"We all were."

"Well, I know you weren't about to be arrested by yourself. Who's we?"

"Bob Godfrey, Leonard Zellner, and I."

For a moment, Barcus considered hanging up. He would never get any sense out of Little Hamilton, and could easily wait until he had a chance to talk to Leonard or to that other young idiot, Godfrey. Then, the thought struck him that Hamilton had another reason for calling. "Do you want me to get you out of jail?"

"Don't you want to hear why I was arrested?"

Frustrated, Barcus shook his head and tightened his stranglehold on the receiver.

"I was by-standing."

He would have to be, thought Barcus. Hamilton was not the type to do anything else. "Where were you by-standing?"

"Outside of Frantz School."

"How did you happen to be there?" This is like pulling teeth, George thought.

"I went to watch Lennie."

"Why was Lennie arrested?"

"The police had to arrest somebody." Getting no reaction from Barcus, Hamilton added, " Wouldn't have been any trouble if the woman hadn't come over and kicked him."

"Kicked him?"

"Yeah, we were just standing around and watching, by-standing, all these women screaming and yelling, they were pretty ugly. . .

." . . women are." George interjected.

." . . all wearing pants, and pedal pushers, and their hair up in curlers. They looked like dragons, like a teacher I had in third grade. Then they recognized Zellner. Your friend Sergeant Gremillion, he . . ."

"Yes, yes, go on." George said after a moment when little Hamilton didn't say anything further.

"He was talking to the T.V. men. Sergeant Gremillion was. Will you see if I'm on T.V. this evening?"

"I think you'll be out of jail in time to see it yourself. You do expect me to get out you out of jail?"

"You'll get us out of jail, won't you George?"

"I'll consider it." Slowly, the full possibilities of the situation unrolled before him. Unfortunate he would have to parole Zellner and Godfrey at the same time.

"Lennie said you had parole power," Hamilton continued.

"I might have. It depends why you were arrested."

"Oh, we weren't doing anything."

George smacked his forehead with the heel of his right hand. Uh, huh, sure you weren't.

"Everybody in the crowd started singing, you know 'Two, four, six, eight, we don't want to integrate.' The guy from the T.V. station wanted to move his tape recorder into the crowd, but Sergeant Gremillion wouldn't let him because of all the pushing and shoving. In fact, there was this man way over on the other side of the crowd— Lennie says the man was his lawyer once—somebody recognized him and the police had to rush over and form a circle around him to protect him."

"Then, I suppose, somebody recognized Zellner standing next to you."

"Yeah, this woman. And she started screaming and came charging over carrying her baby..."

"And Zellner started dancing around like a silly ass."

"Yeah, and I got out of the way see cause Godfrey was carrying all these pamphlets and we didn't want to lose them."

Barcus reached under the tail of his bathrobe and scratched his ample rear. "So the woman kicked Zellner," he prompted.

"Yeah, and then Lennie started to wave this painting like it was a flag. . ."

"Whose painting? What painting?"

"The one this colored kid in the second grade made, with the squirrel and trees and stuff. You know you made stuff like it when you were in the second grade."

George hugged himself with both hands and swung his upper body to and fro as if trying to break loose from an unseen assailant. "That's not a painting," he roared, "it's just a little drawing with crayon. Probably doesn't even look like a squirrel."

"Oh yes it does. It's a real good drawing. That kid will be an artist someday, you'll see. And Lennie is waving the painting and people are trying to grab it . . ."

"So they grabbed it and stomped Zellner to death and you and Godfrey went home and TELL ME why were you arrested?" Barcus shouted, a deep swell of fatherly indignation rumbling through the bass notes from his chest.

"I went and rescued the painting."

"You did what! It's a fucking drawing."

"I kinda liked it. My little sister made one just like it when she was in the second grade. She sent it to me. It's got squirrels and two trees. And a house. I think it's supposed to be our house."

"This wasn't your kid sister's drawing, it was just some little nigger child's homework."

"Yeah. But I didn't want them to rip it up, so I went and took it away from Lennie."

Barcus screamed inwardly.

"They arrested Godfrey when they found all the pamphlets on him," little Hamilton continued.

"O.K., O.K." George said slowly. "I'll speak to the Sergeant about parole. Now, do you want me to pick you up?" For the idea remained with Barcus, that this was the evening. In Little Hamilton's present excited state, he might be willing, even eager, to come back to Barcus' apartment. Barcus would put a fatherly arm about him, and introduce him to things a father would not ordinarily consider. And there was the matter of gratitude. Surely Little Hamilton would feel somewhat grateful at being rescued from the lice-ridden confines of the city jail. I hope they haven't hurt him, the thought ran through Barcus's mind.

"Oh that's O.K." Little Hamilton said. "You don't have to come all the way down here. Lennie, Godfrey, and I thought we'd go down to Harry's and get a beer and then come home together."

"Harry's!" said Barcus, "What the mother-fucking Christ you want to go there for?"

"We heard the drinks were cheaper. . . . But . . ." (and it seemed to George during the ensuing pause that Little Hamilton might actually be thinking) "I'll come over to your place afterwards. You'll phone Sergeant Gremillion won't you George?"

"You bet! I'll wake him out of bed if I have to. Shut up!" said George to his mother savagely, for she had begun mumbling behind him as he hung up the phone.

"George, you ought to wear slippers," she shouted, determined to have the last word. "Now, where are you going? You haven't had supper."

"Police station."

"Police station. Those goddamn beatnik friends of yours."

"Shut up," George said with penultimate finality, slamming the street door behind him before he realized he was still wearing just his bathrobe.

Chapter 32 (Brownlee)

I decided to go to the Den for that last cup of coffee before going home. Lately, I have been getting up early in the morning. Ostensibly to do some work, although I am not really awake until after ten o'clock and a second cup of coffee. I usually have two or three cups of coffee after breakfast and before lunch.

Coffee used to be just an excuse for conversation, but I find I have run out of things to say. Not that there are not important things to talk about. Students here seem to have so much to communicate. I love to hear them talk about their ideas. But I am afraid to contaminate them with my despair.

At first, I was envious when younger people received the doctorate before me. Now, with my years in the Service, the years in industry, the year of teaching high school, I am so much older that I feel almost responsible for them. And I cannot, strictly speaking, talk with my professors though some of them are younger than I. Too big, too formal a gap persists between us. More and more, I find them unwilling to discuss their research with me. Perhaps, they feel I am too old to impress or, uncertain about their ideas, they are afraid of betraying this uncertainty to me.

I talked for a while with Mrs. Gresham at the cash register. She has been here almost as many years as I have, including the years I was away. I enjoy her company. Only when a line formed behind me did I finally walk away.

The Den is crowded now of the morning and I cannot find a table against a wall. I sit in an extra chair, at an angle to a table full of boys and girls, freshmen, commuters who live in the city; I am not part of their group, but I do not wish to intrude on the privacy of a boy and a girl who sit holding hands nearby. When Dr. Frankel of Economics calls to me, I sit with him for a while. He does not stay in the Den long, and leaves behind the impression he feels I too should have important things to do.

I am not really thinking about my dissertation but about the work I will do afterward. I am afraid I have taken the wrong direction again.

Miriam walks by. I wave to her but she does not see my wave. She is escorted by one of the men in the history department— Professor Mason, I think.

Dave Parsons comes over and starts a conversation, though, as always, he is not really listening to what is said to him in return. Very nervous, his crane-like head constantly swivels to look at the girls around us. I ask after his roommate who interests me very much. He is a boxer, and I used to be a boxer too, and now follow all the fights on television.

Parsons says his roommate has gone away with a girl and stolen one of his shirts. He starts to say something else about his roommate, but stops in mid-sentence when a tall dark-haired girl with a tight, form fitting yellow-blouse walks by. He gets half up from his chair to follow her, but sits down with me again when a much younger boy joins her. My bulging middle is not very attractive, but I can have a very good conversation sometimes with these girls. I am a good listener and most of the boys their age are too impatient to listen. Parsons leaves finally to sit with a girl who is married to another friend of mine. He will probably be back to hop away again.

Mrs. Gresham waves to me from the cash register and I see Barcus standing beside her. Like me, Barcus is much older than most of other the students here, but he is younger than I. He is about my build but has no interest in boxing. It takes a long while for Barcus to thread his way between the tables. He seems visibly annoyed with some of the youths whose feet stretch out into the aisles. His first words to me are "that goddamned #$ jukebox." Actually I have not noticed the sound, it is just another background noise like the students chattering. The jukebox does not seem to have any real tunes anymore, though once in a while one of the songs I used to play has a revival. I will occasionally play a song myself when the Den is not too crowded. "Lousy coffee," says Barcus.

Parsons comes over to talk with Barcus for a minute, but, as predicted, he is off again immediately. "Idiot," says Barcus, "wastes his time on girls." I smile. I do not think Barcus is as down on women as he says, though I have seen his collection of pictures and do not feel he can have much respect for them.

"What are you doing?" he asks me.

"Nothing much."

"How's your thesis coming?"

"Slow."

A female student, fresh out of high school, and not much taller than the chairs in which we are sitting, comes and stood near us. I'd seen Parsons looking at her before. She wears pants instead of a dress and her little behind is outlined smoothly by the jeans. I point her out to Barcus and he just sneers.

We are both waiting for someone else to come sit at our table, so that Barcus can have someone to argue with. I like to listen to Barcus debate. He is the living embodiment of all my beliefs about the politician, although I think a man of good character will maintain public respect regardless of the techniques used against him. People do occasionally rise above their own petty interests. Barcus does not have that much faith in people. Rather, I think he does not allow himself to have much faith in people. His misanthropy will probably prevent him from becoming too powerful.

"Sergeant Gremillion arrives," Barcus says. "I wonder what he wants?" An older man whom I do not recognize stands at attention in the doorway. George says he is a New Orleans policeman although he is not wearing a uniform. Plain clothes, then. I am surprised he has so military a bearing.

He marches toward us still looking far more the army officer than the policeman. Both he and Barcus have the characteristically flushed face, the veined nose, which seems to be so common down here. The Sergeant's hair is starting to grey somewhat and he speaks with the rapid cadence that is so common across the canal.

"Seen your friend Lennie around?" the Sergeant asks, as he sits down, straddling the chair backwards.

"No I haven't. I thought he was your guest for awhile." The implied question is obvious from the tone of Barcus' voice.

"He was. But he got away before I could have a chat with him. Actually, I really didn't wanted to speak with him. I wanted to speak to you and have you communicate."

"Fire away then," Barcus says with a rumbling chuckle.

"Zellner's used up his welcome. He's got to leave. Maybe, he could go back to where he came from. Greenville, Jackson, up that way."

"He can't leave; he's got a trial coming up."

"Let him jump bail then. Those 'grationists got plenty money. They's a lot mo' whea'hit came from. And they's only one of him."

George does not reply. The jukebox is playing one of those new songs that sound almost like a song you've heard before except the words do not make sense.

"It's like this," Sergeant Gremillion begins, "Peterson thinks he's a trouble maker."

"Peterson is an ass-hole."

"That's true George. I won't argue with you. But Judge Peterson's got a lot of money. And..." Gremillion pressed on ignoring Barcus' protests, "He's got quite an organization. Quite an organization, George. It's building up. Good people are behind him and they too think Zellner's got to go."

"I see," says Barcus. His voice has a thin edge, but it is quite rich really. He manages to speak from the diaphragm, and his voice moves through his chest before it comes out. When I listen to George, I constantly hear an echo, slightly deeper in tone, a little behind the words.

"They want to get rid of Lennie any way they can. And I'd just as soon...

"Just as soon..."

"He went away."

"You like Lennie don't you?" Barcus asks him. Barcus' hands that are normally held interlaced behind his large pockmarked head cradling it, have been brought forward and placed palm down on the table.

"It's not a question of liking, George. Now I never gave Lennie any trouble when I arrested him. Some of the boys were all for slamming his balls in the drawer a couple of times, but I says shit on that. He don't make no trouble, no more than he planned to begin with. It's a little extra work for us having to pick him up along with the colored, but it's not as if it were a surprise. No. Dr. Peterson is just something I can't handle. I don't like what they're planning. For everyone's sake, I think it would be best if he just went away."

"No police protection." The words come out very flat and very angry, angrier than I'd ever heard Barcus before. Sergeant Gremillion stands up from the table. He shakes his head and looks off a little to the side. He walks away a few steps and turns to look at Barcus again. Parsons dashes across between us, his hand on a girl's elbow. She is a cute little thing with small breasts in a pink sweater, somewhat like a girl I used to know. She's married now, my girl I mean.

"You tell him, won't you George?" Sergeant Gremillion asks, almost as if he were begging. The jukebox is playing that colored woman, Nina Simone, again and she is real sad.

"I'll tell him," Barcus says. The Sergeant looks relieved, but still he walks away with a slight slump to his shoulders, not erect as when he came into the cafeteria.

George's face is a dead white. I had not expected Parsons to stay with the girl very long and am not surprised when he returns to our table. George gets up as Parsons sits down and leaves almost immediately. Parsons starting talking about the girl, not really listening to what he is saying but looking around him as he always does when he talks. Dr. Frankel and some of the other instructors from his department have come back into the Den again, so I see it is time I should be going too.

Chapter 33

In the large room above the cafeteria, Peter and Miriam sit facing each other, knees touching, in big over-stuffed chairs.

Located just off the flight of stairs that lead from the cafeteria to a series of conference rooms and offices on the top floor, bookshelves separate the stairway from the room itself. The shelves are empty, so that anyone looking toward and through them will see a series of moving sculptures as students pass up and down the stairs.

One wall of the large room overlooks the swimming pool so that the changing patterns of light reflected from the pool create a never-ending lightshow on the ceiling above. The wall facing the pool is hung with pictures of past presidents of the University. The pictures hang at eye level near the stairway, but because the wall spans two floors, few actually look at them. Those in chairs look into the room, those standing look away toward the stairs or the tall curtains opposite.

The remaining wall, a true wall that separates the building from the campus, is covered by tall curtains that cut out the light and absorb the noise from within and without. Because of these curtains, the room has a hushed intimate feeling almost as if one were in a private club. And it is here the young people come, couples in the main, who want to be alone, who want to hold long intimate conversations even as Miriam and Peter are doing now.

Miriam hoped to talk about her pregnancy, not art, as they had done at first, nor Peter's vacation trip through the Eastern States (who cared anyway), nor the continued sit-ins and boycotts of the stores downtown, and especially not the scene of ax handles and blood in the Jackson Mississippi bus terminal the previous evening. She wanted to talk about them, the couple, Peter and Miriam, and what her pregnancy would mean to them.

She had slept with Peter once, only once, a few weeks before, a single short gesture of friendship. Not the first time she'd slept with a boy, but the first time anything had come of it, the first time she'd had to consider the future as well as the present.

She pictured her breasts growing larger. Twins she thought. My aunt had twins and she was never able to fit into any of her dresses again. She couldn't even fit through doorways. Was this the way it began?

But Wood seemed distracted, dissatisfied. What Miriam and he had done together, was to him both forgettable and immediate, so that while he attached no particular importance to the act, he clearly expected to sleep with her, that very evening, as if no curtain of time had come between.

He's changed, she thought, or worse, he's just the same. Wood's grumbling was of the sort she associated with her father, "the deal hadn't come through," "Marcus (her brother) had not been there on time to meet him." She'd always thought of Wood as a wide-eyed traveler. As with Eustachia Vye's imagined trip to Paris with her future husband, Miriam visualized herself traveling with Wood to the Bahamas, to the Yucatan.

She had second thoughts now about the sort of husband Wood would make; he did not seem determined enough. Rather than being different from, he was too much like other boys she knew.

But if she didn't tell him about her pregnancy, then she would have to get an abortion. She couldn't tell anyone else, her sister, perhaps, so she would have to go alone to the clinic. The thought that she would have to go alone irritated but did not frighten her. I am the seed and the husk, she thought, remembering the poem. I have sown and reaped. My body is a barn full of ripe grain that my work has harvested. I can wait my time.

"After all, what are you?" she said aloud to Wood. "You're not working. You're not in school. You're just hanging out. Or would hiding out be a better word for it?"

"Hiding. I'm not hiding." Wood replied.

This is where the hiders live, Miriam thought. The tourists who come to be entertained. Young men who seek the Quarters pretending to write novels, who spend their mornings sleeping, their afternoons doing their laundry and gossiping, and their evenings drinking, while the pages of their books — so they would like to imagine, fill with words. And even those of us who live here, who've lived here since birth not of ourselves alone but of our parents and our parents' parents are dimly aware that in the world outside the present we've never experienced is becoming the future.

It had been twice, not once, she'd slept with him she realized; she had not thought of the time in his car, but obviously it would have been as possible for her to get pregnant in a car as in a motel bed.

They had met on the stairway that evening, she coming down, he walking up from the cafeteria. To her surprise, he kissed her. It was so unlike him to be affectionate without a long period of introspection. It was so unlike her to embrace someone openly in public. "Careful," she said, "The campus is like a small town." But she didn't pull away immediately.

She had walked him to the mezzanine, leading him without speaking past the pictures of the presidents, bringing him to an alcove that was as hidden as anything could be in an open room, an alcove where, if he kissed her again, the only onlookers would be other couples lost in their own conversations or a solitary professor asleep in his chair.

For most of the past half hour, they had sat in silence, like an elderly married couple. Her thoughts were of marriage and weddings, and surprisingly, of going to school. His thoughts were of a train. He could still remember the muddy fields slipping away behind the caboose, the tap-tap of the brakeman's hammer as he lay on his back on the stiff bench seat looking out at the stars. The reassuring click of the wheels. Almost asleep, he was surprised to hear Miriam's voice berating him.

"You're a hider," she said. "Not seeking, not exploring but running away from. What scares you? Or are you merely afraid of knowing what you will be? A secret genius, whose flaws go as undiscovered as his virtues.

"Your mother must have been proud of you, and told you so. So much promise, little Peter has. No one understands you the way she does, and no one has such a steady stream of excuses for Little Peter's failures."

"Miriam!"

"You know a little bit about everything. Enough to cut others down who don't know as much as you, but not enough to contribute anything of your own.

"A man who goes looking after the wilderness stone, never satisfied with lucky days. Did you come to find? Or did you come to run away?"

"Much can be said for not growing up too quickly." he inserted into the pause.

"'I have an elder daughter that I love,'" she quoted, "'And having loved from childhood, would not tame. Because I once was tamed.'"

"And I'm not alone," he said, "I'm part of the integration movement. Godfrey says. . ."

"You're not part of the integration movement any more than you are part of this University. You're watching the movement, the way you'd watch a ball game, or a Mardis Gras parade. And the people who care, the ones who want to stop it and the ones who want to make it work, mean as little to you as actors."

Anger, fear, delight played across his face, but he could not convey his feelings in words.

"You've not lived here all your life. You've not lived anywhere. Montreal, California, New Orleans. Hiding, hiding under the pretense of exploring. You've never been part of a community, never shared its fears. Never been part of one side or the other. How can you say you're committed, when at any moment you can simply run away?

"New Orleans is a community. I live here. My family live here. What happens here affects us. And although I want to get away, I won't creep off like some thief. I won't abandon those I leave behind.

"People deserve . . ." Wood began, but she had no further need of him and his empty phrases.

"You can't just change one thing without changing a whole lot of others. This is the beginning. The sit-ins, the boycotts, the arrests are like the burning of a forest. Afterwards, the long slow process of growth begins again. It will never be the same here, never. Not just in who sits down at a lunch counter, who buys at Woolworths, but in how we deal with one another.

"People will lose their homes — they'll have to move from one part of town to another or think they have to — people will lose their jobs, their status, the things they think make them a little better or a little less worse than those around them. But you won't be affected. Not at all. You'll have moved on.

"Hider!" she spat.

A tall couple who had just entered the room, the girl a long head of hair, the boy a lanky frame against whose shoulder she rested, looked on at Miriam with amazement. And for once, Wood too found himself staring instead of being stared at as Miriam, eyes blazing, carriage erect, stalked regally from the room.

Wood remained frozen in his watchers position. The girl with the long hair and the lanky southern boy grew more intimate, with a kiss, with a touch. Wood looked on at their intimacy with amazement.

"Hiding," he thought, "I'm not hiding." He would go back to school and get his professorship. But not alone. He would take Maggie with him.

Chapter 34 (Barcus)

As a matter of custom, Barcus did not devote much time to the affairs of the crackpot or the deviate, the politically inconsequential. But Leonard had won Barcus' admiration by writing to the Mayor—a brief note, not more than a page, submitted from the Parish prison. Leonard asked that the Mayor take steps to integrate the jail in view of the changing times. This notion warmed the cockles of Barcus' heart; he treasured his copy of the Mayor's reply, which began "Dear Jailbird:."

He would like to have seen this correspondence perpetuated, but Sergeant Gremillion intercepted a message from the Mayor's advisors to Lennie's fellow prisoners informing them their new companion was a goddamm communist nigger-lover. And it seemed, Sergeant Gremillion noted acidly, Lennie had already gone to great pains to tell them on his own.

"Now the sheriff's leaving his cell door open at night. Get him out. Get him out of theah!"

Bail was raised, a team of attorneys followed Leonard around on his ramblings and, whenever possible, Sergeant Gremillion permitted Barcus to whisk Leonard away from the scene of his crimes.

In the months that followed, the lawyers had been summoned one by one to other crisis areas—in Selma, Jackson, and Atlanta. Barcus, obliged to help Leonard all by himself, was worn to a frazzle when the Sergeant found him in the cafeteria, passed on the word that "Leonard was accident prone."

As soon as night fell, Barcus boarded the Freret-Street bus for downtown. Crowded and smelly, the bus had been nicknamed "The Ark," by the Tulane students. When it stopped outside a grocery store, Barcus lip-read the flyers on the store window. This smell, he mused, is just what one would expect of a people that dined off "muskrat, pork chittlings, and riber bass." Not that Barcus condemned the foods themselves any more than he would condemn the foods of a good German restaurant. But, no question , niggers and Germans were the most odiferous people in the world. Fortunately, the spread of Barcus' posterior was such he seldom had to share his seat with other than a rail-like nigger who, in a world ruled by obese germans and fat negro women, had long since learned to "hunch hisself up."

Barely a mile from his destination, a St. Charles trolley swung out ahead of them and the bus slowed to a crawl. Barcus checked and rechecked his watch. Little more than an hour remained before he was due back at his apartment for the date he'd finally arranged with Little Hamilton.

The department stores remained open on Canal street for Thursday night shoppers, the Salvation Army rang its bell, and Gospel Reverend Earlison late of Greenville, Alabama harangued a small crowd on the median between the trolley tracks. Barcus moved into the Quarters along Royal past the tobacco shop, accepting acknowledging waves, head movements, and the occasional jostle from the passing crowds, though, more often, he planted his own elbow in the herd. Outside the Maison Blanche, he found himself exchanging blocks with Sonny Wilburtson, a hulking football player of a man who served on the Mayor's Harbor and Works Commission. "I'll be Goddamned," they said, circling each other in the manner of florid-faced alumni everywhere. Arms extended across the walk, two huge hands met in a bear clasp. "Why say!" "Why, hi!" Their cheeks reddened and puffed up as their grips grew ever tighter.

Three shine boys proposing to walk beneath their linked arms stopped and one extended his hand to Barcus. Barcus gave it a feeble tap with his left. The boy then offered his hand to Sonny who refused it with such a look of horror as to erase all memories of the Sonny Wilburtson Barcus had known in his student days.

"You should have shaken the kid's hand, Wilburtson," Barcus snarled sarcastically, "'Could have snapped his wrist, that way."

"Well, I'll be dammed. The nerve of that little darkie. Goddamn, I'm a member of the Mayor's Harbor Commission.

Barcus smiled. "I heard that. I also heard you had a little trouble with the Fed's. On account of they think the Army Corps of Engineers already completed some work you fellows went and got bids on."

"Oh . . . I'll tell you confidentially Barcus," Sonny said leaning his head close to Barcus' ear without changing the level of his voice ('Why do fat men sweat so,' Barcus wondered), "Them Feds, and O'Reilly in particular, are going to get put in their place." Barcus waited, but Sonny did not reveal more before slipping his moorings and merging with the crowd.

Barcus turned in at a penny arcade and slipped a nickel in the phone. He dialed the number of Lennie's apartment and again no

176

one answered. Overcoming the temptation to play the pinball machines, he continued his stroll. Up Conti, along Bourbon. His pace was slow, casually deliberate. A large fat man with flushed face and pockmarked cheeks, Barcus resembled one of the younger Longs, and the easy grace with which he walked recalled older brother Huey as well.

The cops on the beat gave Barcus the nod, barkers fed him gossip about what they knew or guessed. He moved easily the length of the street. (He would have preferred to wait in one spot and keep watch, but behind the curtains, in back of the bars they expected a glance not a cober, what had they paid protection for?)

He didn't find Zellner, though he walked the length of Bourbon Street twice. Later, to rest his tender feet, he got three shoeshines in two hours. He thought he might gain an eye or an ear that way, but the simple shine boys hadn't heard or seen, didn't know Leonard Zellner, white integrationist. Finally, Barcus stood indecisively outside the Paddock Lounge, listening to the cabbies hustling on the corner and trying to ignore the sounds of Disneyland Dixie that came from all about him.

They were old cabbies, licenses renewed and secure, and they knew enough not to give two bits for Barcus or his connections. They may not have been keen analysts of political trends, but they knew a twenty-block detour to take a tourist to a whorehouse two blocks away. They remembered every detail of the intricate bargainings with their fares — "'No,' he says, 'By the clock not the meter,' and I say, 'Fuck the rate card.'" — but had few other interests besides their fares, the horses and the weather. Rumor had it one of their number could produce pictures of the Mayor topsy-turvy under a red-haired whore named Zada, but Barcus had owned the same pictures back when the other boys on his block were completing their stamp collections.

Barcus rubbed his palms together briskly, the fingers widespread and not touching, and thought about his date with Little Hamilton.

Across the street, the waiters moved quickly between the candle-lit tables. Barcus watched them, mentally putting a napkin to his throat, shouldering the tourists aside and devouring the trout almandine, the crawfish etouffe that had been set before them. Barcus had a few choice words for tourists, less derisive phrases like 'chuckle-head' and 'tit-lapper' he reserved for friends like Lennie. "I'm going to write a long letter to that boy when he's out in the country," he thought. Assuming he would find Lennie and get him out in time.

A stick figure sidled up to occupy the place next to Barcus on the wall. Like Barcus, the wall's new occupant seemed to be waiting for someone, his eyes flicking from restaurant, to cab drivers, to passersby in a jerky series of head movements. Tourist? No, not a tourist. But he was from out of town all the same.

The boy went through his pockets in an intricate stalling ritual. He smiled and tried to catch Barcus' eye, then he crossed over to the cabstand and tried to borrow a match. For sure he was from New York, Barcus thought, and a fool. The boy returned matchless; with the same fawning air he'd tried unsuccessfully upon the cabbies, he turned to Barcus. "Do you have a match, George?"

Barcus stared at him.

"I'm Parsons' roommate." Barcus looked the boy over carefully. This match business, this phony chatter — the fellow was trying to camouflage an interest in the club across the street. Parsons' roommate? It was possible. Everything was possible. This was the guy that was supposed to be off on a honeymoon at Niagara Falls or someplace. Very well, he was back. What was Barcus supposed to do about it? The wife eliminated him from Barcus' list.

." . . thrown off a freight in Greenville, coming the way I chose to come... packed my wife on board the Panama Limited and she turned our tinted picture of the Bayou to the wall. . . Can't find Lennie, Parson's won't let me stay in his apartment, what am I going to do next month?"

Should Barcus have played Trantor to Wood's Odysseus? Wandered with him half a hundred thousand miles, like some T.V. hero, curing evil and delivering babies?

Barcus gave Wood the matches and told him to get lost. The two stood eye to eye for a moment till, with Wood failing to get the hint, Barcus turned and walked away. He walked out of the Quarters toward Dixie's apartment. A slim possibility existed that Zellner, chuckle-headed Zellner, might be there.

Wood raced after Barcus trying to keep pace with his long rolling strides. The crowd soon separated them and Barcus went on alone. Outside Dixie's door, a blond sailor fell heavily against him. The sailor was worth a second look. Barcus rang the bell. Two short, two long. He leaned his whole body against the door and it fell inward just as an indignant husband whisked the sailor away.

Panting heavily, Barcus climbed the long steep flight of stairs to Dixie's apartment. The scent of mimosa was overpowering and grew stronger as he reached his destination. The apartment door gave readily and he stepped inside, shutting the door quickly and opening it again as his feet encountered broken glass. He paused for a moment on the balcony. A single banana leaf probed the stair wall, its roots lost in the gloom beneath. He stepped back inside, shuddering.

The apartment was as he remembered, a schizophrenic's dream complete with broken perfume bottle. Rows of bare book shelves; other shelves with children's books the owner hadn't had a chance to read when young. Souvenir programs picked up from the street after a Mardi Gras ball. A set of encyclopedias. Vases and antiques, not expensive, not cheap, the gifts of uncounted Johns, scattered as freely as parade throwaways about the room.

Lately, Dixie had been in with an arty crowd. She hung their paintings when requested and was readily pressured into paying for them. A charcoal of her, a gift from a nonpaying friend, hung in the bathroom. Taken from the rear, it made her look like a boy. The only discordant notes in her apartment were an ironing board in the centre of the living room and a buxom Jewish girl waiting in the corner as if afraid.

"Dixie's not here." Barcus said. It was more of an assertion than a question.

"No, I'm afraid I've kind of taken over." the girl replied, "I love to come here and sew and cook. That is, I don't live here, I go to school."

"A Newcombe girl."

"Uh, huh. I hope I don't look like a Newcombe girl." She blushed, rose on olive. Barcus was embarrassed, for her not for him. "My name's Miriam Finestone. Won't you please sit down.

"I'm sure Dixie will be back soon. I just came here to do some cooking and, oh, some ironing. I'm all through with that. I made gefilte fish today. Do you like that? I love gefilte fish. Would you like some gefilte fish?"

"Fish?" Barcus made the word sound like sweaty negroes on a bus.

"It's quite good. All different kinds of things. It's Jewish. Would you like some?"

The fish had taken on unappetizing mimosa-scented proportions, but, not wishing to be considered anti-Semitic, Barcus consented. He ate several balls.

"You try it with the horseradish."

Barcus shot her a puzzled look.

"With fish. You always eat horseradish with fish." She giggled; her breasts bounced.

He tried it with the horseradish and finished the plate. "You'd make somebody a fine wife."

"Oh, really."

"I'd marry you myself only I'm not Jewish."

"You're kidding. You're . . . you're Barcus aren't you?"

(She meant, "You're that way, aren't you." He wondered how and how much she knew about him.)

"Yes I am. Do you know Leonard Zellner?"

"Un, huh. He comes here all the time. He's crazy."

Crazy, uh. The girl was perceptive if not tactful.

"You know I believe he has integrationist tendencies. He came here one day with a colored fellow."

"Well we all have tendencies."

She blushed instead of giggling. "He got arrested, you know."

"For his tendencies?" Barcus smiled. He could be very warm and compelling when he wanted to be.

"No, it was one of those sit-ins. It must have been terrible. He was in jail. Do you know he once asked me to invite a colored person to a party I was giving."

Barcus motioned with his hand for her to continue.

"I don't know any colored people."

"None of us do. Just Lennie. You haven't seen him tonight, have you."

She shook her head.

"Well, look, why don't, no. . . I'll stay and . . . damnit I've got a date tonight."

"A date!" Miriam repeated, and then giggled.

Against his better judgment, Barcus found himself apologizing. "What's wrong with that? Because I'm that way? It's with a boy actually."

"Little Hamilton?"

"Good God, does the whole world know the story of my life?" Barcus shouted, but he had an inward smile. "I've got a message for Zellner; can you give it to him?"

"Uh huh, sure. I got an A in all my courses."

"Very commendable." A distinct and enjoyable possibility existed that this girl was making fun of him. She'd done an awful lot of talking for a creature that was hiding in the corner when he first came in. If she'd been thinner now, hips like those of Dixie in the painting, he might have seen how far he could go.

"Y'all tell Lennie he is not to come to this apartment any more, that he is not to come to my place, and that he is to go to that spot in Lafayette Parish we talked about, immediately. And tell him, tell him that Goddamnit he made me miss a date with Little Hamilton because I've got to keep on looking for him."

Chapter 35 (Wood)

He ought to go home. He ought to call Maggie now.

Fleeing the sullen antagonism of Barcus and the cabmen, his stomach fluttering as if he'd had too many drinks for too many days, with hands seemingly plucking at his sleeve from each passing doorway, he stumbled into Dixie the bargirl. Despite the hour and the day, Dixie wore a long red afternoon dress and a floppy, Sunday-go-to-meeting straw hat with artificial flowers and a long red trailing ribbon. The dress hung about her loosely.

She'd always been slim almost boyish, but now she looked thin and emaciated. Dixie's sick, Wood thought.

Dixie said, "It's Peter. Pete, old boy, how are you?" said it in a booming after-service voice at midnight on the edge of Bourbon Street.

She was drunk. Drunk or not, he was glad to see her, glad to see someone he knew after so many days among strangers. "Let's go get a cup of coffee, Dixie. Down at the French Market."

"Let's go to the Kings Room."

"We can get a drink later. I was just goin fo' coffee. Fo' the change." he said, mimicking the local accent.

"Peter. You're no damn good. Now let's go to the Kings Room."

"I've got it. We'll go get some coffee, meet Lennie, and we'll all three go to the Kings Room together. What'd ya say?"

"Let's go to the Kings Room."

Though she'd stood as if holding up the wall, it took only a few steps to convince Peter the wall had been holding up Dixie. He caught her on the first lurch. She twined her arm around his—"like a lady," she laughed—and leaned all her weight against him till he thought his arm would snap.

Away they strode toward the King's Room. Sailors stared at them, jabbering in a foreign tongue; barkers closed their curtains. I should get clear away from her, Wood thought, but he needed a place to stay.

Outside the King's Room, Wood made a final plea for coffee, but inside they went, Dixie slightly in the lead. She released her hold on him and staggered the length of the room heading midway between the Ladies and the bar. The colored girl at the piano looked up at her and smiled. Dixie threw her coat on an empty chair near the piano, perched on the edge of an occupied stool, apologized profusely to the smiling Chinese gentleman she'd displaced and, skimming her straw hat the length of the bar where it collided with a scotch on the rocks, announced (unnecessarily, Wood thought) "Dixie's here.

"LaVerne," Dixie said, interrupting the pianist at the climax of her song, "Play something for me."

"What'll it be honey?" LaVerne cooed to the displeasure of the other customers clustered around the piano. The colored woman's voice was a low alto, smooth and syrup-like; she too, was drunk, Wood realized.

"A scotch for me," Dixie cried to the waitress, "And one for LaVerne."

Wood interrupted. "Public Law 417 forbids the serving of beverages to intoxicated persons."

"Whadaya mean?" the waitress shouted back.

"Don't serve her." He held out a hand to the waitress, but no money was in it. Turning his back, he sat down on the stool next to Dixie's, first removing her coat and placing it in his lap.

"OK Dixie, whatya been doing?"

"Having a good time, Peter, old boy, having a good time. I've got ten bucks left and I mean to have a good time. You don't have money, do ya Pete? Nah, you never have any money.

She turned to LaVerne. "Do you know somebody stole twenty bucks from my purse yesterday."

"That's too bad honey," LaVerne said.

"Where are you working?" he asked Dixie.

"Not. Not working. They fired me."

"That's right, white folks. They fired her after all them years." LaVerne looked as if she were going to cry. The Chinese gentleman asked if LaVerne knew "Melancholy Baby."

"Where'd you get the twenty bucks from?" Wood asked.

"Oh Pete, you ask too many questions. What are you my father? Shut up and have a good time. If you can't have a good time. Go home to New York."

"I'm not from New ..."

"Have a drink. Where's my drink?" She bawled across the room.

"Yeah, where's da scotch," LaVerne screamed in support.

"He said not to bring her anything," the waitress called sotto voice.

"Who the hell is he?"

Wood left the bar hurriedly in search of reinforcements. He ran down the street hoping he could find Lennie. They collided outside the Paddock Lounge where Barcus had stood waiting for Lennie only an hour before. ("The Paddock's got the only genuine Dixie in town," Parsons had said once and leered.) Lennie looked startled, as if a meeting with Wood were not foremost on his mind.

"We've got to go to the Kings Room," Wood cried.

"Not now, I've got a guest." Lennie replied. Indeed, a slight dark figure of pigmy proportions stood close by Leonard's side.

"Dixie's there; she's drunk."

"I thought she was in the hospital."

"We've got to help her!"

"Well, I don't know." Lennie turned to his guest. "Kumar. Something's come up. We could meet back at the first bar we were in." The figure nodded. "You'll be O.K.?" The figure nodded again. "What the hell," Leonard said and rushed up the street after Wood.

They gathered around Dixie's chair, like doctors with a particularly worrisome patient. The first doctor, older and more assured of himself, radiated concern. "I went to the hospital," Lennie said.

"Oh, sure, I was in the hospital." Dixie replied. "Do you know that husband of mine tried to have me committed?"

"And what happened?"

"Are you O.K.?" Wood interjected.

"I was discharged."

"How did you get away? Why did they let you...? Didn't you have to have a lawyer or a doctor or something?"

Dixie smiled and hiccupped loudly, her eyes crossing as she did so. "I had a psychiatrist, three of them. They all said I was sane."

Wood cradled his head in his arms.

"I can prove I'm sane." Dixie continued, "Can you prove you're sane?"

The doctors conferred a second time. "I've got to go catch up with my friend now," Lennie said to Wood.

"For God's sake; aren't you going to do something?"

"What can I do?"

"You can talk to her. She won't talk to me. You're the one that can talk to people. Look, all she's got left is ten bucks. What's she going to do once she spends it?"

"Where do you think she got the ten bucks?"

"No. She couldn't have."

"Sure, that's how Dixie gets her money."

"She works as a stripper, a bar girl."

"Sure she does. Makes all her money from tips."

"Great money in da tips." LaVerne looked up and smiled drunkenly at them. Then her eyeballs rolled up and back into her head and she slumped sideways on the piano bench.

"Help me Lennie, help her!"

They faced each other outside on the street. Lennie extended his hand.

"No hard feelings?"

Wood shook his head, no.

"There is nothing that can be done."

"You'd do it. I know that."

"I've got to go see a guy. Catch you later."

"Dixie's apartment?"

"You're going to Dixie's apartment?"

"I've got to. I need a place to stay."

"Sure. Dixie's apartment."

Wood went back into the bar. LaVerne and Dixie were slumped against each other on the bench snoring. The short Chinese gentleman stood at the piano, playing the Georgia fight song, tapping out the melody with two fingers. Wood picked up Dixie's coat and purse and drew her upright against him. She weighed almost nothing.

"I can walk," she said.

He rang the bell of Dixie's apartment, and then let himself in with her key. Leonard wasn't there. Maybe he would catch him at La Siete later.

The light from a lamp in the back of the apartment cast a dim glow on the living room furniture giving its antiques the same horrendous cast as some of Barcus' anthropological curiosities. She could always sell some of the antiques to get money, Wood thought.

Through the closed door of the bedroom, he could hear Dixie calling, "I'll be out in a moment." He began taking off his clothes, stripping his tie, unbuttoning his shirt.

"Hi."

It was not Dixie, but a second figure standing in the light from the bedroom door, a dimple on her cheek and a scar where she'd crashed against the windshield years before.

"Maggie!" They ran toward each other and crushed each other in a hug. She was wearing only babydolls. His hands played up and down her body; he kissed her face, her neck, her eyelids. His hands quivered. She pressed her thighs against his the way a younger girl experimenting will open her lips to kiss. His pants were still half undone; he could feel all her warmth against him while he fumbled with the zipper. He kissed her forehead; he cupped her breast with one hand while he slipped his other hand and fingers up behind her buttocks.

"I'm O.K.," Dixie said from the doorway. Peter and Maggie broke apart. Peter looked away, embarrassed. His pants were down around his ankles, his penis jutting north-by-north east, first in Dixie's direction, then in Maggie's. Wood knew Maggie would not stop, would want to take him inside her even if Dixie continued to sit, as she did now, asprawl on the big couch watching them.

"You know," Dixie began, "I like Lennie even if he is strange sometimes."

"Sure, sure."

"He likes everybody, everybody you know, everything there is to like, he likes."

"We could go in the bedroom," Maggie whispered.

Dixie stood up. "And you know, I like him." She walked into her bedroom like a stripper exiting down the runway.

"Take me on the couch." Maggie said.

Leonard passed by Dixie's apartment again about two. The lights were all out inside. If Pete and Dixie were there together in bed, they would not want to be bothered. He left the area and walked the back alleys of the Quarters, not quite sure what he was looking for. In the shadows, they watched him as he entered the alleyway and watched him again as he came out. Lieutenant Arnold second-guessed him to a flophouse on Barrone and watched him as he sipped a final beer and went to bed.

Later on that same morning, a police doctor reported that Leonard Zellner, white male, twenty-six years of age, had died of a heart attack. However, secondary bruises could be found on his face and neck and on his body above the ribs where his pericardium had been kicked in.

Chapter 36 (Wood)

Before I left for the laundromat, Maggie had finally started packing for the long trip to her new home. I'd got her to take down three or four suitcases from the attic that morning, but then she found dolls, some old clothing she thought her sister could wear, her high school yearbooks, and a stack of '45's. We made a game of leafing through the yearbook-I picked out all the girls I wanted to marry-she made me close it when we came to her picture. She played all the records, some she hummed along with, some we danced to. She kept asking me if we had to leave so soon.

We'd had lunch with her father that day. I'd slipped into her house late the night before and met her sister and the two dogs and a cat but I hadn't been up then to facing her old man. (We'd taken off from New Orleans in sort of a hurry and only phoned back to say we were married when we reached Virginia.) The lunch had gone well; he accepted me as her husband, almost gratefully. We talked about his work-I got off a good anecdote-rather than our own plans. He even offered to take us to the best restaurant in town that evening, by invitation only, for white wine and trout amandine.

Maggie didn't want me to go to the laundry; it was in Emil's old neighborhood and she didn't want any of his friends to bump into me. I prowled around the house for a while after lunch and picked out a few books and a couple of her father's ties. But when I looked into the bedroom, where she supposedly was packing, she was just sitting among piles of clothing, fondling some old letters and staring out the window. A pile of worn and out-of-style dresses had been set aside for a negro called Nellie; the rest of her belongings were still in scattered heaps.

Someone had to hold a stopwatch on her emotions. I picked up the laundry and headed for the door. "We've got to go, honey. Work like hell while I'm gone, heah," I said in my put-on Southern accent. She didn't look pleased. I gave her a kiss; she smiled; everything was all right again.

A neighborhood of warped wooden houses with empty stretches of dirt instead of gardens. A laundromat located across from a car barn where a few trolleys and a bunch of smelly buses awaited the rush hour. Rings of soap scum coated the floor along with bits of red fluff and grayish sticky threads, the color of the awful fat woman's hair who squatted repulsively before me pushing clothes into a machine.

A Mexican sat beneath a hand-lettered sign warning colored washerwomen to enter only if escorted by their white patrons. Like the blacks, the Mexicans seemed to occupy their own separate territory. Still Maggie wouldn't go out after dark alone. "They'll steal your purse and knock you down for a dime," she said.

Two high school girls entered the launderette. One was fat, the other cute, hair in a neat black ponytail, rising breasts and trim hips. I watched the appealing movements of her backside and almost introduced myself. Oh, well, the hunt was over.

I sprinted for half a dozen steps as I left the launderette, thinking about my own unborn daughters, then dawdled, breathing the magnolia-scented air. I wanted to store every detail of the streets I had come to love, their look, their smell, even the accents in the people's voices.

The front door was unlocked. I let myself in and climbed the stairs calling "Maggie." She didn't answer, and I stood on the landing peering in turn through all the open doorways trying to guess where she was. Still not finding her, I tore through each room, her sister's bedroom, her/our bedroom, the bathrooms, the living room, her father's den, the kitchen, the back porch, calling, then screaming, "Maggie," where are you?"

. . . Somewhere, the back porch, perhaps, I stood for a long time staring fixedly into space. The same thoughts cycled over and over in my mind never making much sense. Where was she? What was I doing in this city? Where was she?

She must have, had to have left a note, must have—but by the phone, nothing. Then, I was in her bedroom looking. Her garments were still strewn across the bed and floor, unpacked. Her black purse was still there! But so, too, were a couple of less familiar purses that she sometimes carried. No note.

I followed myself into the damp hallway, speculating on where she'd disappeared and why. Perhaps, she'd gone for a short walk, to sort things out in her mind or to call on a neighbor and say goodbye.

I repeated, "she's gone for a walk" several times to myself and once out loud, though no one was in the house with me.

I waited in the living room, on the davenport, stroking the cat, unmoving as the sunlight disappeared and the house grew faded and dismal. . . The lights in the living room clicked on unexpectedly. Her father had returned from work. "Where is Maggie?" he asked.

Gone for a walk, I guess. I left this thought unvoiced. What time is it, I wondered. She's gone. She's gone but why?

Her father had taken off his topcoat and changed his shoes for slippers. He sat down with the evening paper, leafing through it slowly, chuckling at his favorite columnist. "Where is Maggie?" he asked several times.

Finally, he put the paper aside. "I didn't buy any groceries; I was planning on taking you kids to a good restaurant and buying you a swell French meal."

It would have been wonderful, thought a callous portion of my mind. I looked at him. He looked hurt and unloved.

How many times have you been hurt like this? Why don't you complain, you lousy bastard? And I thought then of my own father walking away when I was only seven.

Taking charge, I began to speak, carefully choosing my words: "This friend of hers, Emil, I understand he's in some sort of mental clinic uptown."

"That's right," Dr. Mason answered. "He should be there now, though they do let the patients out occasionally on passes. He's about cured. It would be a good thing if you and Maggie didn't bump into him before you left."

I started to ask what hospital Emil was in, when Diane, Maggie's younger sister, came running up the stairs into the living room and shouted breathlessly, "Dan'smotherdrovemehome, I'vegottoeat rightawayandgobacktochurch."

"Where's Maggie?" her father asked her calmly.

"Golly, I don't know. She was here when I left."

"What time was that, sugar?"

"About four."

"What time did you get home?" He turned back to me.

"About four-thirty," I said.

"You know," He began, "Maggie did bump into Emil's cousin on the street yesterday."

Diane interrupted and demanded dinner. Her father fixed her a sandwich. The clock ticking in the hallway, the pair of us sat and watched her eat.

I was angry with myself because I didn't know who to blame, because I'd wasted all that time wallowing in self-pity while she was at the mercy of. . . He's almost cured, I thought.

Meanwhile, Diane prattled on endlessly about the intrigues of junior high. She had the full upper lip that she and Maggie had inherited from her father, but she also resembled someone else, her mother, I guess, whom I'd only seen as a picture on Maggie's bedroom wall.

One thing Diane said was kind of cute. She turned to her old man in the middle of a sentence and asked, "Daddy, if you were on the playground and heard the radio say that the whole world would explode in one more minute, what would you do?"

Mr. Mason thought it over, "I'd run for shelter."

"No, silly, you'd go on playing."

I watched Diane and her father drive off to church, wanting to scream at them to come back and help me. I had to get help, somehow. I threw myself down on the couch in the living room finally and thought of nothing in red flashes. In a sense I was still waiting; but no one came. Finally, I relaxed and came up with the beginnings of a plan. When I heard someone at the front door, I ran out and met her father on the landing.

"Maggie still not back?" he asked.

"No! What's the number of the clinic that Emil's in?"

I dialed the number, hurriedly. The switchboard operator shifted my call to the nurse on duty who told me that Emil was out on a pass.

"What time did he leave?" I demanded.

"At seven this afternoon," was the prompt reply. I looked at my watch; only a few minutes past six.

"What time this afternoon?"

She gave me the same nonsensical answer. She was giving me the run around, but why? Peggy's father, still calm, spelled it out for me. Regulations stated a patient couldn't be released before seven. The nurse had been telling me politely that Emil had already been released, that he'd been out since four-thirty that afternoon!

"Where does he live?" I demanded, though demands were not at all mine to make.

"The clinic, mainly," her father replied.

"Where's his home, his family?"

"He doesn't go there; he hates his parents and his brother."

"Where the hell would he go?"

"I don't really know."

Of course, you lousy shithead, you wouldn't know where the bastard lives who's been playing with your daughter for the past two years.

"Where's this cousin live who spotted Maggie on the street yesterday?"

Professor Mason ran his fingers through his salt and pepper hair. "Him? Do you think he'd have told Emil? Do you suppose Emil would have come up here. . ?

I walked out of the room, letting him ramble on. Jesus! A moment looking out the window into the darkened street and I came back angry and determined and told him we were bloody well going down and talk to the bastard's family. He was worried about Maggie, too, by this time, and volunteered to go alone and talk to them, to keep my identity a secret, he said.

They didn't know who I was, but I didn't know who they were. A picture of Emil was still on Maggie's bureau, its face turned to the wall. I crumpled it up, jammed it in my pocket; then, I searched the house looking for weapons.

I paced up and down looking first in the kitchen, then in the basement. He returned smiling. "They said he wasn't there."

"Where is he?"

"His brother said he didn't know."

I sneered.

"He looked sincere." Dr. Mason continued.

"Christ, don't you care about your daughter at all." He didn't answer. I think he was mumbling to himself. I'd been holding this Sam Browne belt and I placed the buckle between my middle fingers. I drew one loop around my wrist, then brought the loop up and around my thumb three times. The remainder of the turns I coiled around my knuckles; I tucked the end in my fist. It would be a good idea for us to visit the brother again.

Her father looked up shocked. "Look, I don't think violence will do any good."

Right, I thought. "Any other suggestions?"

He didn't answer. He looked very melancholy.

"Let's go find out what his brother really knows." I slapped the belt in my palm meaningfully.

"Look," he said, "maybe Maggie just went out to have a last drink with Emil."

Maybe? God I hoped so. It was easiest to think what her father suggested was true. He said he'd drive me to their usual hangouts.

We walked heavily down the stairs and to the car. He drove out to the boulevard and followed it up twenty or thirty blocks till we reached a neon strip of bars and lounges. We parked and her father led us into the Carrollton Tavern; I was a shadow, a particle of dust blown into the tavern by the wind. Dr. Mason headed for the bar and the dust mote drifted between the empty tables toward the jukebox, drifted slowly, eyes scanning every corner of the room. When the mote returned, Mason was talking to a small man with greasy hair. They were both hoisting a brew.

"Sure, Mr. Mason," the fellow said, "She was in, made a couple of phone calls and left."

"Thanks very much," her father began; I nudged him from behind.

"Ask him what time." I whispered.

"What time?" he amplified.

"Oh, five-five-fifteen. What do you think?" the man asked the barmaid. She nodded her head, added she thought Maggie had phoned the clinic.

We left the tavern, drove a couple of blocks. We walked in and immediately walked out of two more bars.

"Ask somebody," I insisted.

"I tell you," her father replied, "It was just a lucky break the first time; I happened to see someone I knew."

"Ask the barmaid."

He asked. They knew who Emil was. A regular who never had any money but could always get others to buy drinks for him.

"Where does this guy stay when he gets out of the hospital?" I said finally.

"He doesn't. He stays up all night drinking when he's out on a pass."

Where does he go when he wants to lie down, I was going to say. But I didn't want to ask that.

"Maybe she's gone home," her father suggested. We phoned. No one answered.

"Look," Mason said, finally, "I know of a friend he sometimes stays with.

I straightened up, happy.

"They often go out and drink together even though the other guy's married, now."

I nodded eagerly, trying to be encouraging, trying to raise my own spirits.

"I've only been there once but I ought to be able to find the place." We drove for a long time, clear across town it seemed to me. Then we slowed to a crawl as her father leaned out the window of the car and tried to pick out the house. We stopped where three streets met in a Y, and parked right at the joint.

Dr. Mason still wasn't sure which house. He thought it was near a grocery store, but then again he thought the house had two stories. We walked over and scanned the mailboxes in the apartment house near the store, but he didn't recognize any of the names.

"They're upstairs," he said.

I ran upstairs and stopped on the landing. Two doors. I listened, feeling with every nerve in my body for a trace of her. No one home in either apartment.

Descending, I looked for Kleenex on the stairs, any signs she might have left as a guide to me. Her father was talking with a woman on the porch. I joined them silently.

"The couple who live upstairs on the other side have a small child?" he was asking.

"That's right. Their name is Rouse." a plumpish blond woman replied.

Mr. Mason went on methodically. "The woman is tall and blond."

She nodded, yes.

"Well thank you very much. We were just in the neighborhood . . ." But I had walked away from them and around the side of the house to where the mailbox said Mike and Lila Rouse.

Her father came up behind me. "That's right," he said, "Mike and Lila; but their car's not here."

We drove off and went back to touring the bars. We didn't run across Maggie's trail again, and I suggested we telephone the police. Her father didn't like the idea; he said it was no use, missing persons were too common in a twenty-four hour town like New Orleans; the police just didn't give a damn. I looked at him, forty-five years old, scrawny and balding, divorced. A miserable misfit who'd been deserted so often that. . . I stopped thinking. I didn't want to hit him, yet.

I called missing persons. I didn't get to say word one, before they asked how long she'd been gone. I told them and they told me to call back after she'd been gone at least twelve hours. My God, how much can happen in just twelve hours!

I could recall the afternoon I'd first met Maggie, almost accidentally; her coffee break stretched into an hour, we met a second time for supper, walked and talked and... kissed. It had taken me a half hour to do the laundry and a half hour walking home, and in that hour, she'd disappeared. And now, more bars, call, run, think, and wait twelve fear-ridden hours for the police to stir their lazy butts.

I was lucky because anger was replacing the cold fear, and I no longer speculated on Maggie's terror, or if they held her while she pleaded, or whether they were hitting her, or if she screamed aloud or inwardly for me. We made Emil's brother's place again and then went back to his friends the Rouses.

This time, an old Buick was in Rouse's driveway. Dr. Mason and I parked beneath a large oak that shielded us from the street lamp. The streetlight shone on the white house in which the Rouses lived so that the house loomed taller than any other house on the block. The lamplight, filtered through the oak leaves, streamed through the car window casting crazy patterns on the seat backs. We held a war-council, but didn't really agree on anything before we moved on common impulse out the car and up the stairs.

Dr. Mason reached the landing ahead of me and knocked. I stayed on the top stair, flat against the wall near the door. A man's voice called, "Just a minute." The rustle of footsteps, more delay; the door opened finally and a voice said, "We was asleep."

Rouse had answered the door in his stocking feet and shorts. Big but flabby. Tattoos covered his thick arms but the shoulders and biceps bulged with fat not muscle, and his legs were thin. The iron jaw was steel blue, shadowed with beard. His eyes didn't meet Dr. Mason's, though he talked to him politely, calling him Professor, asking after his health and stalling. Dr. Mason began asking direct questions.

"Have you seen Emil?"

Rouse's face didn't flicker a muscle and my eyes never left his face.

"We're looking for Maggie." her father offered.

Again, Rouse remained expressionless.

"Any idea where we could find Emil?"

"No I don't, Professor."

"What clubs do they usually go to?" I asked.

Rouse took his time about answering; his steel-grey eyes flicked toward me, wobbled back without focusing.

"You know, the Carrollton Tavern, the One-Two Club. You've been there with them as often as I have, Professor."

What were Dr. Mason and I to do now we'd finished questioning Rouse? Lay him out? Stomp into his house and ransack

194

the rooms? Or daintily ask his permission to enter and search the place?

I'd read too many detective novels. Professor Mason said, "Let us know if you see Maggie," and we walked unhappily downstairs.

"Let's sit in the car for awhile," I suggested. We waited five minutes till the lights went out in the upstairs apartment, then drove to the One-Two Club.

A half hour later we drove home disgusted. Another weak beer, another group of people who should have gone home, hours before. The lights in Mason's home were partially lit, but we couldn't remember which ones we'd left on ourselves. Besides, Maggie's sister had come home and gone to sleep since we'd left. No message on the pad by the phone and Maggie's bedroom was untouched.

I wanted to go to sleep and be fresh when things broke. Her father wanted to talk. Unwillingly, I lay back on his bed like a psychiatrist in reverse, shut my eyes and listened. He told me more about himself and his former wife and Maggie than I really wanted to know. About his early struggles to get an education and his wife's instability, and so forth.

"Why are you so damned incompetent, Dad?" I said to myself as I fell into a bitter sleep.

. . . I woke at six, instantly awake. A sure feeling possessed me. Emil had taken Peggy away, kidnapped her; she hadn't wanted to go with him, had just wanted to talk with him, to try to calm him down. But he had gotten drunk and struck her; she hadn't wanted to go with him.

Six a.m. and I was alert, fresh. The night before I had woken from the murky depths bathed in sweat. "Honey," I'd said nudging her, "Honey, I had a bad dream." "Uh, huh," she'd said in reply and rolled back to sleep while the White Queen writhed in agony.

A car came down the alleyway, parked beneath the window, then drove away again; no one came up the stairs. I woke enough to realize I'd been sleeping fully dressed, stretched out on the old man's bed.

I got up, prowled around the house. I found Mr. Mason uncomfortably asleep on the davenport and woke him. "Give me the car keys," I said. He handed them over. When I drove off, he was upstairs heading groggily for his own room.

The street was soaked with black pools glistening under the street lamps but it wasn't raining. The air was clean for a change, though still humid and clogging. The morning paper had been tossed carelessly against the Mason's doorsill. The front page held no sign of her name, no stories about unidentified women's bodies.

Before starting the car, I felt for the army belt in my pocket, the long scissors in my coat. I drove carefully, at precisely the legal speed limit, first to the Carrollton Tavern. A cop was lying asleep in a parked patrol car outside the building. I parked in front of him, self-consciously and made a lousy job of it, two feet away from the curb. The tavern was open but deserted; some all-night hangout! I woke up the cop, tried to tell him about Maggie. "You gotta wait twenty-four hours," he said.

Who did I know in that lonely city, I kept asking myself: eight restaurant owners who'd let me wash their dishes, Zellner, wherever he was, Maggie's father, and Parsons.

I drove to Parsons' place. I'd shared his pad for a while; we were friends. I rang the buzzer and pounded on the door; nothing happened, and I let myself in with the keys I'd retained. Parsons sat up sleepily in bed and snapped on the light.

I sketched the story for him very briefly: We'd come back from our honeymoon; we'd been supposed to leave; Maggie had been packing; Emil had kidnapped her. It looked as if I would have to repeat the story; Parsons didn't seem too alert. He snapped suddenly, "Where does Emil live?"

"He doesn't. He stays up all night when he gets a pass from the clinic."

"Does he have a car?"

I shook my head. "He shouldn't have. He doesn't have any money."

Parsons turned thoughtful, reflective as he if might soon have a solution, but he didn't say anything.

"I'm going to go around to the tourist courts," I said impatiently.

"Use my phone," he offered. "Wait a minute, must be over three hundred motels in this area."

"The hell there is," I replied, grabbing at the yellow pages; but he was right, the listings stretched over several pages.

"If he goes to a motel, it would probably be close by, on this side of town, near a trolley line." Parsons suggested. I phoned four or five nearby motels immediately. The first call took a suspicious minute, the next few were completed in seconds. Why so quickly, I wondered? Maybe the clerks weren't looking at their registers; maybe they were lying; why would Emil be stupid enough to sign his real name?

196

I yelled to Parsons, loud and angry, "Have you got your gun back?"

When he told me "No," I snarled a goodbye, and headed for the door, a red mist before my eyes. He stopped me as I left and handed me a hammer-all he could find-all he seemed willing to find for me.

I raced across the lot and into the streets, driving along a route I'd followed only in the dark. I recognized none of the houses or the cross streets; an instinct led me in tightening circles to the Y, and the grocery, and Rouse's house. I parked in his driveway, blocking his Buick, and checked the hammer under my coat. Up the stairs, slowly, then pounded on his door. A sleepy voice answered; a moment later, Rouse appeared, wearing jeans instead of shorts; he was still bare-chested.

We went through the old routine. He was patronizing and uncommunicative. His wife's voice came through from the background, once, to confirm a statement. I tried to get a look at her, but he neatly blocked the doorway. Should I bust him one or slink off downstairs?

I slunk. "I ain't seen him," he'd said. "I'll give you a call if I find out anything about Maggie." Again that iron jaw never quivered.

I circled the block slowly, then parked across and down the street from the house. One question still bugged me. Why hadn't Rouse asked me who the hell I was? Didn't he care? If he knew my identity, who had told him?

I was having a recurring daydream in which I killed the Rouses one at a time for their part in kidnapping Maggie. My mind kept skipping the part where they touched Maggie. I had to find her before they harmed her! Was she upstairs across the street, now, or would Emil try to bring her here later? Or, I could keep looking in five hundred bars and a hundred tourist courts, peer in the face of every furtive passerby.

In all the time I'd sat in my car waiting and agonizing, no one left or approached the Rouses' home. I felt I couldn't wait any longer and drove back home for the reassurance no one there seemed capable of giving.

The phone rang as I entered. I picked up the receiver and didn't say anything. Mr. Mason and Diane stood in the hall watching me, silently.

"Hello, Professor?" Rouse's harsh voice questioned.

"Ye'ar."

"Is this Mr. Mason?"

"Ye'ar." Again, my words and tone were unidentifiable, disinterested.

"You know that kid you was here with last night? Well, look. That kid was here at 6 a.m. this morning."

I breathed my concern.

"Now look, this kid is going to get himself hurt if he keeps bothering people. I got a wife...."

I interrupted Rouse. "Maybe you might get hurt," I said.

."..and I want you to tell him that. . .Say, who is this anyway? Why you! You're that lousy punk kid, ain't you. By God, if I was there you'd get a fucking rod up your ass."

"Maybe you're going to get hurt." I repeated.

"Hah. Look, you ain't nothing but a lousy punk, see. Now my wife is here and she's pregnant and I don't want anybody bothering her. If you come here again, there's going to be real trouble."

"I was thinking of sending the police instead."

My flat statement took the edge off our conversation. A few more muttered threats from Rouse, an assurance he'd be waiting for me at his home, and he hung up.

Maggie's father told me Rouse had already been jugged a couple of times for drunken assault; I didn't know whether to feel better or worse. I phoned Missing Persons again. They told me to call back after nine a.m. That figured; what they meant was call back and tell your troubles to the day shift.

I barely had time to clean up in the bathroom, when the phone rang again. I took the receiver out of Mr. Mason's grasp before he had a chance to speak and waved him back into his bedroom. I held the phone without speaking. I could hear traffic noises and the sound of dishes clattering. A voice whispered to someone standing near the other receiver that we'd answered but hadn't said anything.

The silence was ruptured by an aggressive voice bellowing, "You there mother-fucker?"

I was.

"Listen m.f., I don't want you bothering my friends."

So?

"You leave them alone, hear. You just pack up and get the fuck out of town."

"Tomorrow." I replied audibly.

"Listen, don't give me none of that shit, you lousy mother fucker, you stinking..." His obscenity was violent, exceptionally graphic, but confined to one mode of intercourse and limited to incest.

"Where's Maggie?" I asked.

He began to holler and scream his curses.

I heard Mr. Mason say behind me, "That's Emil's voice, all right."

"Who is this?" I asked next.

"You know fuckin well, m.f." he said.

"Emil?"

Silence.

"Emil, you're yellow."

"Look m.f., when we get through beating on you, they're going to flush you down the John."

"Down the tubes," I corrected.

He repeated his previous offer.

"Afraid to fight me Emil," I challenged.

"You name the spot, m.f."

"Right here."

"Jam'n candy, m.f., cause we're going t'ram you..."

I interrupted. "I'm going to kill you, Emil."

I hung up smiling.

Then the fear came. The noise and the bellowing, the names and the threats had gotten through to me. I phoned Parsons first and asked him to come and back me. He said he'd think about it. I told him we'd drive over and get him. He said not to bother, he'd be leaving the house as of that instant and disappearing for the remainder of the week. Then, he hung up. I phoned him back; no one answered.

I phoned the police next. "Now you're thinking," Mr. Mason commented over my shoulder. I asked for Homicide, and told them the full story.

"What do you expect us to do?" they asked.

"Protect me, for Christ's sake!"

"Look Jack, if we protected every guy who got himself into trouble over a woman, we'd be working our asses off twenty-four hours a day."

"That's what you're paid for," I stormed, but only after they'd hung up.

I worked over the cracked wallboards with my fingers. The paper in the hallway, stained and spotted, peeled off in my hands; it was dusty and drafty where I was sitting.

I had to know someone in New Orleans besides that bastard Parsons!

Mostly, I knew women, I realized forlornly. Each had a song and a story but it did not help now to remember. (A very young girl, a nurse in training at a catholic hospital across town — Mercy Hospital, I think, had never been kissed, she said, before she met me, had been out of the convent for just three months; a thin girl, who clung to me because I was a man. She said, "I don't know enough about the world to marry you now.")

I broke off and snarled at the unmoving father and daughter whose silent fear had invaded my thoughts. I paced the house, raging.

The dogs were whining for their breakfast so I closed a second door on them. Back in the hallway, I unhooked the phone receiver; I went through Maggie's clothes in her bedroom to see what was missing. On the living-room threshold, I stopped and listened to her father pacing in his den with quick steps between his bed and his desk and back. Diane lay on her back, fully clothed, her fists clenched, staring very hard at the ceiling.

I listened for a break in the traffic outside the house. I listened in jumps. My mind raced searching for an easy solution. I needed somebody, somewhere to stand beside me.

I had no one. Yet, I was no longer nervous. It was much easier, now; I did not have to search for the kidnappers; they were playing right into my hands. They were coming to me and I would kill them. Crazy lunatic thoughts.

But how many of them were there?

I flopped out on the davenport in the living room and picked up a novel. I concentrated on the story for a few minutes, then, leaping to my feet in answer to a silent reveille, I stalked into the father's bedroom.

"The kid should be in school," I said. "You had better drive her there." Very noble, huh? The kid could hardly help me fight; all she could do would be to get hurt. Besides how did I know which side her father was on?

They whisked out the front door, as though both of them had been awaiting that very command.

"Honk your horn twice before returning," I told the father, not that I felt he'd have guts enough to return. "I'm going to lay out the first man to put his foot on the stairway."

"No one can get in the back way," confided Diane enthusiastically. (Take away her braces, stop her giggles, and she'd be a doll someday like her older sister.)

Mr. Mason stammered pompously, "This is my house young man. You can't just go bopping the first person who happens to enter."

"I'll send the police a registered letter instead. Better just honk that horn Mr. Mason. And lock the front door."

They quickened their pace out of the house; I had to run down a couple of steps in pursuit to ask, "Does Maggie have a key?" They called back yes before driving away.

I was alone in the house.

I was a hollow man, straining to hear each sound. A floorboard creaked; I caught the sound of a fumbling at the window along with other unexplainable noises. My hand was running smoothly, rhythmically over the rough grain of a tall bookcase; my mind was wildly cycling over the names of everyone I'd ever known; like the gang I grew up with and friends I had all over the country in Chicago, Cleveland, L.A. — the magic names of cities that didn't mean a damn thing for no one could get here in time to save me, only in time to seek vengeance. Anthony was my blood brother, but he was in California. I picked up the phone and asked the operator to call San Francisco.

Five long rings till a disgruntled voice answered "Hello."

"Could I speak to Anthony?"

"He's not here," his old man asserted.

"When will he be back?"

"Later, much later."

"About what time?"

"I-uk, druk-uk, y-huk"

"Hello, hello" I wailed into the receiver. The phone had gone nuts. Cracklings distorted every word Anthony's father said. There were more 'uk's' from his end.

"Hello. Can you hear me? Can you hear me!" We alternated 'uk's and 'hello's in this manner for several minutes, when I remembered where I was and began to look back over my shoulders and listen for sounds again. The static ceased abruptly and I could hear a voice saying to someone by the phone, "If he doesn't says something soon, I'm going to hang up."

"Hello," I screamed.

"Hello, hello," his father's hoarse voice echoed, "Why don't you say something?"

"Anthony!" I screamed.

"He's not here!" his father screamed back across the country.

I lowered my voice and asked, "Where is he?"

"Is this some sort of joke?"

"It's no joke. I'm in New Orleans. I've got to get in touch with him. A mob of guys are coming after me."

"Say, do you know what time it is? It's five o'clock in the morning and if this is some sort of joke I'm going to hang up."

"Don't" I pleaded, "I'm calling from New Orleans."

"New Orleans." He mispronounced the name horribly and accompanied his mispronunciation with grunts and snarls that demonstrated his full contempt for jokers in the next block.

"Let me talk to Anthony's mother please."

He sounded grateful for the opportunity. "Hello?" her voice came through clearly. I suspected the father was so sleepy he had been talking into the wrong end of the phone.

"This is Pete. You must remember me. Listen closely, I'm in Louisiana. I'm waiting at the top of the stairs for an unknown person to climb up and try to . . ." The doorbell rang. ." . .kill me. You've got to . . ." My God, the doorbell rang!

"What's this? What's this!" she said, confused. Why had I called her?

"Call Anthony to the phone!" I screamed. "No, wait a minute. Please. Don't hang up. I've got to answer the door. If I don't come back call the police."

I raced into the front bedroom, dropping the receiver on the floor with a thunk. I peered through the blinds trying to see who was ringing; but I couldn't see the door from that angle. I tore back into the hall, jumped the phone, and went into the living room. The dogs woke up and began racing and barking after me. The doorbell rang again.

From the living room window I could look down on a gray-shingled overhang above the front door, but I couldn't see who was standing beneath it on the doorstep. I reached under the blind and opened the sticky window a crack. I yelled into the street. "You in the doorway, come into the street where I can see you."

A formless horrible yell came in reply.

"Go out to the curb" I commanded. A fat, flustered Negress stepped out from under the overhang, wringing her hands. I raced

202

out into the hall; the dogs were still barking effusively around the telephone. Thank God, I didn't have to pay the phone bill.

I ran downstairs, hammer in hand. I threw open the door, yelling to the Negress, ushered her inside, slammed and locked the door behind. She fairly flew up the stairs. I followed her and told her, the hammer still in my hand, to take the dogs back out on the back porch, feed them, then make me a last breakfast.

I returned to my phone call and repeated what I'd said before; there wasn't much more to say. I found out from Anthony's mom that he wouldn't be back till much later. He was currently stationed at Fort Ord, 3rd Brigade, Infantry. My stomach was knotted in fear; I must have been crazy to have wasted time calling.

What other phone calls could I make? What else could I do now that I was totally alone, except run? And I wouldn't.

I stood pale and empty against the railing. The Negress called from the kitchen that breakfast was ready. Despite all the previous noise and confusion, I looked forward to peppered, perfectly prepared eggs and grits and hot biscuits. A key turned in the front door lock. I stepped, swift as a shadow, to the right of the stairwell and flattened against the wall. They came up the stairs.

A knife blade jutted out from Rouse's left hand, like the protruding claw of the bear. He shambled past me, turning to his right before he bumped the back wall. I swung the hammer just as he realized he ought to have looked back along the corridor before turning. I missed him. He backed down the hall toward the kitchen. I leapt after him and as I passed the top of the stairs I glimpsed Maggie and, in front of her, Emil with a gun.

Rouse stopped backing and stabbed at my hammer arm. I stepped inside his arms, reached across with my left and pinned his wrist. Holding it pinned for a second-I could only have held his thick wrist for a second-I brought the hammer down crunching the top of his skull.

I stepped back in from the side; I turned as Emil screaming "mother fucker" came charging, trying to bayonet me with his pistol. I continued the arc and caught him with a lucky blow to the temple. He dropped his gun.

When he made a leap to retrieve it, I kicked him. He rebounded off the wall and dived for my legs as I brought the hammer down full force on his spine. He held on and began climbing up my legs, throwing me off balance against the wall. I was forced to use my arms as braces and I lost the advantage. He dumped me and I rolled down two stairs still clinging to the hammer.

He moved groggily toward his gun, but I was on my feet first. Maggie moved forward and kicked the gun away from Emil. She stood between us facing me; the search was over, I had her back now.

"I don't love you," she said. "Please, why don't you just plain get the hell out of here."

"Maggie."

"Go on, take the next train out of here."

I didn't say anything. Words rearranged themselves in books unavailable to me. Didn't say anything at all. Her tones were too firm, too determined. They reminded me of a time in the first grade of school, when they'd let us out early and I'd run all the way home and mother wasn't there. . . She'd gone shopping or something, and I had all this exciting stuff to tell her. . . While waiting I cleaned up my room real neat, cause I loved my mother so, and wanted her to pick me up and hug me, and it was dark by the time she came home, and awfully cold. . . I sat bolt upright when she walked into my room and put down my picture book and my mother said, "What are you doing sitting on that clean bedspread?"

I dunno; what was I doing anywhere; I really never thought much about where I was or how cold it was; I just wanted to be near you.

In the end, Maggie left with Rouse and Emil, Rouse holding his shoulder where I'd clobbered him with the hammer. And I waited for Dr. Mason to come for me across the years.

Chapter 37 (Mason)

It appears we will have to let Zellner go. Ironic, but, his dismissal, for academic reasons, comes after we — all of us — expended so much effort on his behalf. In defending him, Henry — Henry Starr — so alienated the other members of our department that Henry, too, is to be let go as soon as his contract expires.

(True, Henry only had a temporary appointment; however, he had been advised by Dr. Kaspers that his appointment could be made permanent.)

A great deal of pressure to expel Mr. Zellner had been exerted on our department over the past few months, principally by the Dean, and it is only through the cohesive efforts of our chairman, Dr. Kaspers, that we were able to resist it. Again, it is ironic that Kaspers, "Papa" Kaspers to three generations of graduate students, should have become the focus of Henry's attacks. Without Kaspers to lead us, without his acting constantly as an intermediary between our department and the Dean, Zellner would have been let go long before. Never mind that the boy's public displays were anathema to Dr. Kaspers' sense of propriety, his own strong sense of fair play and his belief in our department led him to intervene constantly on Zellner's behalf.

I would caution Dr. Booth and the other remaining members of our liberal wing that Dr. Kaspers' seemingly extreme attitude is, in great measure, a reaction to their own polemics. One might say it was Booth's and Starr's behind-the-scenes maneuvering that, in the end, left Kaspers with no alternative but to ask for Zellner's dismissal.

Other, external pressures also left us little room for maneuver. Professor Werme felt slighted he had not been consulted earlier. The old argument that we were already passing too many of our students through the courses, "waving" them on to the doctorate as it were, popped up anew. And, I'd forgotten this, some questions arose regarding discrepancies in Zellner's original admission forms.

In the end, I had little hope that my own proposal to give Zellner an additional month or two to hand in some sort of thesis could meet with any sort of reasoned consideration. If I can't say I am unhappy about Zellner's leaving, it is because I am bitter I earned so much resentment on his behalf.

Our final faculty meeting on the topic of Zellner was a crude parody of all our previous discussions. All eight members of the faculty were in attendance, so that none could say his views had gone unrepresented. (This did not dissuade Henry from later accusations of unfairness.)

Miss Wicks, Dr. K's secretary was ill with the result no coffee had been made and we must forgo the break that so often permits the renewal of discussion with some measure of giving and fair play. Dr. Waxman (he is a Unitarian, incidentally, despite his Jewish name; it is quite common these days I am told for Jews to become Unitarians) made a short speech on the necessity of the professional attitude and the importance of keeping separate one's political and one's academic views.

This was absolutely the wrong thing to say in Henry's presence and he made the first of his many interruptions. Kaspers was forced to call for silence and thus, from the very beginning, the calmness and temperate attitude Kaspers had prayed for was lost.

Dr. Flanders again asked that we stop and consider the possibility of adding a statistics course to the undergraduate curriculum. (Flanders, in the course of his investigations on the disputed authorship of the Federalist papers, has become something of a statistician himself.) Obviously, we were in no mood to consider his proposal (not that it ought to be given serious consideration in any case) and our rejection may have turned Flanders against Zellner.

Dr. Brown said he thought Zellner was a poor student. To Dr. Brown's credit, this is the only "fact" as such we were to receive at the meeting, though, in my opinion, the boy is not a poor student, but has simply been under a great deal of stress. Rather than berate us, Henry would have been far more effective had he spent ten minutes or so outlining the boy's academic background, the splendid record the boy had assembled as an undergraduate — at a small Baptist college to be sure — his demonstrated capacity for original work, and his obvious and excellent communication skills.

Henry, of course, did nothing of the kind. He was going to make a speech and did so, filling it with lively anecdotes from sixteenth century France (his period). Dr. Kaspers finally interrupted when the allusions to the profligate Bourbon kings grew too pointed. And, however amusing I found Henry, I was obliged to vote with the rest to silence him. Besides, Henry is entirely too free with his allusions, creating enemies out of poor allies, heaping abuse on those who are merely undecided, and making fun of those who, like Professor Werme, are unfamiliar with the facts of the case.

Starr argued correctly that Zellner had too many outside activities during the semester. But what he couldn't do was convince us that Zellner would have fewer activities and spend more time on his courses during the semesters to come.

If Henry had one telling point, it was, I feel, that departmental meetings to determine graduate status and to discuss the award of fellowships are normally held in March rather than November. Reiner and Benjamin try to make light of my insistence on precedent (thankfully, I am backed up by the majority of the members of our department) but the integrity of our institution relies mainly on our traditions. The force and credit that will be given to our departmental decisions and the respect in which our department will be held by the outside world rest on the consistency with which our judgments are rendered.

In this instance, Dr. Webb, our longest resident (apart from Kaspers of course) was able to show from previous minutes that while discussions of the fellowships themselves might take place only in the spring, usually in April, but occasionally as early as March or late February, graduate status could and has been the subject of discussions at many different times of the year; however, my point on precedence remains.

In the end, it was Kaspers who suggested we simply leave it up to the administration. Henry reacted immediately with cries of Pontus Pilate, a vicious and unwarranted accusation that did not go unnoticed.

Before a vote on Kaspers' motion was taken, I rose to present my own views. I began, I think fairly calmly, pointing out the ups and downs of the boy's academic career and, what seemed to me, his ultimate promise of excellence, but I was interrupted so often by cross-talk and whispered asides, that finally, as the meeting broke up into little groups, I simply sat down and refused to vote one way or the other.

I wanted to help. Once, when I was midway through my own academic career, I failed a pre-doctoral examination. It is not on my records, of course. The committee said they would consider it only a trial exam, but I knew that I had failed. It is a terrible thing after seven, no seventeen, years of education to realize suddenly you are not fit for your own chosen profession.

I over dramatize of course. But, at that time, my friends and I tended to over dramatize everything that happened to us, to feed excitement back and forth until we were exhausted, unable to cope with the present for fear of the future. "For me, it is the end of the world," I wrote. "Soon you will rise like the Phoenix from the ashes," a friend wrote back. And my reply, which makes no sense now, was something about Job and the dung heap. (Suicide never occurred to me or to any of my friends, probably because it would have meant an end to the drama.)

At any rate, though my major professor told me not to worry and to go back and prepare for the next examination, I dropped out of school. After spending a few unsuccessful weeks in and out of employment agencies, I left New York and went to stay on my Uncle's farm near Scranton. (Looking back, I realize I set out in quest of work during the greatest depression in history, with thousands of men begging for the opportunity to wash dishes or dig ditches, the humble jobs I had picked out for myself so deliberately.)

My intention was to ingratiate myself with my Uncle by working at chores and things so that I would be asked to stay and, eventually, after many years of hard labor, who knows, inherit my Uncle's farm. My Uncle, of course, had plans of his own. He spent the first afternoon I was there grandly showing me about the estates, as if he were a gentleman farmer rather than a small businessman, and after that he left me alone with my aunt. I used to rise fairly late in my student days (perhaps I should write, in my bachelor days) and my aunt, I imagine, let me sleep to my heart's content. The result was that I woke about ten or eleven in the morning at a time when most of the heavy labor on the farm had already been completed. If I tried to join my uncle and his workers in the field, they would entertain me for a few moments (or let me entertain them), and then, with a glance at his watch, my uncle or one of his foreman would say "well there's work to be done," and start the tractor, so I'd no chance to discuss my own role in the work.

In the evenings, we'd sit before a roaring fire — are there any of those enormous King James' fireplaces still left in this country, I wonder — and my uncle would ask me about school and about my mom and dad (about whose comings and goings I knew hardly more than he did), and I'd try to ask my uncle questions about farming, not knowing quite what to ask. We had just so much we could say about my parents, while farming it seemed was something one did, not something one talked about, and, in the end, the conversation get back to my studies again.

I soon discovered my Uncle had a completely wrong idea about what historians do (though no more ridiculous I'm sure than my own notions of farmers and farming). By the time I'd explained the job to him properly — my uncle was really quite a good listener, no matter how bad he might be as an explainer — I realized how much I liked the idea of being a historian.

(But I realized too that no matter how much I liked the idea, I was not and could never be one.)

My uncle thought of history as something to do with teaching and high school, which, of course, is where his last contact with history had been, and insisted on congratulating me on my high-mindedness, filial loyalty, and deep moral commitment in wanting to devote my life to educating the young (and in following in the footsteps of my father, a similarly high-minded, if impoverished individual). Strangely, I'd never before considered the idea of being a teacher. For me, history had been something you studied, not something you taught.

I went back to school with renewed vigor (after all the country was in a depression and, however much my aunt and uncle may have admired the scholar, they weren't about to praise an idle one) and a new sense of purpose. I audited several courses for prospective high school and elementary-school teachers though these seemed somewhat lacking in particulars. And I took my exams again thinking that even a narrow pass might help me to get a job teaching school. They passed me, I imagine mainly on the basis of friendship ("Mason has been around a long time, can't just dump him"). I had a semester to kill before the public-school term began and since I was offered a bit of money to help one of my advisors on a WPA project, I stayed on at the University and, incredibly enough, soon found I had a thesis (a rather creditable thesis I've been told), a doctorate, and an offer of a teaching position at a university. In fact, I received two offers. I'll confess I took the one at Tulane more out of a desire to see just what the South was like than for any other good reason.

The thing is: I still don't feel that I am a historian. I go through the motions. I write papers. I attend lectures at society meetings. I'm even the associate editor of a small historical journal. But I'm not a name that future students will learn about. Zellner, in contrast, had promise. His was a very original mind. He lacked training in the discipline (the Baptist college he went to as an undergraduate was an awfully poor one) but he was quick to pick up whatever techniques he was shown. A pep talk or two with someone who would stress the importance of good grades in all courses (not just the ones he favored) and he would have been one of our top students. Perhaps, a small amount of money could even have been arranged for him.

But the facts were that since the beginning of the semester, Zellner has not been doing the work. Oh, we covered up his lack of application. We were so busy stressing our department's independence from the University that we had no choice but to cover up. But it wasn't that he hadn't been doing much of the work or even most of it, he hadn't been doing any. When he'd get back to the University from those damm fool expeditions—going to some integrationist meeting, sitting with negroes in lunch rooms and being arrested, or just horsing around with Henry—why then he'd spend the rest of the night drinking or playing cards. (I didn't find this out directly. I learned it from Maggie and she learned it from the boy Peter she'd been living with.)

Let Henry dramatize Zellner's activities if he wishes, but I sometime feel Zellner's activities were a ruse to cover up Zellner's own uncertainties. Zellner's insecurity manifested itself in other ways, too. For example, however well Zellner might get along with the undergraduates he served as a teaching assistant, he was routinely obnoxious to many of the faculty. And I wonder if Henry knew that Zellner had been heard saying, "My name is Zellner, not Zellerman, what do you think I am, some sort of kike?"

"Zellner never backed down." Henry said in justification.

No, Henry, I suppose he didn't. Zellner endured and he endured alone. The department had been behind him, but he never really knew the extent or even the existence of our support. He endured and he survived without us, and he will survive without us in the future. But Henry, did you ever think, maybe he really didn't want to?

Epilogue

If looking back I see
No more trains,
Desert that was $5 an acre,
And lakefront properties without a lake,
Five condors, only two a mating pair,
King Canyon, a place to park Mickie and Minnie with the kids,
My nation's focus outward to
Lebanon, Ethiopia, South Africa.
Every express a local:
Chuga-a-chug-a
Candy butcher come to sell you
CaNDY coffee doughnuts papers magazines.
"He orders one coffee; fills the cup with sugar. Says
He is a railroad man."
"I said I worked for the railroad, in public relations."
"Public relations! Now I ask you."
Candy butcher got off in El Paso
The humiliation, hunger remain
Through Las Cruces, Deming, Tucson, Phoenix.
As the young ladies
Carrying tennis rackets, smelling of horses,
Board the train,
I saw the Indians selling pottery,
some cracked, some with hidden defects,
All with racial memories
Hidden in the swirling patterns of their hands.
I loved her,
Loved her then.
We'd have been riding my cycle through
Reflections in train windows
Joshua tree, saguaro, magnolias, and the climbing vines.
Wood remembers everything about New Orleans;
He has learned nothing about himself.

Outside Parsons' apartment, wet and cold,
He took the cycle apart, piece by piece,
Following a set of scrawled instructions,
that disintegrated in the rain.

Removed the cylinder sleeve,
Greased it lightly;
The rain shattered on the oil-soaked pavement,
Dancing in a thousand colored fragments.

He had had to move several times;
Once, the first time,
When he tipped the cycle over to remove the generator,
The oil dripped hot and thick on the pavement;
The gutters thick with the dirty black oil
That had already stained the concrete,
That would give Parsons (and the University maintenance crew)
Something to complain about for months to come.

The van came and took the cycle away.
He boarded the trolley,
Oil-soaked saddlebags over his shoulders,
Sat, as always,
Ahead of the unmarked division between white and black.
A crack in the window
Where someone had shot the trolley with an air rifle.
They said it had something to do with integration; He
Thought it had more to do with simple hate, the need
To shatter and break something
Over and over, the need:
Maggie, he whimpered, Maggie.
A black woman stared at him, thinking
Crazy white man.
The black woman spoke to her neighbor,
Laughed, who could tell,
Staring faces filled with hate,
Blackbirds waiting in the rain.

Was there time for a last beignet in the Quarters?
A rich oyster-filled poorboy, a muffaleta smothered in olive oil,
A bowl of crisp red shrimp,
Molting tender crabs served on a piece of toast,
Crunchy and crisp?
Instead,
a line inside at the counter,
pausing to pay their checks,

To grab paper cups with coffee to go.

From Houston to Odessa, he mixed sugar packets in plain hot water;
Stole crackers, ketchup.
His ticket commanded him to leave at such and such a time,
To arrive Las Cruces, Barstow, Modesto in accordance with the
schedule.

"I drove through here on a motorcycle,"
Wood said to no one in particular,
Pointing to the vast expanse of Sonoran desert:
Snuck around the mountains, took the Southern route,
Phoenix, Needles, across the LA River
and under the palm trees —
I loved her
Loved her then.

In Berkeley,
No recognition, no ranking with the heroes of the past;
And from the supervisor of my department
Not, "Where did you go?," but
"Did you have important business?"
So the days and nights go on now as before
Though I have stories, memories too;
And after every rain,
The pungent smell
Is a reminder of New Orleans.